Totally Bound Publishing books by Tiffany Aaron:

Fallen Volume One
Detroit
Reno

I0680783

FALLEN
Volume Two

New Orleans

Chicago

TIFFANY AARON

Fallen Volume Two
ISBN # 978-1-78184-691-9
©Copyright Tiffany Aaron 2013
Cover Art by Posh Gosh ©Copyright 2013
Interior text design by Claire Siemaszkiewicz
Totally Bound Publishing

Published in 2014 by Totally Bound Publishing, Newland House, The Point, Weaver Road, Lincoln, LN6 3QN, United Kingdom.

NEW ORLEANS

Dedication

To all my readers who have enjoyed my fallen angels, because even angels should be able to love. And to my awesome editor for making this a better story.

Chapter One

The hustle and noise of the French Quarter disappeared as Dominic LaFontaine stood on the sidewalk outside Ryder's Bookstore. He stared through the plate glass window at the dark-haired woman standing behind the counter. It had been a long two weeks away from New Orleans, but it wasn't the city that had called him home. It was Teresa Ryder, the woman he called his best friend and the one his heart called his love.

She glanced up at that moment and caught him staring at her. A joyous smile broke across her face and she waved him in. It was embarrassing how his heart jumped at the sight of her racing across the floor to him, and scary how at home he felt when she wrapped her arms around him and her laughter filled his ears.

Crushing her tight to him, he whispered, "God, I've missed you."

She pulled back from him, her violet eyes sparkling with happiness. "It's only been two weeks, Dominic."

"A minute away from you feels like a lifetime," he stated truthfully.

"Quit your flirting and help me close up." She led him back to the register. "How was your trip?"

"Productive," he murmured as he eyed her bottom. He had to stop himself from reaching out and squeezing those luscious cheeks. *Great way to greet her after being gone for two weeks*, he thought.

"Did you get all your business taken care of while you were out there? I didn't know you knew anyone out in Reno." She started counting the till.

"He was more of an acquaintance when I went out there, but I'd like to think we're friends now." As he started shutting off the lights, he thought about the routine they had established years ago.

"I'm sure you are. Who wouldn't like you after they met you?" She tucked the last of the money into a bag.

He laughed. Teresa had always seen him as a sweet person. She didn't know that he was one of the most feared men in New Orleans. He had never told her about his past—he didn't want to destroy her innocence. "William never does what you would expect him to do, but he's a good man." He took the cash bag from her and opened the door. "Will you join me for dinner? I've missed talking to you."

She blushed. "I can't. I have a date."

Disappointment rushed through him. "That's great, sweetheart. Who's the lucky man?"

"His name is Vincent Delacourte. He came into the store the day after you left and we just hit it off. We've gone to dinner a few times since then." Her face was glowing with happiness.

"Does he treat you like the lady you are?" Dominic shivered as fear trickled down his spine. Was he too late to confess his love? He didn't know what he would do if he lost her.

"Yes, he treats me almost as good as you do." She laughed up at him, not seeming to notice that his heart was in danger of being broken.

"That's good. I don't think anyone could care about you as much as I do," he said softly. She studied him in puzzlement. "I'm going to the club. Why don't you bring Delacourte by after dinner?"

"I'll see if he wants to. If not, I'll see you tomorrow morning like usual, right?" She gave him a kiss when he nodded.

"I'll drop this off for you." He waved the cash bag and gestured to the limo waiting at the curb. "Go enjoy your dinner. Looks like your ride is here."

She waved goodbye and slipped into the car. He wasn't thrilled to see that no one held the door open for her — where was the respect everyone should show her? He put a black mark against Delacourte in his mind.

* * * *

"Hey, man, your little hottie's here," Randy said as he poked his head into Dominic's office.

"She's not mine. She's out on a date and I told her to stop by."

"Your hottie's got a date and it isn't you, man? That's shocking." Randy's voice still held a hint of the islands he came from.

"Shove it," Dominic said nicely. "Take her to our regular table. I'll be there in a minute."

Randy grinned before heading out. Dominic followed a few minutes later. He was surprised to see Randy standing next to the table he and Teresa usually used. If his friend had been a cat, his back would be up and he'd be spitting. A blond man slightly shorter than Dominic sat next to Teresa. She was flushed from something Delacourte had whispered to her. Dominic clenched his hands in anger when he spied Delacourte slide his hand up her thigh. She pulled away before he got too far.

He tried to stifle the raging jealousy inside him. He couldn't believe Delacourte would try to grope her, especially in public. He managed to ignore the little voice in his head that said he would do it in a heartbeat, if he had the chance.

When Dominic approached the table, Teresa's eyes light up. Before he had a chance to say anything, her date said, "Finally. The service here is atrocious. I'll take a Jack and Coke. My date would like a glass of white wine."

Teresa opened her mouth to protest. He knew she hated wine. Turning, he flagged down a waiter and gave him the order. He didn't sit at the table yet.

"Do you find the club lacking?" he asked, as Randy blended back into the crowd. Dominic knew if he needed help, his friend would be available, but for now, he had things under control.

"Yes, I do. If I knew the owner, I'd make some suggestions."

"I never talk about business when there's a beautiful lady I can enjoy." Dominic bowed in Teresa's direction.

The waiter returned with their drinks. He smiled at the man's frown when a Martini was set down in front of Teresa.

"I ordered white wine," Vincent complained.

"Teresa doesn't drink wine. Do you, love?"

"No, I don't and I would have told you if you had allowed me to order for myself." Teresa finally found her voice.

When Dominic had walked up to the table, she had been surprised to see what she thought was a flare of jealousy in his eyes. It had to have been shadows from the flickering lights, because she would never believe he would be jealous of any man she went out with. She drank in the image of her best friend. She hadn't had much time to talk to him when he'd stopped by the bookstore before her date. His dark hair wasn't as neat as it usually was—she got the feeling he had been running his fingers through it. His chiseled features held a sharp sorrow in them and his blue eyes were the color of the ocean—they bore mysteries she had always been too leery to ask about. She knew he kept in shape because she had gone to the gym with him a couple of times. She had wondered if he had asked her to go with him because he thought she needed to lose weight, but when she'd asked him, he'd looked at her in shock. He'd told her he loved the way she looked and the only reason he'd asked her to go along was that he wanted her company.

There was a different feel about him tonight. He was eyeing her like she was a juicy peach and he wanted to take a bite. She shifted her gaze from his before the look in her eyes gave away how much she wanted him.

"I'm Dominic LaFontaine and I own The Fallen Angel." His voice was smooth, almost like how silk felt rubbing against her skin.

She had been embarrassed when Vincent assumed Dominic was the waiter. Of course, Vincent's inability to see beyond himself hadn't allowed him to notice the

Armani suit and linen shirt Dominic wore with such ease.

She had asked Dominic once why he chose such expensive clothes. He had said in a serious tone, "Life is too long to wear uncomfortable clothes." She'd assumed he was joking, but a feeling told her he believed it.

She jumped when a man appeared beside her—seemingly out of nowhere. He towered over the other men in the room, even Dominic, who was the tallest man she knew.

"May I have this dance?" He bowed slightly. His unusual silver eyes danced in amusement at Dominic's snort.

She looked at Dominic, who shrugged. "He's harmless to you."

Vincent started to protest and the man's eyes turned icy. The protest died away. She didn't mind dancing with the stranger, since Dominic wasn't worried about him. Delacourte and Dominic stared at each other while Teresa walked away. She glanced back, not sure she should leave them. She was afraid Dominic would take Vincent apart.

"Don't worry, Teresa. He won't hurt your date." The man must have read her mind.

She wondered who he was. It wasn't often that she danced with someone other than Dominic.

"I'm sorry, I didn't allow Dominic to introduce us. I'm Mickey O'Flynn." He inclined his head.

"I'm Teresa Ryder. Dominic has never mentioned you." She wasn't surprised—Dominic had told her very little about his life. If someone had asked her, she would have sworn he hadn't existed before he arrived in New Orleans.

"We are acquaintances, mostly, so there would be no need for him to say anything to you about me."

"Like William was?"

"I think he and William became friends while they did business together."

"It sounds like it, from what he told me while he was in Chicago. How long have you known Dominic?"

An odd look came into Mickey's eyes. "Some days it feels like forever."

She laughed. "I know exactly what you're talking about. He does have a habit of getting underfoot, doesn't he?"

Mickey smiled down at her. "Underfoot has never been my problem with him. I only talk to him when I have a business proposition for him."

"Oh, so you do business together as well?"

"Yes, we're in the same line of work."

"I've never figured out what Dominic's work is."

"I'm led to believe he has his hand in many different businesses. He doesn't like to tie himself down to one type of work."

Teresa looked back at the table and saw Dominic lean forward to say something to Vincent.

"Don't worry, Dominic won't hurt your man. He'll only threaten him with bodily harm if he hurts you. He takes your friendship very seriously, Teresa. You are the most important thing to him. He has no real family of his own."

"So he sees me as a sister." She couldn't hide the disappointment in her voice.

Mickey's laughter drew Dominic's gaze. "Dear, if you were his sister, it would be illegal for him to think of you the way he really does."

Blushing, she ruthlessly crushed the flash of hope in her heart. She'd been trying to get Dominic to notice her from the moment they'd met, but he never seemed to see her as anything other than a friend.

"He is scared, just like you. His heart is a fragile thing, so he wouldn't risk it without a hint that you might accept him." Mickey looked over his shoulder at the two men at the table. "I think he discovered something while he was away. This discovery has helped him make a decision about you. If I were you, I wouldn't be surprised to see Dominic looking at you in a very different way. He's feeling a little off balance now because he has competition. He wasn't expecting that."

Teresa had the strange urge to apologize. "I didn't know he had any sort of feelings for me. He's so hard to read sometimes."

"He has never had an easy life. For more years than he cares to remember, he's been alone. Don't apologize, Teresa. Competition is good for him."

As Mickey swept her into the rhythm of the dance, she allowed her worry to seep away for a little while.

* * * *

Dominic stared at Delacourte. There was a darkness surrounding the man that he didn't like, but he couldn't figure out exactly what it was. He would have to talk to Randy to see if the bouncer's reaction was from the man's self-absorbed arrogance or if there had been something else that had set Randy off. He was glad that Mika'il had shown up to distract Teresa, even though he couldn't help but wonder what the archangel was talking to her about.

"I've been trying to talk Teresa into selling her business." Vincent twitched the French cuffs of his shirt to a perfect inch outside his suit's sleeves.

Control was important in any business deal and Dominic saw this as a negotiation. There had been other reasons for Vincent to start dating Teresa. Most men would see her beauty and giving nature and treasure her, but Vincent didn't strike him as being that type of man. Delacourte saw her as a trophy and a potential business deal. The man thought he could talk her into selling her bookstore for less than market value, letting him get the historical building the bookstore was in. Dominic couldn't tell from the man's thoughts why he wanted the building.

"Why should she sell? She enjoys the business and makes a good profit." Dominic swirled the bourbon in his glass around, studying the man across the table from him.

"She's a young, beautiful woman. She shouldn't be working so hard. She should be out enjoying life and seeing the world." Vincent straightened his tie.

A laugh washed off the dance floor. Dominic glanced over at Mika'il and Teresa in surprise. It had been several centuries since he'd heard the archangel laugh like that. He couldn't help but smile at the pride he felt knowing it was Teresa who had made him laugh. There was a dark emotion buried deep inside Mika'il's heart. If Dominic didn't know better, he would say that the angel had loved and known loss that would have broken a weaker heart. Maybe someday he would ask him about it.

"On the other hand, maybe you should just stay away from that question." Mika'il's voice echoed a warning in his head. He turned to see Mika'il staring at him over

Teresa's head, and he bowed in acknowledgment. For now, he would hold onto his curiosity.

"What does Teresa say to your business proposition?" Dominic wondered if she was considering the offer.

"She won't even listen to me. My business partners and I have some good ideas of renovating the building into a bed and breakfast."

"Is that really what the city needs? Another hotel?" He took a sip from the glass. The bourbon was the best money could buy, but it didn't matter. There had never been any taste or kick from it. He could drink every bottle in the club and never get drunk. He drank because it made him feel mortal and less like the freak that he was.

"Do you really see yourself as a freak, my friend?"

"Yes, I always have."

"What is it with you and William? You're not freaks just because you are different from them. You're another one of His creations and that makes you worth as much as they are."

"I don't think you're qualified to be handing out advice to fallen angels, Mika'il. You don't know what it's like to lose something you would give anything to have back."

Sadness flooded his mind to such a degree that tears welled in his eyes. *"You don't know all that I've been through, LaFontaine. Never think I don't understand what you've lost."*

Vincent smiled at him. Dominic wanted to wipe the smirk off his face.

"Law of supply and demand, my friend. New Orleans is a very popular destination for travellers. I think there is always room for another hotel. She's not being cooperative at all."

"That's because she knows her business partner wouldn't go for the idea." Dominic saw the look of surprise on Vincent's face. Ah, so the man didn't know Teresa had a partner. Damn, his lawyers were good. "Her landlord wouldn't think about selling that building either, even if she wasn't there."

"How would you know? I'd only need one meeting with the guy to convince him that my ideas are the best money-making deal he could make."

Dominic leaned forward to study Delacourte. Could Vincent really be that blind to all the currents around him? "It wouldn't matter if you could guarantee the man would be a billionaire by the end of the year, he wouldn't sell to you." He held up his hand to stop Delacourte from talking. "I know because I'm Teresa's partner and her landlord. I don't need any more money. If the time ever comes when Teresa wishes to sell her business, she'll sell to me because it's in our contract."

Standing up, Dominic motioned for the waiter to bring Delacourte another drink before looking around the dance floor to find Teresa smiling up at Mika'il. That did it. No archangel with heartbreak eyes and a killer smile was going to steal his woman away. He went after her without looking back.

* * * *

Teresa sighed as she laid her head on Dominic's shoulder. He hadn't said anything to her since he had cut in on Mickey's dance. Dominic wrapped his arms around her waist and pulled her tight against him. She had never danced this way with him. She curled her arms around his broad shoulders and she couldn't help but tease the hair at the nape of his neck. He moved his thigh in between hers, causing her pussy to rub against his hard muscles. Dominic rocked his hips into her and she gasped as she felt the ridge of his cock graze her stomach.

She was amazed. No man had ever been this hard for her, and to have that man be Dominic was a dream come true. For five years, she had fantasized about having him in her bed. She knew it would never happen, but she'd always believed in dreaming big. From the size of the bulge in his pants, she hadn't dreamt big enough. She grew wet as he slid one of his hands down to cup her ass while he stroked her back with his other. Teresa buried her hands in his dark hair. A moan passed her lips as Dominic touched the side of her breast with his thumb. He was seducing her on the dance floor in the middle of his club and in front of her date.

The thought of Vincent Delacourte washed over Teresa like cold water. She jerked away from Dominic and stared up at him in shock. What had she been thinking? Here she was, practically making out with her best friend while her date sat drinking by himself. When had she become such a tease?

"What's wrong, love?" Dominic's voice caressed her just like his hands had. More moisture made its way between her legs.

"What are we doing?" She turned to walk back to Vincent. Dominic reached out and grabbed her arm.

"We're getting to know each other on a more intimate level."

"Why?" Vincent wasn't at the table anymore. She looked around for him.

"I want you, Teresa. I always have. I'm not going to let some self-centered prick steal you away from me." Dominic pulled her to him again. Cupping her chin, he lifted her eyes to his. "I'm not playing. You, of all people, should know I don't play games."

"I don't understand. What happened in Reno to make you decide that you want me all of a sudden?" Teresa was confused and scared. Did everyone's heart race when all their dreams came true?

"I found the truth. I found the courage not to be afraid anymore."

"Afraid of what?" She would have never thought that Dominic would be afraid of anything.

"I was afraid of the future and my place in it. I learned that my future is with you, and my place is beside you and inside you."

Her skin flushed. Holy cow, the man could bring a woman to orgasm with just the honey smoothness of his voice. It snuck into the hidden corners of her heart and lit a flame under her. Vincent pushed through the crowd to stand next to her, his face red with anger.

"Teresa, I think it's time to go. I have an early business meeting." He pulled her away from Dominic.

She glanced back at the man who had set a blaze burning in her stomach. His brilliant blue eyes followed her as she crossed the floor. She had the feeling that he wasn't done with her. More seduction was forthcoming and she wanted to shout for joy.

Wait, a cautionary voice chimed in Teresa's head. *Would Dominic be so interested if you hadn't already been dating Vincent? Maybe it's the possessive thing that all men go through when their female friends start dating. He has been drinking. Maybe he just doesn't have as much control? He's probably just reacting to the fact that you're a woman.* Teresa couldn't deny the voice that whispered those depressing thoughts in her head. Was there a reason she needed to be practical tonight? For one night, couldn't her heart just accept the fact that Dominic had gotten hard because she was in his arms?

Teresa let Vincent help her into the limo without saying a word. She tried to feel embarrassed by the whole episode, but she couldn't. Dominic had turned her on faster than any man had in a long time. She had never been overcome with desire for Vincent, but she knew that didn't mean anything. Teresa was still getting to know the man, unlike Dominic, whom she had known forever it seemed. She turned to apologize when Vincent grabbed her chin and crushed her mouth with his.

Teresa whimpered in pain as his hands slid down to grip her arms. Trying to pull away proved futile and she found herself pressed between Vincent and the inside of the door. His lips were devouring hers, but there was no seduction in his mind. There was anger and possessiveness in the kiss. Her legs were pinned beneath him so she couldn't kick out. The windows of the limo were tinted for privacy and the driver worked for Vincent. Teresa was trapped, and cried out as Vincent bit into her bottom lip.

Suddenly she was falling backwards and would have hit the pavement if Dominic hadn't caught her after he'd wrenched open the door. He kept one hand wrapped around her waist while twisting Vincent's shirt under his chin with the other. Shaking the man like a terrier with a rat, he swore at him.

"If you ever hurt her again, I'll forget every vow I made and hunt you down like the monster you are." He threw Vincent back onto the seat and slammed the door shut, but not before Teresa got a look at the madness burning in the eyes of her date. As the limo drove around the corner, Dominic pulled her into his arms and buried his face in her hair. "Are you okay, love?"

She had never thought about the endearments Dominic called her. She had always figured they were just his way of showing friendship, but now she wasn't sure. Maybe he had meant them and she was the one who hadn't believed them. Her hands shook as she snuggled close to him. "I am now."

Dominic looked down at her and his anger rose again. Caressing his thumb over her bottom lip, he spied the teeth marks and swore. "He bit you."

She ducked her head, but not before he saw an embarrassed flush staining her cheeks. "He was angry because of the way we were acting in the club."

"Anger is never an excuse to treat a woman like that." He whispered a kiss across her forehead. "I'm sorry, though. I should've been in control and not tried to seduce you in front of him. I've missed you so much that I forgot myself for a minute or two." Tucking a strand of chocolate-colored hair behind her ear, he stared down into her violet eyes. Even though Teresa was scared and hurt, a sense of belonging filled him because she was in his arms. "I'll take you home."

As Dominic led her around to where he'd parked his car, she shivered. Reaction was setting in and she had to be realizing what might have happened if he hadn't rescued her. He didn't think that Delacourte would have gone further than just kissing her, but there was a touch of uneasiness in Dominic. When he'd grabbed Delacourte, he'd felt the presence of another spirit in the man's mind, but it wasn't like the demon possession he was used to. The spirit he had touched was dark and malevolent. It had the feeling of being very old, but very human. He decided to start looking into Vincent Delacourte the next day. Dominic noticed Teresa shivering again.

"Hang on, love. I'll get you to your apartment and you can take a warm bath." He opened the car door and helped her in. After shutting the door, he stood outside for a minute, breathing deep to bury his rage. She didn't deserve to be bombarded by Dominic's anger and he knew at times that his mind would leak his emotions to others who were receptive. After the years they had spent together, he knew Teresa was very open to him. He stalked around to the driver's side then got in.

Teresa had her head lying against the headrest and her arms were wrapped around her waist as she shivered. Dominic turned the car on and did something he had never done since coming to New Orleans—he turned on the heat. Positioning the vents to blow on her, he leaned over to buckle her seatbelt, bringing his face close to her breasts. An immediate blast of lust surged through him and hardened his cock. He wanted nothing more than to bury his face in those two mounds, to roll Teresa's nipples between his fingers and suckle them as hard as he could. She took a deep breath, causing her breasts to rise even closer to his face and he looked up to see her eyes on him. Dominic wasn't embarrassed at being caught eyeing her. His gaze aroused her—he could tell by the way her nipples stood out through her dress. He finished fastening her seatbelt and sat back with a groan. Adjusting his cock in his pants, he grimaced softly.

"You do realize there is nothing I would love better than to take you home, spread you out on my bed and fuck you all night long." His voice came out harsh and frustrated. She nodded. "I won't, because you've just gone through an assault and you're not ready to take our relationship to that level."

"Vincent didn't assault me."

Dominic could tell she was avoiding the last part of his sentence—Teresa would deal with it when she had recovered from the night's events. He was pushing her too hard and too fast, but he didn't want to waste any more of her life without being her lover. Mortals lived such short lives with all sorts of danger willing and able to cut them down before it was time—he didn't want to run the risk of losing her before he had her. "Yes, he did assault you. You have bruises to prove it." After pulling out into the street, Dominic headed for her apartment.

"He was just upset. I'm sure he would have stopped before he went too far." She didn't sound too confident about that.

"Thank God we'll never find out." Though he'd never been much of a praying angel, Dominic sent a short prayer of thanks up to the Father.

"How did you know I needed help?"

He'd wondered when Teresa would get around to asking that, but he didn't think she was ready to hear about the Fall and all the powers he had. Someday he would tell her and let her make the decision about whether he was crazy or not, but tonight he would dance around the truth. "I just had a feeling when I saw that the limo hadn't pulled away from the club. I thought maybe something was wrong." He pulled up in front of her building. Teresa's apartment was above her bookstore. "Let's get you inside."

Chapter Two

Teresa sighed as she sank into the hot water. Dominic had carried her up to her apartment, left her in her bedroom then ordered her to undress while he drew a bath for her. She had slipped on the red silk robe he had given her for Christmas last year. His eyes had lit up when he'd walked in the room.

"Go take a bath. I'll make some tea." He had pushed her gently toward her bathroom.

She had gasped as she entered. He had lit candles and placed them around the room. As she settled into the bathtub, the water felt slick against her skin. Taking a deep breath, she inhaled the scent of lilies — Dominic had found her bath oils and mixed some into the water. She started to lean back when she bumped her arm against the side of the tub. A faint hint of pain emanated from her arm. Raising it, she stared at the bruises Vincent had left there.

Teresa knew his anger had been justified. She had gone to the club with him and ended up dancing with two other men. She thought about Mickey and how he had warned her that Dominic's intentions had changed toward her. Then Dominic had danced with her like she was the only woman in the club. The minute he'd taken her in his arms, all thoughts of Vincent—or any other man—had flown out of her head. Teresa realized Dominic was the man she wanted—had been from the moment she'd met him. Maybe she had tried to cloud the issue by dating other men, but he'd never done anything about them before. Like a big brother, he would check them out then give his approval. Of course, she'd had the impression Dominic wasn't happy with any of them, but she thought it was because he didn't think any of them were good enough for her.

"None of them were, love." His voice from the doorway caused her to jump.

She sputtered as water hit her in the face. Dominic stopped her hands when she tried to wipe it away.

"Let me." He cupped her chin in his hand and ran the washcloth over her cheeks with the same gentle touch he'd always used with her.

"Are you reading my mind now?" It was the only thing she could think of to ask.

Dominic shook his head. "I try not to invade your privacy like that. Now let me help you."

Their eyes met and held as he reached down to soak the cloth. Teresa saw lust burning in his gaze—his normally cold eyes had melted into warm sapphire flames. Hidden deep within them was hesitation. She could tell he was afraid she would reject him. She wasn't ready to jump into bed with him, not yet anyway. It was too sudden a transition to make, but Teresa would let him court her.

She sighed as Dominic circled her breast with the cloth. He dropped his gaze to stare at her chest. Teresa remembered that he could see everything under the water. For some reason, she wasn't embarrassed. Dominic had seen her in every way throughout their friendship, so she supposed being naked was the next step to here.

He was kneeling beside the tub, his linen shirt unbuttoned with the sleeves rolled up. He took one of her hands and placed it against his chest. She kneaded his warm skin as he ran the soapy material up and down her arm. He rinsed her arm off and did the same with the other. Dominic massaged her back as he cleaned it. Her muscles were turning into jelly with each caress and stroke. As Dominic swirled the cloth over her heated skin, he studied her reactions. As he reached her legs, she leaned back and moaned. He was worshiping every curve and valley of her. Her feet were treated to detailed care.

Teresa arched as his attention came back to her breasts. He cupped them and squeezed softly. He used the washcloth to tease her nipples. When she groaned deep in her throat, he dropped the cloth and stood. The huge bulge in his slacks caused Teresa to smile.

He moved to the door. Looking back at her, he shook his head. "You're not ready for any more of that yet. It might be killing me to walk away, but I'm willing to wait until you're ready."

She wanted to yell at him that she was ready, but she wasn't emotionally ready for their relationship to move so quickly beyond just friends. She nodded.

"Do you want me to stay or will you be okay?" He leaned in the doorway and caressed her with his eyes.

"I'll be okay. You don't need to stay and take care of me. I'm perfectly capable of getting to bed on my own." She blushed at his grin.

"What if I don't want you getting to bed on your own? What if I want to be the one who takes you there?"

"You said I wasn't ready." She threw his statement back at him.

"So I did. I guess tonight isn't the night when all my dreams come true." He blew her a kiss. "Sweet dreams, love. I'll stop by and see you tomorrow."

She sat in the warm water, listening for the front door to close. She hadn't realized how quietly Dominic moved. There was no sound of footsteps through the apartment, no sound of clothes brushing against each other. It was like he just disappeared, but then the door closed. *He's just light on his feet*, she told herself.

She climbed out of the tub and dried off. After wrapping herself in the robe, Teresa wandered into her living room. Dominic had left some candles burning and tea was simmering on her stove in the kitchen. Her French doors were open to the evening breeze, which brought in the humid, earthy smell of the bayous and the tang of the ocean. She poured a cup of tea then moved to stand just inside the doors. The curtains billowed in concert with the gentle wind blowing in. When one of the curtains touched her calf, she jumped. A cold shiver ran down Teresa's spine as the soft velvet fabric seemed to wrap itself around her ankle and cling to her. A cold, harsh wind burst into the room, bringing with it the stench of rotting food. She gagged and stumbled back. Fighting the wind, she closed the doors and sagged against them.

An eerie sound came from the night. She told herself it was an alley cat, but a small voice in her head told her no alley cat sounded like that. After blowing out the candles, she quickly checked all the locks on the doors and headed for her bedroom. As she climbed into bed, the phone rang.

She hesitated answering it. Finally, she leaned forward and grabbed it. "Hello?"

"Are you okay?" Dominic's deep, smooth voice came over the line.

"Yes." She collapsed against her pillows. "Why are you calling me? Didn't you just leave?"

"I got a strange feeling something was wrong and I wanted to make sure you were okay."

"Do you get these feelings often?"

"Often enough that I usually listen to them. So are you okay?"

She thought about the cold wind and strange sound she had heard. She managed to convince herself it was just a delayed reaction to Vincent's actions. "Yes, I'm fine. I think I'm a little jumpy from the incident this evening."

"If you want, I can come back and stay. I'll sleep on the couch."

Teresa grinned at the thought of Dominic trying to fit his tall body on her little couch. "I'll be fine. I'm going to bed now anyway. After a good night's rest, I'll have forgotten about the whole thing."

"You better not forget about it. If you see Delacourte again, be on guard. I don't trust him."

"What have you got against Vincent?"

"Aside from the fact that he attacked you?" She could hear the shrug in his voice. "I'm not sure, but something about him makes me uneasy."

"It wouldn't be jealousy making you uneasy, would it?"

He laughed. "Sure some of it is plain old jealousy, but some of it is my instincts telling me he's dangerous."

"And you're not?"

"I'm dangerous in a good way."

She curled up on her bed and pulled the blanket around her. She loved his voice. It touched a place she had never known was there. It was the first thing she had noticed about him. Okay, it was the second thing she had noticed, right behind how great he looked in a three-piece suit. When they had met, she'd spilt coffee all over him and he'd apologized so sweetly for running into her. Like a true gentleman, he had taken the blame for the accident. When he'd asked her to join him for dinner, she hadn't been able to refuse. She smiled at the memory of their first dinner. "I didn't know there were different kinds of dangerous."

"Trust me, love. There are several kinds of danger out there in the world. My kind of dangerous is intriguing because you know I'll never hurt you."

"How do I know that?"

"Look deep inside you and you'll see what I'm talking about. It's the little voice in your mind saying you should take a chance and go out with me. It's the same voice making you unsure about staying involved with Delacourte."

It didn't have much to do with the fact that Dominic was showing an unusual amount of interest in her now. Teresa hadn't been feeling the burning attraction to him she was looking for in the guys she dated. She had almost reached the decision to stop seeing him when Dominic had returned home and started hitting on her. Vincent attacking her was the nail in the coffin of their relationship. Teresa wasn't about to put herself in that kind of danger again.

"Dominic, what happened in Reno?"

"Why do you ask?"

"You've changed. I've never seen you as forceful as you were tonight."

"I know and I'm sorry. I think I got scared."

"Scared?"

"I never thought I'd really have to worry about you finding someone else. I didn't stop you from dating other men because I guess I always thought you knew we were meant to be together. After I saw you at the bookstore, all I heard about from our friends was how wonderful Delacourte was and that you made the perfect couple. All of a sudden, I saw all my plans for the future disappearing before my eyes. So I got scared."

"Oh, Dominic."

"I promise to move slower, Teresa. I don't want to scare you away and if you want to keep seeing Delacourte, I won't stop you."

"It's hard for you to let me choose, isn't it?"

"Yes, it is, but I've learned the value of free will." A note of sadness touched his voice for a moment. "I've also seen the folly of free will, so I hope you don't mind if I keep an eye on you if you decide to keep seeing Delacourte."

She laughed softly. "I'm not surprised. You can keep an eye on me. I've grown used to you being around."

"Sleep well, my love. I'll see you for breakfast tomorrow."

"Goodnight."

Teresa hung up then snuggled under the blankets. Warmth filled her and she knew it was because Dominic was home again. Tomorrow she would break it off with Vincent and see where this attraction between her and Dominic went. She fell asleep to dreams of her and Dominic entwined on a bed of white satin sheets.

* * * *

While she dreamed erotic dreams, she didn't hear the strange sounds coming from the street below — the same sounds she had dismissed earlier as an alley cat. In the sudden cold wind that blew, a chuckle could be heard. If someone had glanced out of their window, they would have seen a sharply dressed man standing on the street across from her building.

"She'll be ours soon."

"Yes." Vincent laughed. *"So will that lovely piece of property she owns. I want that for my hotel."*

"I want her. Her soul is pure. It's perfect for me."

The part of his soul not corrupted by the spirit baulked at the thought of offering Teresa up as a sacrifice to this evil thing. *"Why does it have to be her? Can't any of the other women I've dated work?"*

"No. There is something special about this one. I haven't figured it out yet, but I know that she must be the one. The only thing that worries me is the man she was dancing with tonight. You didn't tell me she had a business partner."

"I didn't know. Nothing in the research I had my assistant do told me she didn't own her business and the building outright. LaFontaine makes me nervous."

"As he should. You will never be in his league, no matter how much I help you. There is something strange about him. He doesn't have the same feel as the rest of you."

"What does he feel like?"

"He has a touch of the infinite in him, I think. It's strange because I don't sense the presence of another spirit in him."

"That should be good. He shouldn't be that hard to take down then."

"You would think that, but I have the feeling he'll be harder than anyone else I've dealt with. He will protect her fiercely as well. We'll have to be cautious."

"That's a good plan. I'll have my assistant start looking into his background. Maybe we'll be able to find something to blackmail him with."

"I don't think we'll find anything and, even if we did, I don't think he's vulnerable to blackmail. He strikes me as a man who doesn't care what others think of him."

"But he might care what Teresa thinks of him."

"Not enough to risk harming her. If it comes down to you revealing all his secrets and her getting hurt, he'll take out the ad in the newspaper for you." Another cold breeze blew down the street. "It's time for us to go. We need to plan."

Vincent walked away. He didn't see the tall figure step out of the alley behind him. Eyes narrowed, the man watched the departing shadow and wondered about the blackness he felt in the other man's soul.

* * * *

"We might have a problem with Delacourte, LaFontaine."

Dominic wasn't surprised to see Mika'il show up later that night. The club had been closed for an hour and he was going over the receipts from the night. Not glancing up at the angel, he waved him to take a seat across from him. "Do you want something to drink?"

"No. I don't need to make myself feel mortal by pretending to drink. Did you hear what I said?"

"What's got you so uptight?" Dominic focused on Teresa for a moment, then smiled. "Right now, Teresa is curled up nice and warm in her bed having sweet dreams of me."

Mika'il twitched his shoulders. "I don't like this town. There are too many spirits still existing here. I also get nervous when I'm around Vodou practitioners."

"Vodou? What do you have against that?"

"Nothing, except it freaks me out. I prefer the clean and traditional Catholic ceremony."

"Ah, all smoke, incense and Latin. It's a little stuffy for me." Dominic waved a hand and two glasses of bourbon appeared on the table. "Have a drink, Mika'il. It won't affect you, but it'll give you something to do besides obsess about this town. That's the magic of New Orleans, my friend. It's beautiful and ugly. It's deeply religious, but the mixture is exotic and pagan as well."

Mika'il sipped his drink as he watched Dominic with enigmatic silver eyes. "Is that why you like this place so much? I never thought you would settle down in one town for so long."

"I do like the feel of the faith that permeates this town, but there is also the decadence. I don't have a problem with all the different religions here."

"Good, because I think our problem with Delacourte doesn't have anything to do with the usual religions, but the fringe ones."

"Has Delacourte done anything to her?" Dominic started to stand. "I'll go over and check her."

Mika'il waved him to sit back down. "No, she's fine. I just left her apartment. Vincent was standing outside on the street, mumbling to himself. I can usually see the souls of the mortals. The odd thing about him was it looked like he had two souls inhabiting his body."

"Spirit possession?"

"Yes. It's not a true demon, though. Both you and I would have sensed it when he was here earlier. I haven't had any experience with this type before. We're going to have to learn as much as we can before they do anything to Teresa."

"I'll see what I can do." Dominic shrugged. "I might have some employees that know about Vodou. I'll check with them first."

"I'll look up a few sources I have. I'll get hold of you if I find anything." Mika'il disappeared as Randy came around the corner from the bar.

"Hey, boss man, are you talking to yourself again?"

"I must be. I need to ask you something." He waved his bouncer to take a seat.

"Sure, boss." Randy didn't glance at the second glass on the table. He had gotten used to the unusual ways of his boss.

"Randy, do you believe in God?"

The big man looked at him. "Sure. I believe in God, but I practice the island religion."

"Island religion?"

"Vodou. The real kind, not the tourist bullshit they sell in the French Quarter." Randy's lip curled in disgust.

"So you believe in the power of spirits?"

"Yes. Good and bad. The spirits of our ancestors are all around us."

"What do you think of Vincent Delacourte?"

"Why are you asking me? You usually have better judgment about people than I do."

"You're closer to the 'other' world. Your Vodou religion gives you more of a sense for evil than I." He knew he had lost some feeling for the spiritual world. Living for centuries, he had become more like the mortals he had once ridiculed. *I'm more experienced with demons than spirits,* he thought.

"Delacourte is bad news. I've seen him at some of the ceremonies. He came looking for something. I was hoping he didn't find it, but the feeling I got from him tonight said he found exactly what he was looking for."

"What do you think it was?"

Randy shrugged. "If people don't know the true power of Vodou, they come looking for zombies and Vodou dolls. They expect us to be doing curses and things like that. I'm not saying that stuff doesn't exist. It does, but for any of the bad stuff, you have to go find a sorcerer or *bòkò*. I don't know any of my people who would tell him where to find one."

"If the stuff being peddled to the tourists isn't the real Vodou, why aren't you and the religious leaders trying to educate them?"

"This isn't a religion for the man who has always been free, Dominic. There are reasons why it's called the religion of the slaves. My ancestors practiced it in Africa before their enemies sold them to the white men. Vodou isn't even the true name for it. It's a form of ancestor worship."

Dominic started to ask another question when Randy held up his hand.

"I'm not saying anything more. I trust you, man. You've been a good friend and you won't use anything I tell you to get me in trouble, but for anything else, you'll need to talk to a *mambo* or *oungan*."

"Do you know one I can talk to?"

"I'll ask mine and see if he knows anyone who will talk to you. It might take a little while to convince him."

Dominic pulled out some cash. "Take him a token from me. If he can use the money for his community, that's fine. If not, get something he can use. Maybe by showing respect, he'll be willing to talk to me."

"Thanks, man. I know just what he'll use it for." Randy took the money and stood. "I'll head over and talk to him right now."

"Isn't it a little late to be dropping in on someone?"

"He doesn't sleep much anymore. I think he's on his way to the ancestors' land."

Dominic watched his friend head out of the club. He wasn't sure what would happen, but he would keep a close eye on Teresa. If the Father's warrior angel was worried, things weren't looking good.

Chapter Three

Dominic was sitting at their usual table at Peter's Bakery, a tiny shop tucked in the French Quarter of the city. He had ordered her a cup of chicory coffee, though he didn't know how she could stand drinking the thick, rich liquid this early in the morning. He sipped his tea and looked out at the crowd of people passing by. They all seemed to be in a hurry to get somewhere. He envied them having the dedication to keep going every day, but he knew the truth. There was no point in rushing because nothing ever came of running around unless it was an early grave. These mortals couldn't afford to die any sooner than they had to.

Maybe he was just getting tired after all these centuries of living. Dominic never got up early unless it was for breakfast with Teresa. He didn't rush anywhere, because he did have all the time in the world. Dominic heard the bell over the door ring and looked up to see her walking toward him. His heart constricted as he thought of how much he loved her.

She wasn't fashionably thin—she was always complaining about her hips and her thighs. Dominic had told her several times he loved her the way she was. When he held her, he wanted to feel curves and softness, not bones and angles. She smiled and laughed at something Pierre had said to her as she made her way through the crowd. He couldn't help the smug little grin he gave the other men in the bakery as they shot jealous glares at him.

After standing, Dominic pulled her into his arms. Crushing her to him, he kissed her hard. She gasped and he took advantage by sliding his tongue in and stroking hers. Melting against him, she wrapped her arms around his neck. As he devoured her lips and caressed her back, he wondered how long it would take before she remembered where they were. Then he lost himself in her touch and the soft moans coming from her throat.

The sound of clapping broke into his fogged mind and they pulled apart. Dominic smiled down at Teresa as she blushed. She slugged him while the other customers cheered. He held out her chair and brushed her hair out of the way to kiss her neck. She shivered.

"Dominic, I thought you said you'd take it slow."

"I don't think kissing you is really rushing things. Actually, I've wanted to kiss you like that since I first met you."

"But here in the middle of the bakery?"

"I couldn't help it. You make me glad to be alive and no one has done that in a very long time." He pushed her coffee over to her.

"You don't really expect me to believe that, do you?" She took a sip and sighed. "My coffee never tastes like this. Why is that?"

"You've never made coffee." He grabbed a beignet the owner of the bakery had brought over for them.

"I'm sure if I ever did, it wouldn't taste like this."

"So have you done any thinking about Delacourte and whether or not you'll be seeing any more of him?" As much as he wanted to demand she stop seeing the man, he knew there was no better way to make her mad than by issuing an order.

"I'll call him later and let him know I don't want to see him again. I think after the way he acted last night, he'll understand why."

"I'm not sure. Do you want me to be there when you tell him?"

"I can take care of myself. I don't need you there to hold my hand."

"Take a step back, my friend. Pushing her isn't the way. Tell her how worried we are for her," Mika'il's voice cautioned him.

Sighing, Dominic shoved his tea away. Grabbing Teresa's hands, he lifted them to his lips. "I'm sorry. I know you don't need me to take care of you. You've proven you're more than capable of taking care of things by yourself. I'm worried about Delacourte. I don't think he's quite the nice guy you seem to think he is."

"Have you had someone gathering information on him?" She didn't sound happy.

"Not any of my people. My business associate, Mickey O'Flynn, has been doing a little digging of his own. I didn't ask him to." He shrugged. "You don't really ask Mickey to do anything. I guess there was something about your date that he didn't like. So he checked a few things and let me know."

"What things?"

"It seems he's into Vodou."

"That doesn't mean anything. A lot of people practice that religion." Teresa bit her bottom lip at the news, even though she tried to act casual about it.

"Of course, it wouldn't mean anything if he was into the regular Vodou, but he's into the bad *mojo*, Teresa."

"*Mojo?*"

"The black charms that can harm you if he wants them to."

"I didn't think those things happened. I thought all that stuff was just for the movies."

"It has its good and bad side just like every other religion. If he knows what he's looking for, he'll be able to find it."

"You really think he'll harm me in some way?" Teresa didn't seem convinced.

"Not really. I just want you to be careful while you're around him. Don't make him mad."

"It wasn't me making him mad last night. It seemed to me someone *else* was pushing his buttons."

Leaning forward, Dominic caught her gaze with his. He hoped she got the point he was making. "You and I could have made love on the dance floor. Even that isn't an excuse to attack you like he did."

"Are you telling me you wouldn't be angry?"

"Sure, I'd have been furious if my date started kissing some other guy, but I wouldn't take my anger out on her. I'd probably be tempted to punch the guy moving in on my territory," he admitted.

She laughed. "Totally a male response."

"Is it? How would you feel if some woman came over here and started hitting on me, especially after seeing our kiss?"

Teresa curled her lip. "I'd want to scratch her eyes out."

"See, it's a territorial response, not just a male reaction."

"What would you do or say to your date if she did something like that?" She studied him.

"I'd chalk it up to fate and walk away. She obviously isn't the right one if she's kissing someone while she's on a date with me. I'll take her home if she wants me to, and say goodbye. Life's too long for me to waste my time on women who don't want me."

"Don't you mean life's too short?"

"Do I?" Dominic shrugged. "I mix those sayings up sometimes."

Standing, he offered his hand to her. He helped Teresa to her feet then threaded her arm through his as they made their way through the morning crowd. As they stepped outside to walk down the street, he hugged her closer to him. He found himself thinking about how different his life had been since he'd met her. She made the days brighter and more joyous.

Before, he'd gone months without laughing because he hadn't discovered anything good in the world for so long. Then one day he'd heard Teresa laugh and found himself smiling again. Inside her heart, she held a small piece of his soul. When they were together, he was complete. Nothing was going to happen to her — he wouldn't let it. He had a feeling that if she were to be hurt, he might cross the line he'd been walking between sanity and the darkness.

"You're so serious all of a sudden. What are you thinking about?" She tugged on his arm.

He looked down at her and smiled slightly. "I was thinking about what I'd do without you."

"I don't think you'll have to find that out. I don't plan on going anywhere." She glanced at her watch.

"Shoot. I have to go. I hired a new girl while you were gone. She starts today and I have to train her."

Leaning down, he kissed her quickly. "Do you want me to come by for lunch?"

"No, I'm going to be busy all day. But I won't say no to dinner."

"Then I'll stop by and pick you up after the store closes. We'll have dinner at my place."

"Wow. Who's doing the cooking?" At his affronted look, she giggled.

"I'll have you know, I'm a gourmet cook. I only cook for very special people." Tugging her close, he nuzzled her cheek. "I can't think of anyone else I'd like to cook for more."

A shy light came into her eyes. "You're going to spoil me if you keep treating me this way."

"That's the point, love. You deserve to be spoiled." He kissed her hard then pulled away. "You have to get going. I'll be there tonight to get you."

As he watched her hurry away, he knew that the night would be special. He had tried to be patient, but he wanted to make her his as soon as possible. His instincts were screaming that something was going to happen soon, and he was afraid of what that might mean for Teresa.

* * * *

"Teresa."

She couldn't stop a shiver of fear from running down her spine at the sound of Vincent's voice. She turned to see him approaching from the door. Glancing around, she realized they were the only two in the store. She had sent her clerk out for lunch. *Don't worry*, she thought. *He won't hurt you.*

"Vincent."

He handed her a dozen pink roses. "I want to apologize for my behavior last night. It was unforgivable of me to treat you like that."

She took the flowers and hid a grimace—she'd never liked roses. Setting the bouquet on the counter, she smiled at him. "I understand why you were angry, Vincent. My behavior with Dominic was inappropriate. I don't know what came over us."

"Men like LaFontaine and I hold a certain allure, cast by our wealth and power"—Vincent touched her hand—"I can see how a girl like you could get carried away by it."

Thank goodness Vincent didn't seem to lack confidence, but Teresa didn't feel like arguing about the truth. "You're probably right."

Vincent leaned against the counter. "How long have you known LaFontaine?"

"I've been friends with him for five years. Why?"

"Have you ever met any of his friends?"

"Sure. The people who work at the club."

He dismissed them with a wave of his hand. "Those are his employees. You don't become friends with the people who work for you."

"I met Mickey O'Flynn last night."

"Ah, the tall, rather unpleasant fellow."

She hadn't found Mickey unpleasant at all. In fact, he had been rather charming.

"He's a business associate. Never socialize with business associates. They'll try to take advantage of you."

Shaking her head, Teresa pointed out, "You must be a lonely man. His friend, William Bradford, lives in Reno. Dominic spent a couple weeks out there helping him with some things."

"Or so he says."

She shrugged. "Why would he lie to me?"

"All men lie, sweetheart. It's in the blood."

"If he has lied to me, why should I care? He's an adult and we aren't exclusive, so he can go where he wants to."

There was a flash of impatience in his eyes. Teresa didn't intend to play his game. There was no way he would get her to doubt Dominic. For five years, he had stood by her. He had been a friend during times when she'd felt there was no one out there for her. He held her while she cried and laughed with her when she was happy. She might doubt he could want her as more than a friend, but she could never doubt that he loved her.

"Vincent, I'm glad you stopped by. I was going to call you."

A smug smile came over Vincent's face. "I'm glad to hear that. I forgive you for last night. I blame LaFontaine."

She couldn't believe he really thought she was going to call and apologize. "Actually, I was going to let you know that we couldn't see each other anymore. I don't think we're right for each other. I think what happened last night just reinforced the truth."

Anger and something more sinister skated over his face. She took a step back then silently berated herself. *Don't show fear or weakness. He'll attack.* She wondered why she thought of Vincent like a rabid dog—maybe because there was a wild look in his eyes.

"You were going to break up with me?"

He leaned over the counter and reached for her. Grabbing her arms, he jerked her toward him. Teresa gasped at the yellow streaks swirling in his brown eyes. For a moment, she had the strangest thought that another soul stared out from those eyes. Was that what Dominic's warning had meant? He snarled at her and she couldn't help but cringe away from him.

"No one leaves me without my permission. You're mine, Teresa. You need to accept that I won't give you up. Your soul is pure and just what I'm looking for. I'll win you from him. I'm warning you, don't make me fight for you. You won't like the way I do it."

The bell over the door rang as a brunette woman walked in. Her quick glance took in the scene at the counter. Whether she sensed the danger or not Teresa didn't know, but she thanked her silently for having the courage to come up to them.

"I was wondering if you could help me." Her voice held a hint of the Midwest in it. She looked at Vincent, acknowledging the fact that he was trying to intimidate Teresa.

Vincent shoved Teresa away from him. "Remember what I said." He smiled "There's always help for a beautiful woman. If I can be of any service to you, please don't hesitate to call me. Here's my card."

Teresa couldn't believe he'd had the nerve to try to charm another person when he had just been threatening her. The stranger took the card, but didn't say anything until after Vincent had left. Calmly tearing it up, she looked at Teresa.

"Are you okay?"

"I will be. Thank you for stepping in like that."

"Men like him are a dime a dozen. Think they're God's gift to women and don't believe any of us can resist them. He doesn't realize God made us smarter than that." The lady rolled her eyes.

Teresa laughed. "Some women find him attractive."

"Those are the women who make the rest of us look bad. He's not my type at all."

"What is your type? If you don't mind me asking." She couldn't help but be intrigued by her.

"My type is more outdoorsy, I guess. Tall, dark hair and very rugged." It was clear she had a very specific person in mind.

"What does he do for a living?"

"He's an archaeologist." The woman smiled.

Her clerk returned at that moment while Teresa studied her new-found friend. "My name is Teresa Ryder. If you don't have any plans, would you like to join me for lunch?"

"I'm Danielle Weston and I'd love to take you up on your offer."

Teresa grabbed her purse then they left. They were halfway through lunch when Teresa realized she had never laughed so much with anyone besides Dominic.

"I think I know what your type is." Danielle sipped her glass of wine, returning to their earlier conversation.

"You do?"

"Sure. Your type is like the jerk in the store, only about a hundred times better. He's sophisticated, but not snobby. He has money yet isn't obvious about it. Most importantly, he loves you beyond all reasoning and will do anything for you."

"Boy, did you hit it." She smiled.

"Then what's the problem?"

"We've been friends for five years and all of a sudden he decides he wants to be more."

"Are you opposed to the idea?" Danielle sounded a little surprised that Teresa might be resistant.

"Not at all. I've been lusting after him from the second we met, but he's so much more than any other person I've been with. I'm afraid I'll disappoint him."

Teresa blushed. "I can't believe I'm telling you all of this."

"Don't worry. I don't know anyone in New Orleans except for you, so your secrets are safe with me. Just think of me as your guardian angel." A smile slid across Danielle's face. "Has he ever indicated he wants to change you?"

"No. He's always told me I'm perfect the way I am."

Danielle frowned. "You've known each other for five years. That's plenty of time to learn a lot about each other. Does he have any annoying habits?"

"None that I've seen. Something worries me at times. Dominic suffers from bouts of depression. I know he has nights where he doesn't sleep at all. At times it seems like he's hearing or seeing things that I can't."

"Does it scare you?"

Teresa shook her head. "He would never hurt me or harm himself. I just feel so helpless because I can't do anything but talk to him."

"I'm sure that's the important thing for him. I've had moments like your friend and just knowing there's someone out there to talk to helps keep me from the edge."

"So you think I'm silly to worry about disappointing him?"

Danielle reached out to touch her hand. "In the years I've lived, I've figured out that regret is the hardest emotion to live with. Never do anything you'll regret because you'll never forget it. I think you'd regret not taking the chance to fully love Dominic. Grab what he's offering with both hands and enjoy it to the tiniest moment. You might be surprised to learn that your world will be complete when you're together."

The sincerity in Danielle's voice brought tears to Teresa's eyes. She knew that whether Dominic chose to seduce her that night or not, she would grab hold of him and never let go.

"Thank you, Danielle."

"You're welcome. Now I must be going. I have a business meeting in a few minutes." The brunette stood before smiling at her. "I enjoyed our talk."

"Would you like to have lunch again tomorrow?"

Danielle shook her head. "I'm sorry. I have a business lunch."

"If you're free tomorrow night, why don't you meet me at The Fallen Angel? It's my friend's club."

"I would love to. Say around nine?"

"Great. I'll let Dominic know and he'll reserve us a table."

Danielle said goodbye to Teresa, then headed in the opposite direction from her. As soon as Teresa turned the corner, Mika'il appeared beside Danielle.

"Why, Danielle, getting involved in a mortal's life? That isn't like you."

"Go away, Mika'il. I have mortal friends."

"I know, but Teresa is a stranger. I must admit your speech about not living with regret was quite stirring."

She stopped and turned on him. "Do you think I don't regret what I did?"

"I've never seen much remorse from you."

"I repented. I got down on my knees and begged. He chose not to forgive me. Fine. I'm not letting His refusal drive me mad. I'm not letting guilt eat me alive either. I'll live the life I've been given, but I'll live it my way. I won't become the hunted or the hunter." She walked away from him.

"Good for you, Danielle. Most mortals don't even have the courage to live," Mika'il said softly then vanished.

Chapter Four

Dominic wiped his hands on his pants, not believing how nervous he was. It was silly really—he'd taken Teresa out for dinner a million times before and never felt like this. *That's because you were never going to end up in bed with her.* He didn't want to think about what he was planning for after dinner. It was a huge step they were about to take, even though he knew it was the right one. Ever since he had first talked to her, he had wanted her. Need built inside him, and it wasn't just lust. That emotion would have burnt out early on. His love for her had grown over the years to become the most critical thing in his life. When he was with her, he was home. It was as simple and as complicated as that.

Teresa opened the door and his mouth dropped open. She had always been beautiful in his eyes, but tonight she glowed. Dressed in a white silk gown, she looked like an innocent virgin...until he noticed the slit in the skirt going to the top of her thigh and revealing glimpses of her stockings. The plunging neckline displayed the tops of her breasts. She wasn't overly endowed in that area, but he had never been much of a breast man.

She was wearing stilettos that brought her closer to his height. The diamond and sapphire jewelry set he had bought her for her last birthday graced her skin. With a trembling hand, he held out the single lily he had brought her. Her bright smile made him feel like he had given her the moon.

"You're so beautiful. You make my heart ache," Dominic confessed in a husky voice.

She wrapped her arms around his neck, then pressed her lips to his. He savored Teresa's warm, moist mouth as if she were the finest chocolate. He dipped his tongue in and stroked hers with a soft, velvety touch. Never once did he demand or take from her. His goal was to give her all the pleasure.

The closer he pulled her, the deeper the kiss went. They became lost in the taste and texture of each other. In a final moment they pressed together so close, their shadows became one.

A bitterly cold wind rushed around them and forced them apart. Dominic looked at Teresa and saw that she'd heard the voice in the wind as well. He pushed her into her apartment and turned to search the night. Someone was hiding in the shadows and hating them. He hadn't felt anything until the wind, so it was easy for the watcher to hide in the dark.

"Are you ready to go?"

She handed him her jacket and he held it out for her to slip on. He slid his hands over her shoulders and she shivered. At her sharp intake of breath, he knew she was anticipating their night as much as he was. He escorted her from her apartment to his car, waiting at the curb. Usually he drove himself, but tonight he wanted to focus all his attention on her. He was taking her to his house outside the city, instead of his apartment, and he wanted everything to go right. His chauffer, Terrance, held open the door for them.

"Thank you, Terrance. We're going to Paisible."

Before Dominic climbed in beside her, Terrance stopped him. "Sir, something isn't right around here. All my instincts are screaming alarms."

"Thanks. Keep your eyes open." Dominic slid in the car.

"Yes, sir." Terrance shut the door then climbed behind the wheel of the Rolls before pulling from the curb.

"Where did you find Terrance?" she asked as she settled into his arms.

He smiled. "Terrance found me, actually. He used to be a mercenary."

"A mercenary? Why would you hire someone like that?"

"Why not?"

"His loyalty can be bought. How do you know he wouldn't turn on you if someone gave him enough money?"

"When did you get cynical?" Dominic shook his head. "I don't keep Terrance around because I need a bodyguard. I can take care of myself. I hired him to give him a chance to regain his humanity."

She gave a puzzled frown. "Regain his humanity?"

"He decided being a mercenary wasn't the right thing for him anymore. When he stopped caring about the people he was fighting for, he knew it was time to get out. While I'm sure he has several talents, I figured the best thing for him to do was what he had been doing. He's another set of eyes for me. I don't truly think anyone is out to get me, but sometimes crazy people become obsessed and it pays to have someone there to watch your back. I trust him with everything important to me, even you."

"That's high praise from you. It's strange to think I'm so important to you. It scares me in so many ways. I'm afraid I'll disappoint you." Teresa frowned slightly.

"The only way you could disappoint me is by not taking a chance on us." Dominic rested his hand on her thigh.

"I met a woman today who told me the worst thing is to live with regret. I don't plan to do that. We're going to start learning everything about each other. There can't be any secrets between us."

"Do you have any earth-shattering secrets?" He laughed.

"I might. Are your secrets deep and dark?"

His smile disappeared and he turned to look out of the window for a moment. Dominic saw their reflections in the glass — her eyes glowed with love. He found himself doubting he deserved her. If he couldn't receive God's forgiveness, there was no way he was good enough for this wonderful woman.

"Stop it, you fool." Mika'il's voice shot into his mind. *"How do you know God didn't have this planned from the very beginning? Maybe He knew she would need you."*

"She needs me? Did He plan for how much I seem to need her? I can't go a minute without thinking about her."

"Ah, love is a wonderful thing, isn't it, my friend?" A laugh echoed through his thoughts. *"Trust me, as the years go by, it'll only get worse."*

"Have you ever been in love?" He couldn't imagine an archangel in love, but God had allowed stranger things to happen.

"*That isn't important. You deserve her and every good thing that's going to happen to you. You've proven your faith. I don't think He could ask any more of you.*"

"*Thank you, Mika'il.*"

He turned back to her. "Tonight isn't the night for secrets. We'll have all the time in the world to tell each other our pasts." Dominic slid her onto his lap, then wrapped his arms around her waist. Laying her head on his chest, she kept quiet. There wasn't anything else to say until they pulled into the driveway of his house.

Teresa stepped out of the car and gasped. Staring up at the three-story plantation house, she couldn't find the words to describe her reaction.

"I felt the same way when I first saw it," Terrance said as he winked at her.

"Do you like it?" Dominic pulled her close to him as they stared up at the wide veranda.

"Like it? Oh, Dominic, it's beautiful. What did you call it?"

A sad smile graced his face. "I call it Paisible. It means peaceful."

"Peaceful. I can feel it." She hugged him. "Will you show it to me?"

Dominic nodded. "Thank you, Terrance. You can have the rest of the night off."

"Thank you, sir. Goodnight, miss." Terrance got in the car before driving it around the side of the house.

Dominic led Teresa up the sweeping front steps to the huge double doors. In the light of the porch lamps, she could see the intricate leaded glass panes in the doors, which depicted several people kneeling on a mountain. Their arms were raised to the skies and tears ran down their cheeks. In the sky above them floated an angel dressed in armor and holding a sword. He was pointing behind him at a gleaming golden gate. There was such sadness in his eyes, Teresa had the feeling he was denying the people's pleas. There were piles of wings all around the people. Reaching out, she touched the face of a man who looked strikingly like Dominic. She had a feeling this stained glass window held the secrets to Dominic's heart.

Tears filled her eyes. "This is so sad. What does it represent?"

He wiped her cheeks, then stared at the glass. "It's a reminder that everyone can make a mistake."

"It depicts the Fall, doesn't it?" Teresa remembered learning about the rebellion in Heaven during one of her Sunday school classes when she was a child.

"Yes. Even angels can make mistakes. They aren't infallible. No matter what any priest wants you to think."

She didn't comment, but the certainty in his voice convinced her that he was speaking from experience. The ageless understanding he often exhibited made her think he was more than a mere human. If she believed in vampires, she could almost accept that he was one, but he never gave off the menacing presence those legendary creatures were said to. Dominic often made her think of a guardian angel, in the way he took care of her.

He pushed open the door and waved her inside.

Teresa marveled at the exquisite marble staircases climbing toward the second floor. Done in deep jewel tones of sapphire, emerald and burgundy, they sparkled like precious stones under the crystal chandelier that graced the ceiling, which was created out of pale gold tiles. Though the staircases and chandelier were awe-inspiring, it was the fountain in the middle of the main floor that held the eye.

Made of obsidian, it formed a large, natural cross. Water cascaded down its front in a bubbling waterfall. She went to stare down into the basin. The bottom was lined with rose quartz.

"It's gorgeous."

"Here is where peace begins. In this house, there has never been conflict or pain. When it was a working plantation, no slaves were held here. There were only free men and women of every race. They shared in the profits."

"That was very generous of the owner."

"I had… I mean, he had no need for money and even if he did, he wouldn't have made it on the backs of others." Dominic led her up the stairs to a door just a few steps away from the top step. Swinging the dark mahogany open, he allowed Teresa to enter first.

The room was dark at first. Then candlelight appeared. Soon a hundred candles illuminated an intimate dining table where two plates were set across from each other. He went to a chair before pulling it out for her. As Teresa sat, she admired the pale blue china and sparkling silver. She reverently touched the elegant crystal wine glasses. Another single lily graced the table.

"You remembered I love lilies."

"I remember everything you tell me." Dominic poured her some wine. Lifting his glass, he toasted her. "You are perfection. There will never be another lady like you, Teresa. You've touched the darkest place in my heart and brought it into the light again."

Tears welled in her eyes. "Tonight has been wonderful."

"But it doesn't end here, my love. This is only the beginning. We have all night."

Dominic guided their conversation, and Teresa was happy to let him do so while she ate the wonderful meal he'd prepared for her. It touched her that he had made all of her favorite foods. After they'd finished, Dominic stood, then offered her his hand.

Teresa knew it was her last chance. If she had qualms, she could say no and he would show her to a guest room. He wouldn't berate her or make her feel guilty. Dominic would simply continue to love her. It was that knowledge that gave her the confidence to take his hand. As they left the room, Teresa glanced back one last time and the candles went dark. She thought it was a pretty neat trick—she'd have to ask him how he did it.

They went up the next flight of stairs, side by side, though this time they stopped in front of a door made from ebony. He swept her into his arms as the door swung open to reveal a room illuminated by two small Tiffany lamps. Soft shadows danced in the corners, but she didn't fear them because, tonight, she would rely on Dominic to keep her safe.

He set her down near a large sleigh bed made of ebony as well. Angels were carved in minute detail into the headboard, and Teresa ran her fingers over the one closest to her.

"You believe in angels."

"Yes, I must believe in them."

"Why?"

"The world would be too bleak a place without something good to make it worth saving." He stared at her, but she wasn't sure he was seeing her.

"Yet you believe in the Fall as well."

"Yes, but the reasons why are too deep for us to discuss tonight." Dominic reached for her.

She agreed silently and offered her lips to him. Tonight was about making love for the first time, not about the demons that haunted Dominic's past. Teresa was willing to wait to hear about those. He took her mouth gently, with patience and love. Pressing her body tight to him, she found out how much he wanted her—his erection was huge and she rubbed her mound against it. Teresa couldn't help but grin as Dominic moaned softly.

"You think torturing me is funny?" He growled as he slid his hands down to cup her ass. He lifted her so they fitted perfectly together and they both groaned.

"Dominic." An urgency came into her voice.

"Hush, love. Tonight we have all the time in the world to explore each other." He kissed her again.

This time, the kiss was a little more demanding and a little rougher. She loved it. As much as she wanted him to take her quickly and hard, she found she was enjoying him taking his time with her. She could feel him pulling the hem of her dress slowly up her legs. She gasped when his rough hands stroked the tops of her thighs left naked by her stockings. They drew a deep breath together as he lifted the dress up over her head.

She knew he had seen her naked before, but it was different tonight. They were going to have sex and she was afraid he wouldn't like what he saw. She dropped her gaze nervously. He lifted her chin and smiled at her.

Kneeling, he slid her shoes off. She tried to focus on his touch as he caressed her knees and her inner thighs. She waited for him to take her stockings off, but a shock rippled through her when Dominic placed a gentle kiss on her hip. Leaning forward, she put her hands on his shoulders and spread her legs a little more. He pulled her panties off and stared at her for a moment, his shoulders rising and falling with his breathing.

Throwing her head back, Teresa whimpered as he settled his mouth on her. She braced herself on him and he held her steady with one hand on her ass, using his other to reveal her clit.

He hummed his appreciation against her and she jumped as he licked her with his tongue. While he continued to kneel, he urged her backwards until her knees hit the edge of the bed and she sat suddenly.

"Relax and enjoy. I know I am."

He spoke against her and the warmth of his breath and the vibration of his voice made her wetter. He licked her slowly, savoring her.

"I knew you would taste good."

She leaned back on her elbows and watched him. His wide shoulders forced her legs farther apart, giving him better access. Dominic had a very talented tongue. She'd had several lovers go down on her before, but it had always felt like they didn't enjoy it and that they were only doing it to impress her. Dominic seemed to be enjoying every taste of her as he sucked harder. Moaning, Teresa dropped back onto the bed, becoming lost in the sensations he was creating.

A scrape of his teeth and her hips were arching off the bed. A flick of his tongue and she was moaning. The touch of his finger and she was begging. He was relentless. He slid his finger into her tight passage then pulled it out slowly. Her inner muscles clenched in disagreement. She wanted it to stay. When Dominic thrust it back in, the tip of his finger teased the perfect spot inside, causing her to tighten everywhere. The pressure kept building as he tasted, teased and licked every inch of her. Just when she thought her head would explode, he pushed two fingers inside her and Teresa came.

Dominic held her, caressing her back as she slowly stopped trembling. When she could finally speak, Teresa looked at him and said, "Please."

Through half-lowered eyelids, Teresa watched him strip. Dominic's black shirt went flying across the room and she admired his flat stomach. She knew he worked out often to maintain his athletic body, and she sent up a silent thank you to God for that. The light dusting of hair on his chest tapered down to a thin line leading to the waistband of his slacks. When he reached for the button, she sat up and gestured for him to come to her. He smiled and moved closer.

Reaching out, Teresa unbuttoned his slacks, brushing her hand over his erection as she pulled the zipper down carefully. Dominic groaned, but didn't try to stop her. His cock sprang free and she licked her lips. Teresa wanted to know how Dominic tasted. She'd been dreaming about this moment ever since they'd met, and having him standing in front of her. It was obvious he wasn't going to stop her from doing whatever she wanted, and his submitting turned her on even more.

She pushed his slacks down his lean hips, but she must not have been moving fast enough. Dominic shoved her hands away to finish pulling them off. Then he stood in front of her so she could drink in the beauty of his body.

She studied him from head to toe. There wasn't a flaw to be found, except for a curious, cross-shaped brand on his chest. She had never noticed it before.

Then she realized she had never seen him without a shirt on — even when he worked out, he wore a T-shirt. There were black markings along the tops of his shoulders and around his biceps. In the faint light, she couldn't make out what they were, but she wasn't too concerned. She wanted him pressed tightly against her and inside her.

She ran a finger lightly up and down his length, watching it jump and tremble with desire. She leaned forward and took him in her mouth. Licking him, Teresa swirled her tongue over the head of his shaft and enjoyed his salty taste. Teresa cupped his balls and he widened his stance as she rolled them around, then squeezed them while she milked his cock. Soon he was thrusting into her mouth, fast and deep. She knew his climax was getting close when his breathing quickened and he reached out to grab her shoulders. Instead of coming in her mouth, he pulled away from her.

"Someone's a little overdressed for the occasion."

He pushed her back on the bed before stripping her stockings off. Dominic flung her pretty lace bra behind him, and Teresa couldn't help but laugh. He pressed her back into the mattress as he crawled over her. She wrapped her arms around his neck while he moved his hips between her legs.

Dominic looked at her. "Do you want me to use a condom?"

Teresa shook her head, not worried about getting pregnant since she was on the pill, or catching something from Dominic. She trusted him to take care of her, and he wouldn't suggest not using a condom if there was a possibility he'd hurt her.

He sighed as he positioned the head of his cock at her opening then slowly sank in. It was like he had finally come home. She had been made for him. Staring into her eyes, he began to rock gently. Dominic didn't want it to end.

It was a perfect union between two souls, and Dominic realized she had been meant for him all along. His climax ripped through him, bringing with it an epiphany of how truly arrogant he'd been. He had never trusted that God knew what He was doing. Teresa cried out as her orgasm hit her.

He cuddled her close and vowed he would never let anyone hurt her. He couldn't afford to lose her. Dominic waited for her to fall asleep.

As they lay in bed he held her tight to him. Stroking her back, he reveled in the pleasant tiredness engulfing him from their lovemaking. She was asleep for now, but he didn't plan to let her sleep for too much longer.

A sudden restlessness struck him, and he slipped from the bed before walking to the French doors that led to the balcony. Dominic strolled out into the dark night and listened for the sounds of the forest around him. He had loved this place from the moment he stepped off the boat onto the land. The animals and the spirits of these bayous had spoken to him, making him welcome. Two hundred years ago, he'd been among the first white men to settle in this place, and didn't plan to ever leave it. The total silence of the night warned him things weren't right.

A voice intruded in his mind. *"Dominic, help me."*

He tried to ignore it. There was no way he was leaving Teresa alone and unprotected. Even in his own place of peace, evil could intrude—he wasn't going to take the chance of something happening to her.

"The pain is terrible and I want to die." The voice was ragged and exhausted. The fallen it belonged to had lived too long, and the madness and suffering it had endured made it yearn for death. A tug at Dominic's soul told him where the fallen could be found.

"It's difficult to ignore their pleas." Mika'il joined him, appearing out of thin air like usual.

"Is this what you hear?"

Mika'il nodded. "They're similar. They have the same hint of desperation."

"He's decided to make me his executioner." Dominic grimaced.

"Yes. He calls out to you for forgiveness and redemption when all you can give him is death."

"That's all I can give any of them."

Mika'il nodded. "That is the way it should be. Only the Father can forgive him, and if he doesn't ask Him for it, he'll never get it. We must humble ourselves to get forgiveness and most of us are too proud to ask for it."

Dominic nodded. He remembered how it had torn him apart to beg when he had been one of the most powerful creatures God had created. He also remembered the heartbreaking pain he'd felt when God had denied him and Mika'il had taken his wings. "There are times when I understand their madness. It's been hard at times to continue on."

"You are stronger than they are, Dominic. All of the Enforcers are. You are the ones who have found a way to survive in this mortal world without hurting anyone else."

Teresa murmured, and Mika'il smiled at him. "You should go back inside. She'll be waking up any moment and you don't want her to see us talking together."

Dominic returned, then slid into bed. Pulling her into his arms, he warmed his cold soul with her body and love.

Chapter Five

The next morning, Dominic picked Teresa up then carried her into the bathroom, waking her up with the pulsing warmth of the shower. He smiled as she gasped with pleasure when the water hit her. She leaned against him as he held the massaging showerhead between her legs. He fondled her breast, tweaking her nipple, tugging and squeezing. Dominic lifted Teresa's head from where it lay on his shoulder, then he kissed her. He drove his tongue into her mouth to stroke hers with passion. He wedged his leg between hers, grinding his erection into her hip.

Teresa began to move and he groaned. Her soft skin against him built the pulsating pressure higher and higher. He hung the showerhead up so that the water beat down on both of them. After grabbing the soap, he lathered his hands before running them over her body. He stroked, teased and played with every part of her. The torture continued as he knelt to wash her legs. She cried out when he reached her clit to run his fingers across the hard nub.

"Dominic," she moaned.

He pressed her against the shower wall, then lifted her up. Teresa wrapped her legs around him. He kept one arm around her waist and lowered her down onto him, loving the tightness as her inner muscles gloved him tightly. He pulled out then thrust in again. Bracing one hand on the tiles beside her, he set a fast pace. He rode her hard, loving the wetness of her pussy. Teresa slid her hands smoothly over his skin and increased his pleasure.

He tilted her hips slightly so the head of his cock could scrape against her sweet spot. She screamed as her orgasm rocketed through her. Dominic's climax exploded and he bit the tendon on her shoulder, crying out as he filled her emptiness with his wet heat.

While she stood limply, he washed them both. He turned the water off before helping her out of the shower and gently toweling her dry. He took her into his bedroom, where a clean set of clothes was waiting for her. She stared down at the clothing then looked at him.

"I picked them up for you yesterday."

"You were that sure of me?"

"I hoped you would stay the night, but it wouldn't have mattered if you didn't. It would have happened eventually. I just couldn't wait anymore." He pulled some clothes out of his closet. "I'll drop you off at the bookstore before I head to the club. Will you join me for lunch?"

He watched her dress as he did, making sure she didn't see his back. Teresa would want to know what the tattoo meant, and he didn't have time to explain it to her. She caught him unaware, though, when she walked up to him and traced the cross branded into his chest.

"What's this for?"

He winced. "A group of friends and I received them to remind us about the past."

"What kind of past did you have?"

He glanced at his watch. "I promise to tell you soon."

"All right." She didn't ask any more questions, just continued to get dressed.

He knew he had never told her much about his life, but he could never think of the best way to explain that he was a fallen angel and had lived for centuries. There never seemed to be a good time to bring it up in conversation, but he did know he had to tell her soon.

Terrance had the car waiting for them. Dominic helped Teresa into the vehicle, holding her hand while they rode into the city. When they pulled up in front of her store, Dominic climbed out, then, after she had joined him on the sidewalk, he kissed her.

"I'll stop by around one to take you out to lunch, okay?" he murmured against her lips.

"That'll be fine." She went to the door then turned to wave.

He smiled at her. Glancing down the street, he couldn't see anything out of place, but there was an uneasy feeling about the neighborhood. He wasn't sure if Delacourte was hanging around, but he wasn't going to give him easy access to her.

"Terrance, after you drop me off, I want you to come back here and just keep an eye on things. I don't have a good feeling about leaving her alone today."

"Fine, sir. To tell you the truth, I was going to ask if I could do that. Something's not right around here, and my gut's telling me she needs to be careful."

* * * *

"*So she spent the night with him. An interesting development, but it doesn't change anything. She's still mine and I won't be letting her go.*"

"*She's scared of us. If you hadn't grabbed her, we might have gotten another chance, but now she won't let us near her.*"

"*I don't care. No one breaks up with me. I'm the one who does the leaving. She has to learn that.*"

"*What do we do now?*"

"*We wait a while and when their guard is down, we'll make our move.*"

Vincent moved down the street after he had watched Dominic drop Teresa off. No one looked at him twice, even though he was mumbling to himself.

* * * *

"Are you ready for lunch, love?" Dominic came into the bookstore. He had been ready for lunch from the second she'd left his side.

"One second." She finished unpacking a box. Grabbing her purse, she told her assistant she'd be back.

As they got into the car, she laughed. "Where are we going?"

"A little restaurant I found the other day. They serve great Cajun food."

When they arrived, they were seated in a cozy corner booth. They sat chatting about their day while they waited for their food to arrive. As he was taking his first bite, her hand slid up his thigh. Dominic stared at her in shock as she cupped the bulge in his pants. Teresa looked back at him with an innocent smile, but he saw the gleam in her eye.

Leaning over, he said, "Have I created a monster?"

"I don't know what you're talking about." She squeezed him lightly.

Biting back a groan, he spread his legs a little to give her better access. "This might not be a good thing. How am I supposed to get out of here without embarrassing myself?"

"I'm sure you can find a way." She stroked him while she took another forkful of salad.

He hurried up and ate while Teresa teased and played with him. She hadn't even eaten half her food before he stood up and gestured to the waiter.

"Put it on my tab." After grabbing her gently, he pulled her from the restaurant.

She was laughing the entire time as he glared at her.

"You think this is funny, huh? I'm just one big joke to you." He ruined his seriousness by winking at her. "Luckily, my house is close by."

Dominic and Teresa climbed into his car, and he told Terrance to drive them to Dominic's house. Once they were settled in the back seat, Dominic dragged Teresa onto his lap, then plundered her mouth. He got so lost in her kisses that he didn't even notice when the vehicle stopped. Terrance's knock on the window drew Dominic's attention, and he managed to get Teresa and himself out of the car, then onto the porch without completely letting go of her.

He didn't wait for the bedroom. Slamming his front door shut, Dominic pulled her into his arms and kissed her again. He tried to take her breath away with each stroke of his tongue and nibble of his teeth. Teresa struggled with the buttons on his shirt while he unsnapped her pants. Once she got her fingers to work for her, she pulled his shirt off as he pushed her clothes down. She stepped out of them while he stripped his off. After pushing her against the wall,

Dominic wrapped one of her legs around his hip, then slid his fingers in between her legs to test how wet she was.

"Have you been this way all day?"

Teresa nodded, then leaned her head back while he eased his shaft inside her. Dominic was thrilled that Teresa didn't want him to use condoms.

Dominic thrust hard and fast. There wouldn't be gentle touches or long lovemaking this time. She had primed him with her caresses at the restaurant. He set a quick pace and, a few breathless minutes later, they both yelled as their orgasms ripped through them.

He lowered her leg, but held her tight to him. Dominic let the wall support them because his legs felt like limp noodles. He kissed her softly and whispered words in a low voice, even though he knew she couldn't understand them.

After a few minutes, he straightened up and said, "I think we need to clean up and head back to work."

She agreed and they made their way upstairs to his bathroom. After the shower, they dressed and Dominic had Terrance drive them back to Teresa's store.

"I met a new friend and we're getting together at your club around nine. Can you have a table reserved for us?" she asked, leaning in through the window after climbing out of the car.

"Sure, sweetheart. Anything for you." He couldn't help but feel a twinge of jealousy. He really hoped her new friend wasn't male. He told Terrance to take him to the club.

Randy was waiting for him when he returned.

"Hey, boss. I talked to the *oungan*. He said his mother would be happy to talk to you. His mother is a very powerful *mambo* – or priestess, as you would call her – but it has to be tomorrow."

"Fine. Tomorrow will be fine. Thanks, Randy. Oh, could you put a reserved sign out on nine? Teresa is coming with a friend tonight and I want her to have a good table."

"Sure, boss."

* * * *

Dominic felt a tug on his soul when Teresa came into the club. What worried him was the feel of another fallen that had arrived at the same time, though there wasn't despair in the mental touch, like there would have been if the fallen had turned to madness. He would have to keep track of the pull and see what developed, but right now, he had to greet his woman.

A knock sounded on the door as he stood up. After Dominic gave permission to come in, Randy stuck his head around the edge of it.

"Your girl's here, boss. Something must have happened last night because you're both smiling."

Dominic shook his head at Randy's cheeky grin. "Thanks for letting me know, but whatever happened is between her and me."

As he made his way out to the front of the club, he scanned the crowd, just double-checking for any trouble. He went to table nine where Teresa sat with her friend. He couldn't stop his snort of disbelief – who would have thought Teresa's new friend would have been another fallen? That was where the pull had come from. The brunette's gaze jerked up to meet his and an ironic smile crossed her face.

"Dominic, I'm glad you could join us." Teresa jumped up and threw her arms around him.

As he hugged her close, he studied the fallen over her head. There wasn't any hint of darkness in her blue eyes—he would have taken Teresa away at that moment if there had been any. Yet there wasn't any sign of her being an Enforcer either. Her low-cut shirt bared a great deal of her chest and there wasn't a brand to be seen. He kissed Teresa and smiled at her.

"I've been missing you all day, love."

The brunette stood and offered her hand. "Danielle Weston. I believe we have a mutual friend, Mika'il."

"Yes, I believe we do. It's nice meeting you, Miss Weston."

"Please, call me Danielle. You have a nice club here, Dominic. A very fitting name, I would think."

"I thought it was appropriate." He could tell the undercurrents racing between him and Danielle puzzled Teresa. "How did you two meet, anyway?"

"I stopped by her bookstore to look for a guide book. She was being accosted by some strange man and I interrupted before anything could happen."

Dominic looked at Teresa. "Was it Delacourte? Why didn't you tell me?"

"Yes, it was and I guess my mind was on other things last night. He didn't do anything but threaten me. I told him I didn't want to see him anymore and he told me no one broke up with him. That he was the one who did the leaving and I would regret having done it." She shrugged. "I was scared, but Danielle came in before he could do anything to me."

He glanced at Danielle. "Thank you for helping out. I know you didn't have to."

"It wasn't for you. I did it for her. That man is creepy and you might want to find him before he does anything else. Something isn't right about him."

"I know. We're working on finding out what we can do. Right now, I would like to dance with you, Teresa. It's been so very long since I held you in my arms."

She laughed. "It's only been five hours."

"It felt like a long time."

Danielle waved them to the dance floor, saying she was going to get a drink.

It was a little later when Dominic heard the call of another fallen—the same one who had tried to contact him last night. He rubbed his forehead and tried to block him out.

"It's exhausting at times," Danielle commented as she moved to stand by his side.

"What is?"

"To try to block out their voices when you don't want to hear them."

He glanced at her. "Whose voices?"

"The unrepentant ones."

"How can you hear them? You're not an Enforcer."

"I'm neither prey nor predator, but that doesn't mean I can't hear them. It doesn't mean I can't release them from their pain. It just means I choose not to."

"Can you be that cruel?" He turned to check on Teresa, who was sitting at the table talking to Randy.

"Cruel because I choose not to end their suffering and pain? Maybe you have to convince yourself you're doing something good in the world. You're ridding it of monsters, but I see it as playing God. We got in trouble once for wanting to be like Him. I'm not about to make the same mistake again."

She had a point. He pulled a card from his pocket. "Even though I'm sure you can handle anything that comes your way, here's my card in case you need me."

Danielle took it and the card disappeared as she grinned up at him. "I think Mika'il's been holding out on you Enforcers. He hasn't been telling you the whole truth."

"You're right. I think the cagey bastard likes to keep us guessing."

They laughed and Teresa thought how perfect they looked together. Both were tall and beautiful with startling blue eyes, with the same expression in them. It was as if old souls looked out onto a world they had seen too much of. They made a wonderful couple.

"I'm glad you and the boss man finally got together, Teresa," Randy said as he slid her drink over to her. "He's been panting after you for years. I never thought he'd make a move on you."

"I guess I never thought about the fact he might want me."

"It always amazed me. You seemed so oblivious at times. The man's tongue would hang out of his mouth when you walked by." Randy laughed. "You're good for him. You make him laugh and enjoy life. Before you met, he was pretty unhappy, I think. Don't get me wrong—he's the best boss I've ever had. He really cares about his employees, but I had a feeling something was missing. It was you."

She smiled at the club manager. "Thanks, Randy. He does seem happier." She gestured to Dominic and Danielle. "What do you suppose they're talking about?"

"Nothing important, I'm sure. He'll be back to get you in a moment."

Dominic kissed Danielle's hand before turning to come toward them. There was a strained look on his face. He stood at the table, looking down at Teresa. Dominic wore a tired smile.

"Are you ready to go, Teresa?"

She didn't ask why he wanted to go, and what Danielle was going to do. Waving goodbye to Danielle, she grabbed her purse, then they headed out. His car was waiting at the curb for them. After they got in, he looked at her.

"Where do you want to go? My house, your apartment or out to Paisible?"

"Why don't we go back to your town house? We can sleep a little later tomorrow because we won't have the long drive into the city," Teresa suggested.

Dominic nodded, then told Terrance before turning back to Teresa. "Sounds good. We have a meeting with a *mambo* or Vodou priestess tomorrow night. Randy set it up for us."

"Why?"

"My instincts are telling me that Delacourte is messed up in the dark side of Vodou. We'll need expert help if we're going to get him to leave you alone." Dominic rested his hand on Teresa's thigh.

"Vodou scares me." She shivered at the thought of going to a Vodou priestess for help.

"Only because you don't understand it. Like every religion, it has its good and bad side."

"I'm willing to try to keep an open mind."

"That's all I can ask."

After Terrance had dropped them off, they walked into his house and, without turning on any lights, he led the way to his bedroom. Both of them stripped, scattering their clothes on the floor, then Dominic fell face first onto the bed. Teresa noticed the dark markings on his back, but there wasn't enough light to make them out. She straddled his butt to start rubbing his shoulders. Tension had knotted his muscles.

"You're so tense. What are you worried about?"

He groaned as she worked a particularly hard knot loose. "Mostly a problem at work. It'll fix itself at some point."

"I hope you're not overly worried about Vincent. I think he'll lose interest in me when he finds another woman." Teresa stayed focused on the massage.

"Maybe, but I've learned the hard way it's better to be prepared for any emergency."

She slid her hands from his shoulders to his shoulder blades. There were two thin vertical scars on his skin, where the markings originated. He stiffened when she ran her fingers over the scars.

"Another reminder of the past?"

"Yes."

She chose not to ask because Dominic would tell her when he was ready. Teresa moved to his feet and worked her way up, taking her time with each muscle. When she squeezed his firm ass, his groan had a slight hitch to it. She slid her fingers down between his legs and lightly stroked his balls before urging him to roll over and her mouth watered when she saw his erection.

"I still can't believe this is for me." Teresa grasped his cock softly.

"Only you can get me hard just from the sound of your voice, love. It's all for you."

"Maybe I should call you for a little phone sex one day. See just how far my voice can take you." Palming his balls with her other hand, she rolled them with her fingers.

"Do whatever you want."

It was obvious he wasn't interested in talking anymore. "Oh, I will."

She lay down between his legs to lick him. When Teresa blew a puff of air on his wet skin, Dominic lifted his hips. She tasted the pre-cum pearling at the tip. Arching his back, he tried to push deeper into her mouth, but she wouldn't let him.

"Please, Teresa," he begged.

She finally granted his plea and slid him deep into her mouth. She sucked him, enjoying every taste and texture. His groans told her he loved it as well. His head was tossing from side to side. Right before he came, he pulled away from her. Rolling Teresa over, he took her, and she welcomed him in.

"We're going over the edge together. I won't go there alone anymore." His voice was harsh.

They came together and Teresa saw a glimpse of Heaven, or at least what she thought it would look like.

* * * *

On the other side of New Orleans, Vincent Delacourte stood in Chalmette Cemetery staring at the shifty little *bòkò* he had contacted. The sorcerer had performed a ceremony earlier without Vincent being present, not wanting to reveal his secrets and spells.

"Now, you're paying me one hundred thousand dollars for *voye lamò*. Are you sure you want this person dead?" The *bòkò* glared at him.

"Yes, I'm sure. She's denied my right to own her. She has forfeited her life."

The *bòkò* shrugged, and Vincent knew the bastard didn't care as long as he got his money. "Okay. I've performed the ceremony and cast the spell. The dead will find her soon."

Vincent pointed to the briefcase he had set on the ground beside the tombstone. "There's your money."

"It was nice doing business with you. I hope you achieve what you've set out to do."

Chapter Six

Dominic had just finished paying for breakfast when Danielle arrived at the bakery. She walked up before gesturing to him.

"I need to talk to you for a moment." She smiled at Teresa. "I won't keep him long."

Teresa nodded and walked toward St Mary's Church down the street. The other two watched her for a few minutes before Danielle turned to Dominic.

"There was a killing on the east side of the city last night. We both know who did it. You need to deal with this right now before any more die."

"I can't leave her alone."

"You do what you have to do to keep her safe, but you also have another job—to keep this city clean from the unrepentant. You can't continue to ignore him. Mika'il isn't inclined to send another Enforcer to help you out right now."

"I'm working on it."

"Work faster."

* * * *

Teresa ducked into the soothing coolness of the old church. There were signs of neglect—the wooden pews didn't shine with fresh wood wax and the altar cloths were frayed on the edges. She sat down in one of the side pews and sighed. The noises from the street were dulled into a distant rumble and she began to feel a tranquility settle into her, a peace she hadn't felt since she had woken up in Dominic's arms. She imagined Danielle and Dominic standing side by side and she thought about how perfect they looked together. She bit back a sob.

"There now, child. What are you crying for?" An elderly voice came from the shadows behind her.

Gasping, she whirled around. Tears blurred her eyes and she wiped them with her hand.

"Take my 'kerchief, child. A pretty girl like you shouldn't be doing any crying." A white handkerchief appeared in the shaky grip of a wrinkled hand.

She couldn't tell if the speaker was male or female. The voice sounded like its owner had a two pack of cigarettes daily habit with a hint of a whiskey accent. The shadows bathed the hand in darkness so all she could see were the wrinkles—she couldn't even get a shape of the body out of the blackness. The handkerchief fluttered at her, so she took it and dried her tears.

"I'm sorry for disrupting your prayer time," she said.

"Don't be sorry, child. The Lord and I have had many talks before you got here and we'll have a bunch more after you leave. It's good to see someone use this old church. It hurts to see God's places forgotten." The stranger was silent for a moment.

Teresa held out the scrap of linen. "Thank you for the handkerchief. I'd better be going."

"Oh no, you stay seated, little child. I heard your sigh when you came on in here. There's no better place to lighten a load than this. Lay your problems down at His feet, child, and the world will be a brighter place."

She hesitated.

"Do you believe in Him, child?" The voice was compelling.

"Yes, I do." She was surprised at the conviction in her voice and soul.

"Then tell me your problems and He'll listen in. Maybe between the two of us, we can help you."

"I'm not sure where to begin." Teresa wrapped the linen square around her fingers. "It's all gotten complicated."

"And dangerous." The voice added. "Start with your man, child."

She jerked in surprise. "How did you know it was a man?"

A husky chuckle dashed across the pews. "When a pretty child like you cries, there's always a man involved. Tell me what the rat's done."

"He isn't a rat."

"Then why are you crying?"

"He says he loves me." Tears welled again.

"Oh well, that would make me cry too. Is he mean?" There was a touch of concern in the listener's voice.

"No."

"Does he hit you or say things to hurt you?"

"No." Teresa shook her head.

"Does he run around on you?"

"No."

Her interrogator snorted. "Then you're right not to want him, child. He sounds too perfect to be true."

"He is perfect. That's why I'm crying. A person as wonderful as he is can't really be in love with me. I've seen him with another woman who would be just right for him." She wiped her eyes again.

"And why not? There's nothing wrong with you, except maybe you cry too much."

She laughed. Dominic always said she was a marshmallow inside. "He loves me, but I can't help thinking that it's just because I was there."

"Ah, opportunity."

She nodded.

"Do you really believe he slept with you because he was bored and you were available? Do you think he's the type of man who would use you, then leave when someone better came along? Would he tell you he loved you just to get you in bed with him?"

She shrugged. "No, he's not that type of person."

"Why do you doubt his feelings?"

"We've been friends since I moved here. In fact, he was the first person I met. We ran into each other at a coffee shop. I wasn't paying attention to where I was going. He stood there, staring at me in shock with chicory coffee dripping down the front of his cashmere coat. I was mortified."

"That's what the man gets for wearing cashmere in New Orleans." Another rough chuckle. "I still don't see why he would sleep with you out of boredom. There are plenty of women he could sleep with without screwing up a wonderful friendship."

"I know. He says he loves me, but I can't bring myself to tell him I love him back."

"It sounds like you're doubting yourself. There shouldn't be any doubt in your mind about his love. He's risking more than you know by loving you."

Teresa sat straight as the thought hit her. "You're right. I am doubting my own love for him. I've wanted him since I first saw him. How do I know it's not lust?"

"Lust and love are two sides of the same coin, but lust doesn't make your day brighter by knowing he's alive. Lust burns out fast, but love grows slowly. Think about all those moments you spent together. How you've laughed together and cried together. Imagine what your life would be without him. Do you doubt you love him?"

Teresa couldn't imagine how empty and lonely her life would be without Dominic in it. She didn't want to imagine it. She did love him and, by admitting it to herself, she could finally say it to him.

Dominic stood in the doorway of the church. "Teresa, are you in there?"

"Yes, I'll be right there." She turned to the figure behind her. "Thank you so much for listening to me whine."

"You're welcome, child. Now go to your man and tell him you love him."

Teresa jumped up and ran to where Dominic was standing. She threw herself into his arms and kissed him deeply.

As the couple left the church, the stooped shadow straightened until it was standing tall. A glint of silver came from his eyes and a rustle of feathers was heard.

"Things are only going to get worse, Father. I wonder why we must test them like this." His voice echoed in the empty church as a gust of warm wind caressed his cheek and he nodded.

* * * *

Later that night, Dominic and Teresa went to the home of the *mambo* Randy had told them about. Teresa felt goose bumps on her arms as the door opened to reveal a tiny black woman. It was hard to tell her age because her skin was smooth and unlined. She smiled at them and gestured for them to come in.

Dominic handed her some packages. "If you have anyone in need in your community, I hope these will help them."

"Thank you, child. Gifts given with a good heart are always welcomed. Will you please sit down?" Before they settled in, the old woman asked Teresa to let the woman's daughter know they would require some refreshments. They watched her head toward the kitchen. Once she was out of sight, the woman turned to Dominic and said, "My son is an *oungan* and he says that you might have trouble with a spirit possession."

"Yes, I'm afraid that Vincent Delacourte has messed with spirits he shouldn't have. When I'm close to him, I feel like there are two spirits inhabiting his body. His original one is weakening and should soon be dead. The other spirit is strong. Somehow it has become obsessed with Teresa. I'm not sure if it's a spirit possession or if it's just a split personality, but he's going mad."

"Just like all religions, Vodou can be twisted for personal use," the old priestess told him. She clasped him tightly with wrinkled hands. "Your woman is in terrible trouble if an evil spirit has focused on her. If something isn't done, not even one of God's fallen can help her."

Fear rushed through him. He had never been so scared, because there hadn't been anything he couldn't fight. His power as an Enforcer kept him from being vulnerable to mortal problems, but he rarely dealt with mortal spirits and mortal magic. It was a different form that he wasn't equipped to deal with.

"Vincent Delacourte is a dangerous man. He was ambitious before he meddled in secrets he should have stayed clear of. Now the spirit possessing him will kill to keep his body. His soul is struggling to break free, but he's losing the fight." The *mambo* stared at him. "Vodou isn't the religion people look for when they come to New Orleans. It isn't about zombies and curses, even though we do have those components within it. Don't turn your back on the true lesson in Vodou."

"Which is?"

"There are spirits of our ancestors all around us. They can help us if we are respectful and ask them nicely. Everything in the world has a spirit. We must remember that."

Dominic's phone rang. He was reluctant to answer it. He knew their time with the *mambo* was limited — he could feel her spirit's grip on the mortal world loosening.

Teresa came into the room carrying a tray with cups and a coffee pot on it. She set it down in front of the woman and sat on the couch next to her.

"Answer your phone, angel. I need to talk to your woman." The lady's laugh was deep and full as she and Teresa watched Dominic move away. Grinning at her, the *mambo* said, "That man should be illegal. The thoughts he puts into a good woman's mind just by breathing."

Teresa couldn't argue—she had often thought the same thing. Now that she and Dominic were lovers, she knew he would be even more dangerous if women could see him naked.

"He's a good man. You should never be afraid he'll leave you. You're connected by your hearts."

The old woman took Teresa's hand and held it between hers. The *mambo* stared into her eyes. She felt the sensation of slipping behind a veil and it seemed as if the priestess was studying her soul.

"Delacourte hasn't marked you yet. That is a good sign. You might be able to stay away from him and be safe." The woman looked to where Dominic was standing. "Your man is special."

"Yes, he is."

"He's more than just an extraordinary man, child. There's something in his soul that makes him far more superior to mere mortals." The priestess's eyes widened in shock. "You know this."

Teresa couldn't speak, but she nodded. Though they had never talked about it, she had always understood there was a difference between Dominic and everyone else. It was a difference that had nothing to do with his good looks or his overwhelming wealth. She had tried to explain it to one of her friends, but she hadn't been able to describe the timeless feel he gave her with each moment they spent together.

"He has lived forever, this fallen angel of yours. He has seen friends and lovers die while he endures. It is a suffering brought on himself by inciting the wrath of God. Repenting did no good and his wings were taken from him. Time will tell if you truly believe me, but there's something about you. You were meant for him. From the moment of your birth, God ordained that you and this angel should be lovers." The *mambo* flashed her a smile.

A twinge of recognition flared deep inside Teresa from the woman's words. Dominic came back into the room and the *mambo* let go of her hands. He eyed them with suspicion, like they had been plotting against him.

"I'll ask among my followers to see who might know Delacourte or what *bòkò* has been helping him. Don't be arrogant enough to believe you can handle him, Dominic. Even you need help from time to time."

"There isn't anyone else to call."

"When the time comes, help will be available. Remember love is strong enough to defeat the most powerful of evils and sometimes forgiveness must be earned." She smiled at him.

Teresa saw him nod at the old woman as Dominic escorted Teresa to the front door. She looked back as they were leaving the house. The *mambo* was watching them with tears streaming down her face.

"Why is she crying?" she asked Dominic when they stopped by his car.

Shrugging, he opened the door for her. "Maybe it was the first time she has ever met an angel."

Somehow she knew he wasn't paying her a compliment. "Are you an angel?" Teresa needed to hear it from Dominic to confirm her beliefs.

Dominic turned to look at her. He rested his arm on the steering wheel and hesitated. "Do you really want me to answer that?"

"Yes, and I want you to tell me the truth, not what you think I want to hear." She put her hand on his arm. "I've finally admitted to myself that I love you and there can't be any more secrets between us."

He studied her, and in his blue eyes, she saw the usual arrogance, but for the first time, an unrelenting sadness as well. She wondered if it had always been there.

He nodded. "All right. We'll head to Paisible and I'll try to explain my past to you. I just hope you can believe it."

"Thank you."

Driving to his house, Dominic couldn't believe he was going to tell the woman he loved about his worst mistake. He wondered what Teresa and the *mambo* had talked about while he'd been on the phone.

They were silent as they traveled. He wasn't sure what he was going to say, but he knew it had to be done. Maybe she wouldn't think he was crazy. He pulled into the driveway then parked. Leading her up to the door, he stopped. The lights were on inside so the glass panes caught his attention.

Dominic pointed at it. "Look closely at the people kneeling on the mountain. Do any of them look familiar?"

She studied the people before pointing at the figure closest to the angel. "That one looks like you."

"The people in the leaded glass are William Bradford, Celeste Young and me. We are Enforcers, but more than that, we are all fallen angels. The archangel Mika'il is the one denying us entrance into Heaven."

"He looks so sad," she murmured.

Dominic nodded. "I think he hurt as much as we did when we were thrown out. We were his brethren and, even though we rebelled, he still loved us."

"Aren't fallen angels supposed to be evil?" She looked at him with a bit of suspicion in her eyes.

He opened the door for her before ushering her in. After dropping his keys and her purse on the table next to the door, he led her to the study where he waved her to the couch. He went to the side bar then poured a glass of whiskey for himself.

"It's complicated. There are two factions of fallen angels. On one side are the Enforcers. We are the fallen who repented and asked for God's forgiveness. On the other side are the unrepentant, as Danielle calls them. They are the ones who will never ask God for forgiveness because they don't think they've done anything wrong. They proudly followed Lucifer when he spoke of rebellion and being better than mortals."

"Wait — Danielle is a fallen angel as well?"

"Yes. Only she's one of the few fallen who aren't one or the other. She isn't an Enforcer or an unrepentant. She tries to live as normal a life as possible." He shrugged. "I don't know how she ended up coming into your store when you needed her. Maybe it was part of a plan God has for all of us."

"So only the unrepentant are evil?"

"Yes. As an Enforcer, I'm charged with trying to keep them under control. When they reach a certain level of evil, they start killing and destroying mortals. At that time, an Enforcer steps in and takes them. In reality, we can't kill them. I don't have the power to punish them for their crimes. There are some Enforcers who are given a special power — they're called Avengers. My friend William is one. He takes the unrepentants' immortality. He loops their memories, so that they will always remember the glory of what they once were. It tends to drive them crazy and they end their days in a mental institute."

She flinched. "That seems rather harsh."

"It might seem to you to be cruel, but I've seen what these fallen can do. I've seen the lives they destroy and I'm willing to be cruel to end their reign of terror."

"Aren't you afraid of Lucifer?"

Dominic shook his head. "Most of the time, Lucifer stays out of everyday affairs. He's too busy plotting the next rebellion where he thinks he'll take over Heaven. He hasn't quite grasped the concept of repentance. Also, he doesn't normally lower himself to talk to any of us."

"Why did you do it?" She curled up on the couch as she stared at him.

After going to the French doors, he opened them, letting the humid air of the bayous drift into the room. "I've thought about it for centuries. I think the one thing all the fallen have in common is a very huge ego. We have the arrogance to believe we know better than God. Crazy, isn't it? That anyone—mortal or angel—knows better than God, the being that created the universe. The being that sees the beginning and the end of time. We rebelled. What we thought we would do when we took over Heaven, I don't know. We were thrown out of Heaven and found out how unprepared for mortal life we were. Some of us fell to our knees, begging forgiveness from our Father. Imagine our surprise when God didn't give us forgiveness. Instead He sent Mika'il to take our wings and brand us."

"The cross-shaped brand on your chest and the scars on your shoulders."

"The brand marks me as an Enforcer. The scars are where my wings used to be. I still feel them at times—the way they used to hang from my back. I remember the way it felt to fly. The sheer glory of moving through the sky." A tear made its way down his cheek.

She stood then went to him. Wrapping her arms around his waist, she leaned her forehead against his back. Sighing, Dominic covered her hands with his.

"Why haven't you run out of the house screaming yet? Is it possible you really believe me?" he asked.

"The *mambo* told me. Even if she hadn't, I wouldn't have been surprised. I've known you were different from the moment I met you. There was this otherworldly feel about you. I always had the feeling that you've lived far longer than I've been alive. There's no madness in you, my love. There's only pain and loneliness. I hope I can help with both of those."

He turned before pulling her tight to him. Burying his face in her hair, he breathed deep. A sense of contentment filled him as he cupped her cheeks in his trembling hands and dropped gentle kisses all over her face. She smiled as he brushed his lips over hers. Sweeping her into his arms, he carried her to his bedroom.

He had her get the light switch as they entered. The illumination from the lamps fell on his bed. The angels carved in the ebony headboard were not the cute, winged creatures depicted in art. These angels were tall and beautiful, but there was desperation and a fierce anger on their faces.

Teresa shivered slightly as she looked at them. "How can you sleep with them looking down on you all night?"

He laughed. "I'm used to them. I used to be one of them."

"Why do they look like that?"

"We looked like that right before we fell." He shrugged. "I don't remember much about what things looked like before the Fall. I thought I would have this done to help me keep at least one memory alive."

He laid her down on the bed. After ripping his clothes off, he crawled over her. He quickly stripped her then sat beside her feet, massaging them and playing with her toes. She laughed as he ran his fingers over the arch of her foot. Teresa tried to jerk her foot away, but he held on. He moved up to her calves, stroking and teasing her with his hands and lips. Sighing, she spread her legs as he made his way to her inner thighs. He chuckled when she groaned in frustration as he skipped touching her pussy. He slid his hands up and licked her belly button. Without any effort, he flipped her onto her stomach then started massaging her shoulders. Dominic laughed as he lifted her to her hands and knees. He nudged her knees wider so he could fit between them. Laying her head on the pillow, she sighed when the head of his cock slid over her throbbing clit.

"You'll like this," he whispered as he thrust into her from behind.

Arching her back, Teresa cried out. Dominic put one hand on the mattress next to her head to support himself as he leaned over her. He reached under her with the other, and spread her nether lips to find her clit. Riding her slowly, he built up the tension until she was begging him to speed up. Dominic shifted his angle so the head of his shaft scraped against her sweet spot with each thrust. He pinched her clit and she came apart. Before she was finished climaxing, he pulled out of her, then turned her on her back. Dominic shoved back into her then rushed to bring her another orgasm before he took his pleasure. As her orgasm caused her to tremble in his arms, he came and tears rolled down his face as he shouted out her name.

* * * *

Teresa watched Dominic climb out of bed to walk over and open one of the doors leading out to his balcony. Resting his hand against the door frame, he stared down at the swirling river running along the edge of his property. A cool breeze blew in. She couldn't stand the picture of lonely weariness he made.

She slipped from under the sheet and padded over to him. The single lamp they had left on highlighted the tattoo on his shoulders. A pair of wings spread from his shoulder blades to the backs of his biceps. They were beautiful, and Teresa stroked them tenderly. They originated from the two vertical scars she had noticed earlier. As she traced them, Dominic shuddered.

"What are the wings for?"

He sighed. "Some would say they represent my supreme arrogance."

"You're arrogant, love, but these don't feel like that to me. They feel sad. They speak about pain and loss. What happened?"

With his head still bowed, he spoke quietly. "They serve to remind me of the glorious creature I once was. They also make me remember my fall from grace."

"How could He take your wings? It's like pulling the wings off butterflies." She slid her hands over his shoulders, following the markings to enfold him in her arms.

"You'll have to ask Mika'il. It was his job to take them. At times, I do think it hurt him far more than it did us." Her hands were clasped around his waist and he covered them with one of his own. "He took them so we would have nothing to mark us as different from the mortals we professed to hate."

"Why did you do it? Why rebel against the God who created and loved you?"

Dominic shook his head. "On nights like this when my heart aches, I wonder about it. Maybe it was jealousy. He loved us, but mortals were His true love. He couldn't stay away from you, even when you turned from Him and began to take Him for granted."

"Do you remember what Heaven was like?" As her question washed over him, Dominic trembled. She held him tighter, trying to soothe him with her presence.

"No, I can't. It's been too many centuries and too many lives. Heaven is a vague memory. The closest I get now is when I'm making love to you." Turning, he grabbed her and stared down into her eyes. "In your arms, I get a glimpse of what Heaven is like and I'm content. Being with you makes me happy, but no matter how happy I am with you, there's always going to be a part of my soul longing for my former home."

She felt a sense of loss. She had never thought she was greedy, but she wanted all of Dominic—heart, body and soul. She laughed at herself. The most beautiful and caring man in the world was hers and she wasn't happy because a tiny part of him would always yearn for something she couldn't give him. *Don't dwell on it, girl. He loves you and he's with you now. Every time he starts thinking about Heaven, take him there.*

"So I can give you a glimpse of Heaven, huh?" She pulled his head down to hers. "Then let's go there."

Dominic picked her up then carried her to the bed, devouring her lips as they went.

Chapter Seven

Teresa waved goodbye to Dominic before turning to head into her bookstore. A man bumped into her, spilling dirt down the front of her. She coughed as she breathed in some of it. The man mumbled an apology before running down the street. She tried to brush it off, but it clung to her clothes.

"Great," she mumbled. "Now I have to go change my clothes." She walked through the bookstore and waved at her clerk. "I'll be right back."

She coughed again as she went upstairs. After grabbing a glass, she poured some water to wash the taste of dirt out of her mouth. She smiled when she thought about telling Dominic what had happened. Who would have thought she would get dirt thrown on her in New Orleans, where she was more likely to get wet than dirty? As she pulled her shirt off, she got another lungful of dirt.

"Ugh. This is so gross." After checking out the fabric, she realized there was no way to save it, so she threw it out. Teresa turned on the TV while cleaning up. She paused when a special report came on.

"Another gruesome murder took place last night in the city. This is the third in as many days. The police have no leads and no idea how the victims are related. They do believe it is the same killer for all the murders. Police are asking the public to be extra cautious until the perpetrator is caught."

She shuddered. The thought of a killer stalking the streets of New Orleans made her glad that Dominic was with her most of the time. No one would try anything while he was there. She turned the TV off then headed down to the store after saying a prayer for the victims.

* * * *

"Damn, another murder." Dominic slammed his hand down on his desk. "I can't take the chance of something happening to Teresa while I take care of it."

"You're going to have to do something, friend." William said over the phone. "Mika'il isn't going to be happy that one of his Enforcers is falling down on the job."

"I know, but Terrance found a charm on Teresa's doorstep this morning when he dropped her off. My manager, Randy, told me it was a bad luck charm. Vincent isn't being obvious about what he wants or plans on doing. The charm wasn't going to do any harm to her. Maybe make her sick or have a run of bad luck, but somehow I think something worse is going to happen. I just don't know what and I can't prepare for it," Dominic admitted.

"It's hard realizing that your powers don't make you all-knowing and you're just as fallible as these mortals." William's voice held an exasperated hint of experience. "I'd like to come and help you out, but I can't leave Abby right now."

"Thanks for the offer, but you need to spend some time with your lady. She was a little shaky when I left."

"I know. If things get bad there, call me. I'll come anyway." Hearing Abby speak in the background had William saying, "I've got to go. I'm here for you, though, if you need me, even if I have to drag Abby down there with me."

"Thanks, and tell Abby hi." After hanging up, Dominic slumped in his chair. The feeling of impending danger hung over him like a cloud, but he didn't know where it was going to come from or whom it was going to hurt. All he did know was that he needed to take care of the fallen that was turning his city into a killing field.

Randy knocked on the door before coming in. He sat down across from Dominic and stared at him. "Maybe you'll want to come to one of our ceremonies. You need to get a feel for Vodou and what it can do. Unfortunately, you won't get much information about black magic from the people in the community — we don't like to talk about it. Superstitious lot that we are, we believe, if we talk about it, we'll bring it down on us."

"I don't expect you to give away any secrets, Randy. Maybe Vincent will show up at one of your ceremonies and I can talk to him. That should give me an idea of what he's got planned."

"I'll check with my *oungan* and make sure it's okay for you to come. I'll call you when I find out."

"Thanks, Randy. It's great of you to be willing to open your religion up to us."

"I think a lot of Teresa and you. If showing you my beliefs and religion can help you in any way, I'm willing to do it. Besides, I want to show you that Vodou isn't all about zombies and black magic. We don't worship the Devil and have orgies."

"I've met the Devil, Randy. He doesn't need anyone to worship him to make him think he's important. The creature has an ego bigger than the world," Dominic muttered distractedly.

Randy looked at him with a strange expression. "You don't sound like you're joking."

He stared at the wall behind Randy for a moment and thought about Lucifer then shook those dark memories out of his head. "I'm only repeating what I've heard said about him."

"Here are the receipts from last night." Randy was ready to change the subject.

"Thank goodness I have you. At least I know the club will keep running while I'm busy with Delacourte."

They spent the next couple of hours going over the ordering and by the time he left that night, Dominic was happy to know his club was running smoothly. He drove over to pick up Teresa for a late dinner. When she climbed in the car, he grinned at her, but her return smile wasn't nearly as bright as usual. He leaned over to brush her hair behind her ear.

"Hey, love, are you okay?"

"Just tired, I think. We haven't gotten a lot of sleep lately."

"I'm sorry." As much as Dominic loved having sex with Teresa, he didn't want to wear her out.

"I'm not complaining, but I was wondering if we could have dinner in tonight and just hang out. I don't feel like being around other people." She leaned her head against the headrest.

A fissure of alarm raced through him, but he managed to dismiss it. "Sure. I'll cook us dinner at my place."

"Wonderful." She sighed and closed her eyes.

She fell asleep on the short trip to his town house. After parking the car, Dominic carried Teresa inside. He made her comfortable on the couch before covering her with a blanket. He started getting dinner ready. When the table had been set, he went to wake her up. He leaned down and kissed her lightly on the lips. As Teresa opened her eyes, he saw a flash of yellow in them before she blinked and they went back to their usual violet. Instead of the sparkling joy he usually saw in them, they seemed to be dimmer.

"Dinner's ready, love." He helped her sit up, then they walked arm in arm to the kitchen where he had set a cozy little private dinner table. He served her a portion of the shrimp gumbo he had made before pouring her a glass of wine.

He watched her push her food around for thirty minutes before he stood and took her plate. "You're not hungry, so we might as well put the food away and go into the living room. Do you want to watch TV or a movie?"

She shrugged. "The news should be on about now. I'd like to see if they found any leads on those murders."

Dominic didn't want to hear about them, knowing he could stop them, but every instinct he had told him he couldn't leave Teresa alone or something might happen to her. He sent her to the couch while he put the leftovers away, then entered the room in time to hear the news anchor tell everyone there was nothing new to report. Of course, they didn't know anything new. The fallen doing the killing wouldn't leave clues for mortals to find because he wanted Dominic to come and end his suffering. After settling on the couch, Teresa snuggled close to him. Dominic wouldn't worry about it tonight, wanting Teresa to rest and get better.

His phone rang, and he answered it. "Yes?"

"Hey, boss. There's a ceremony happening tomorrow night and the *oungan* said it was all right for you to come."

"Thanks."

"No problem."

After hanging up, Dominic looked down at Teresa. She hadn't moved one inch while he was talking to Randy. Sighing, he picked her up then took her to bed before removing her clothes quietly and pulling the blankets up over her.

He kissed her cheek, then whispered, "Sweet dreams, love."

* * * *

Dominic had been pacing for hours when the voice broke into his thoughts.

"Why won't you help me?"

Trying to ignore the plea, Dominic wasn't an Enforcer right then, he was a man in love and willing to forsake any promise to keep the woman he loved safe.

"How many more must die before you keep your promise? Or have you managed to fool them all these years? Did you never intend to keep your promise when it came down to choosing something important to you? It's a choice between

keeping your promise to God, or keeping a mere mortal alive."

Dominic didn't answer. He knew he wasn't doing his job. For the first time in the centuries he had lived, he found a conflict developing between his heart and his mind. His mind told him that in the grand scheme of the world, one mortal's life wasn't worth allowing a fallen to continue killing. By allowing the fallen to kill, he was in many ways playing God, deciding which mortal was worth saving and which ones weren't. His heart told him that he had to save Teresa at all costs. Somehow he knew that keeping her alive and with him would save his soul in a way that God's forgiveness never would.

"Trust me, this won't blow over. I'll keep killing them until you stop me. I want this all to end, Enforcer. I've lived too long and done too much. I can't take it anymore."

"I can't either, but I have a chance to make my life better. Why should I let you ruin it for me?"

"It was the same selfishness that got us all where we are today, Enforcer. I left you another gift. See how far your conscience can take you."

A door slammed in his mind and he couldn't find a link to the other fallen. Dominic knew what the police would discover tomorrow. He went into the bedroom, then slipped into bed with Teresa, pulled her tight against him and tried to drown out his guilty conscience.

* * * *

Danielle joined them at the café the next morning. She didn't say a word about the newest murder, but he knew she had heard about it. When Teresa went to the bathroom, he turned on her.

"What don't you say something?"

She shrugged. "It isn't my place. I can't yell at you for not getting rid of him when I won't do it myself."

"It scares me the way I need her and the way I can overlook every promise I made just because I want to keep her safe." He shook his head.

"Maybe you're supposed to make a choice." Danielle twisted a napkin between her fingers.

"What do you mean?"

"I don't know. Who's to say what God wants you to do? Mika'il won't let you in on whatever secrets the Father has given him."

Teresa returned and they got ready to go. Dominic noticed that she didn't eat much of her breakfast. He gestured for the food to be boxed then he handed it to her. Danielle told them she would see them at the bookstore.

"Try to eat it later. You didn't eat much for dinner either." He dropped her off at the bookstore. Danielle arrived just as Dominic was leaving.

"I'll just hang out here for a while. My business meeting isn't until this afternoon."

"Thank you." Dominic was reassured that someone was watching out for her.

"She's my friend as well."

After Dominic had left, Teresa smiled at Danielle. "You're here to take care of me in case Vincent tries anything, right?"

"I'm here to be a friend. I'm not sure what Dominic thinks Vincent will do, but he's afraid the man will do something to you because you turned him down. See, men like Vincent aren't used to being turned down like that. Most of the time, they would just give up and move on to the next woman. Yet there seems to be something different about him. Dominic and I both

sense there is another spirit living within his body."
Danielle set her purse on the counter.

"Like possession?"

"Yes, but not the demon kind. That kind we can
handle. It's the spirit of another mortal and we've
never dealt with that before. I can't say for sure that
our powers will be able to defeat it."

Not wanting to talk about Vincent, Teresa decided to
change the subject to something she did want to know
about.

"What's it like being a fallen angel?" Teresa asked as
she put books away.

Danielle took a while to answer. "There are times
when I think being a fallen is fine. All the things I can
do with my powers and all the centuries I spent
learning about the world. Sometimes, though, when I
think about Heaven, I wonder what the hell I was
thinking all those centuries ago. I think that most of us
rethink our rebellion after a couple of thousand
years."

"What's the difference between what you do and
what Dominic does?" Teresa turned to look at
Danielle.

"He's an Enforcer. He hunts down the unrepentant
who turn against the mortals. I stay out of the fight. I
repented, but God chose not to hear me. I decided I
wasn't going to help Him fight the bad guys either.
No point in damaging my psyche even more for
someone who didn't care enough about me to forgive
me."

"How do you know He doesn't love you? He didn't
destroy you, did He?"

Danielle glanced out of the front window as she
seemed to be thinking. "No, He didn't, but He did
take our wings and leave us in this world where we

will always be different. There are parts of me that still pray to Him and hope He will hear, but most of me knows there's no way He's interested in anything a rebellious angel is praying for."

Teresa decided it was time to change the subject yet again. "Where do you work when you aren't in New Orleans trying to save people?"

"I work in Chicago as an antiquities consultant. The Field Museum is my biggest client, but I've done pretty well for myself."

"Is there someone there you're dating?"

Danielle laughed. "No more serious discussion, huh? There've been a few guys I've dated, but none seriously."

"But you are interested in the archaeologist you mentioned."

"Sure. Who wouldn't be? He's tall, rugged and quite intelligent. Of course, he thinks I'm a pain in the ass. I tend to be called in by the Field when they want some of his artefacts authenticated. That really annoys him. He's not happy when they choose not to believe him about a date."

"He doesn't know you're a fallen angel," Teresa guessed.

Danielle snorted as she rolled her eyes. "Hell no. Do you really think a scientist would believe in something he can't prove? There's no proof that we existed except in legends. All legends have a touch of truth in them, but angels rebelling against God? That's a little far-fetched, even for fiction writers."

"Would you have to tell him if you were involved?"

She shook her head. "I haven't told any of the men I've known over the centuries. It wasn't important for them to see me as I really am. I've outlived them all."

"Do you think, if you could convince him, you might be tempted to tell this archaeologist of yours?"

Danielle blushed. "I could very well be tempted to tell him, but it wouldn't work out. He'd never believe me and I won't risk him thinking I'm crazy." She looked at Teresa. "Why were you so quick to believe Dominic? He said you accepted his story right away without any doubt."

Teresa smiled. "I've always believed in angels. It's not hard for me to believe in the ones who fell. Something about Dominic has always made me think he was different. I'm not worried he's crazy or anything like that—he's been my best friend for years and has never shown me anything other than kindness and love. Maybe I'm selfish, but I'm glad he fell. If he hadn't, I would have never had the chance to meet him and love him." She yawned. "I'm sorry. I've just been so tired lately."

"That's okay. Why don't you go take a nap? I think your clerk and I can take care of things for a while."

* * * *

When Teresa got up, it was several hours later. She rushed downstairs to find Danielle and her clerk doing just fine without her. Danielle grabbed her purse.

"I have to go. Dominic will be here to pick you up in a few minutes. Be careful tonight."

Teresa wondered what she meant, but the woman left before she could ask her. Dominic came in a few minutes after Danielle had left. He smiled at her and helped her close the store.

"We're going to my house for a little while. There's someplace we need to go later on tonight."

She didn't argue, even though she didn't feel like doing anything except going back to bed. They locked up the store then drove to his town house, where they curled up on the couch to watch the late night news, and she dozed. At eleven, his phone rang. He listened for a minute.

"Grab your jacket." Dominic shut his phone.

"Why?"

"We've been invited to a Vodou ceremony."

"You're kidding. Why would they want us there?"

"I'm checking to see if Delacourte shows up."

"If the spirit has possessed him, isn't it a risk for it to come to a ceremony?" She followed him out of the house.

"Tonight is an important night in the Vodou religion. No one misses this ceremony. It's our best chance to observe him."

Dominic's car was parked at the curb, and he helped her in. Making his way around to the driver's side, he wondered if taking her was a good idea. If the spirit possessing Delacourte was fixated on her, it might see this as an opportunity to take her. He shrugged. There was no one he could leave her with—Danielle was busy and there weren't any other Enforcers in the city at the moment. He would take his chances and hope he could protect her.

She reached over and took his hand after he pulled away from the curb. "It'll be fine."

He wanted to believe her with everything in him, but something told him things were about to get worse.

Randy was standing outside waiting for them when they arrived. He helped Teresa out of the car then shook Dominic's hand.

"Don't say anything. Just watch and if anyone looks at you, bow slightly and say *bonsoir*. Just be respectful and see if you find Delacourte here. No one's seen him around lately, but that doesn't mean anything."

"Thank your *oungan* for us. I really appreciate it." Dominic held onto Teresa as they moved into the Vodou temple.

There were already over a hundred people there and the ceremony had started. The drums kept the rhythm for the chants. People began to move as the spirits entered the room. The voices grew louder until there was no difference between the booms of the drums and the chants. Dominic could feel the beat deep in his chest, and his angelic power surged in time with it. Blinking, he tried to clear the images of the ancestors that wove around the attendees. They couldn't distract him because he wasn't there for them. No matter how they demanded him to help them find a way to contact the living.

Dominic tried not to pay attention to the ceremony. He had seen the slaves practice their form of Vodou centuries ago. He kept his eyes on the worshippers. The priest was powerful and Dominic felt the priest's strength, drawing the spirits among the living.

An hour later, he decided to leave. It looked like Delacourte had chosen not to come to the service. He could tell Teresa was getting tired by the way she was clinging to him. He nodded at Randy before they made their way out of the exit and toward the car.

Chapter Eight

Teresa waited until they climbed out of the car. As they were making their way into the house, she couldn't hide her outrage anymore.

"How barbaric."

Dominic glanced down at her with an intrigued gaze. "In what way?"

"All those drums and chants. I thought they were going to start sacrificing something. It was so uncivilized."

"You do know that ancient pagans believed Christians to be cannibals, don't you?"

"You're joking. Why would they believe that?"

Dominic held open the door, ushering her in. "Communion. 'This is my body, broken for you. Eat of it so you may have eternal life. This is my blood poured out for you. Drink.' Why wouldn't the pagans take those rituals literally?"

"Those are just symbols. Rituals we do to help bring us closer to God." Teresa folded her arms over her chest and frowned.

"So are all those chants and drums. The black coffin and the blood. It's all their way of getting closer to their ancestors who they believe will help them in this world. Those who practice Vodou believe in God, but they see Him as distant. He doesn't join in the everyday moments of their world, but their ancestors do and can affect things that happen in the world. I learned long ago, it doesn't matter what religion a person professes to follow, ultimately they're all worshiping Him, just with a different name and customs."

She stared at him in surprise. "Do you really believe that?"

"Yes. Christians call Him God and Jews call Him Yahweh. What's in a name if the meaning is the same?"

"I don't understand how you can be so accepting of this religion. It's hard for me to see God in what they do." She threw herself down on his couch.

He caressed the creamy thigh revealed by her skirt with his gaze. Smiling, he went into the kitchen where a bottle of wine was open and breathing on the counter. He thanked Mika'il silently. He grabbed two glasses and the bottle.

Heading back to the living room, he said, "There are some who would say, as a fallen angel, I should be happy to turn my back on the Father and accept every depravity in the world." He poured her a glass of wine.

"Why haven't you?"

"I admit I went a little overboard for a few centuries after the Fall." He stared into his glass. "I didn't kill anyone, but I used people. I hurt them in ways I'm not proud of. I'm not sure what would have happened if

Mika'il hadn't found me. He came and offered me a chance."

"A chance at what?" she asked then sipped her wine.

"At making my time on Earth mean something. He didn't want my entire purpose to be thrown away because of one moment of madness. He said that he needed help hunting down the fallen that were driven into insanity. Those fallen that had started killing and destroying mortals wherever they found them. Mika'il looked into my heart and soul. He didn't find any madness there, just sorrow and pain. He said I had a choice to make—I could stay the way I was, broken and bitter, using mortals until one day I killed one, or I could help him and maybe find a way to earn God's forgiveness."

"Did you jump at the chance?"

He laughed. "I probably should have, but I told him I needed time to think about his offer. Why should I help a God that had turned His back on me?"

Teresa seemed to be very intrigued by their conversation. "What did you do?"

"I turned into a thief. I stole priceless works of art before anyone knew they were going to be worth millions. I took jewels and paintings. Anything and everything I could get my hands on, I took. There wasn't any way anyone could stop me. How could they when I could appear and disappear at will? I came to America and built my plantation. I used it to store my ill-gotten gains."

"What happened?"

Dominic snorted. "Mika'il happened. Like always, he came to destroy my fun. He does tend to put a dampener on things at times. He made me return everything I stole and he made me make a choice. I chose to help him. I guess I thought it would be interesting and entertain me throughout the centuries. I didn't stop to think about how heartbreaking it would be to capture one of my brethren. Each time I do, I stop and say a prayer because there, but for the grace of God, go I. Each one of the unrepentant could have been me, if Mika'il hadn't been so insistent that I join him."

"Mika'il means a lot to you."

"As the warrior angel, he is busy fighting demons and other troubles, but he also has the utterly thankless job of keeping track of us. He deals with the unrepentant and Enforcers alike. I would never be able to do what he has done for centuries." He drank a silent toast to his friend and leader.

"He sounds like a nice guy." She was silent for a moment. "Have you ever been in love?"

He smiled sadly. "For every century I've lived, there's been a woman I've loved. Eventually, they die."

She laid her head on his shoulder. "I'm sorry."

"Maybe it's foolish to open my heart each time, but I could never convince myself not to fall in love."

"It shows courage."

"In what way?"

"A mark of courage is to keep falling in love even though you know you'll always be the one left alone."

"It might be a mark of insanity."

"If it is, I'm glad you're insane." She kissed him.

Dominic let her take the lead for once. There was a certain weariness in his soul that night. Teresa unbuttoned, then removed his shirt. He lifted his hips when she stripped his pants off him. When she told him to lie down on the floor in front of the French doors, he didn't argue. Teresa opened the doors to let the warm breeze caress their skin.

She ran a finger over the cross on his chest. "That must have hurt."

He shrugged. "It wasn't nearly as bad as when our wings were taken."

Leaning down, she traced the brand with her lips. "Roll over."

He did and groaned when she traced the scars on his shoulders with her tongue.

"My mother always gave me a kiss to take the pain away."

"It works," he rasped out through a choked-up throat. Tears were welling in his eyes. No one had ever taken the time to kiss away his pain.

With each caress and kiss, he could tell how much she cherished him. By the touch of her fingers and stroke of her tongue, her love was obvious to Dominic. In a low whisper, Teresa told him how thankful she was that she'd spilt coffee all over him that fateful day five years ago. She learnt every inch of his body. The spots that made him groan and the places that made him cry out with pleasure.

She suckled his nipples like he had done to her. Teresa explored his shaft and his balls with featherlight touches. He couldn't help but call out her name as she stroked him firmly and swiftly. His climax was building with each touch, but he tried to hold out. Dominic didn't want to come until she went with him.

Straddling his hips, she poised herself above him. As she slid his cock into her moist warmth, she smiled at him and said, "I love you."

He surged up into her and spoke of his love for her in every language he could remember ever speaking.

They rode each other and sought the highest reaches of pleasure. When they both peaked, they found Heaven together and he knew that as long as they were with each other, Heaven would only be a moment away.

She collapsed on him and sighed. "I feel like I could sleep for a week."

He rolled over and climbed to his feet, taking her with him. "Then let's go and see if we can."

He didn't notice how she felt lighter in his arms.

* * * *

While the lovers slept, a killer hunted the night for his next victim. The lust for blood and power raced through him, but hidden deep within his heart was the hope that this time the Enforcer would hear his cry for help and answer it. He didn't care how many he had to kill to satisfy the thirst for power. Mortals weren't important or even worth his worrying about them. He had never understood why the Enforcers had such an empathy with them. Mortals were weak and cynical. Their ability to believe in faith or God had diminished so much over the years, the fallen was surprised He allowed them to live.

From the beginning of the Fall, he had known he wouldn't be able to survive not being in Heaven. He was surprised he had made it this long, but the time had come for him to die—he couldn't take it any longer. The scars on his back burned more and more every day. There were more pains in his head with each sunrise. All he wanted was to rest and the only way he was going to get that was if the Enforcer killed him.

He grinned as he spotted a single woman walking alone on the Moon Walk beside the Mississippi River. How stupid could mortals be? With all the warnings about a serial killer, he couldn't believe some woman would be out walking alone. He wondered if she was looking for someone to kill her. Maybe she'd decided her life should end, but didn't have the nerve to do it herself. He chuckled—hadn't he decided the exact same thing? He had come to New Orleans for that specific reason. Stalking her in the shadows, he waited for the right moment to grab her. It would be his fifth kill and he hoped the Enforcer would finally come to get him.

* * * *

Vincent stared into the dark night. He had followed Dominic and Teresa around all day. He smiled to himself. LaFontaine knew something was happening, but it was already too late to save the woman. Vincent had seen how pale she looked and he knew the spell was working. Soon they would realize how much power he had.

Who would have thought that spells and curses would really work in this day and age? He had always thought the person needed to know they were cursed, that the effectiveness of the spell relied directly on the ability of the person to believe in the curse. If they believed, they would get sick. Yet it looked like the spell didn't need belief for it to work, because Teresa didn't know the curse had been cast and she was starting to waste away.

He laughed softly. Ever since the other spirit had shown up to help him, his every wish had come true. He'd made money by the fistfuls and women were falling over themselves to sleep with him. All women except for Teresa Ryder. Growling, he couldn't believe she had chosen someone else over him, even if that someone else was the most powerful man in New Orleans. LaFontaine didn't have anything more than he had. He didn't know what she saw in the man, but Vincent knew their relationship wouldn't last much longer.

He went inside to his study where he had a set of blueprints spread out. They were prints of the hotel he planned on building on the site of Teresa's bookstore. Once she was dead, LaFontaine wouldn't want to keep the building and Vincent would buy it. One more chance to make money.

Chapter Nine

Teresa awoke with a racking cough. Dominic was worried, but she managed to convince him it was just the flu—she really did think it was just a cold. They had breakfast together and he dropped her off at the store. She worked for only a short time before she found herself falling asleep where she stood. She headed upstairs to take a nap. Several hours later, Dominic woke her up with a kiss.

"Honey, have you been asleep all day?"

"What time is it?" she murmured.

"It's almost eight at night."

"Really? I was tired when I got here this morning so I thought I would take a nap. I didn't think I'd sleep this long."

"It's all right, sweetheart. Do you want to have dinner here?"

"Please. I don't think I have the energy to go anywhere tonight."

"Fine."

He went out into the living room. Before he could turn on the TV, Danielle appeared beside him. She glared at him.

"It's time, Dominic. You can't wait any longer."

He didn't pretend to misunderstand her. "She's not feeling well."

"I can watch her. It doesn't break any vow I made to protect a mortal from one of her kind."

"I don't know."

"You have to do it. He killed two people last night. That makes six so far and he shows no signs of stopping. I can't believe you're thinking about not honoring your vows." She paced from one end of the room to the other. "Mika'il will only take so much of this insubordination before he comes looking for you, Dominic, and drags your ass out to take care of the unrepentant."

"I can handle Mika'il."

"No, you can't. Why are you even thinking like that? No one can handle him unless it's Christian and you know how Christian feels about him. Don't risk his anger. Go and take care of the unrepentant before any more die."

He stopped her and stared into her eyes. "You promise me you'll take care of Teresa and not let anything happen to her."

"Nothing will harm her while I'm here. I promise, and I don't make promises lightly."

"I won't be long." Dominic disappeared.

"I don't doubt that." Danielle headed for the bedroom to check on Teresa. She stared down at the sleeping woman and she felt a shock race through her. Somehow, in the short time she'd been away, Teresa had lost weight. Then she touched her hand to the other woman's forehead. It was cool and clammy. "Mika'il, you better look at her."

Mika'il appeared. He glanced at Teresa quickly and turned to Danielle. "Why did you call me?"

"Look at her again." Danielle gestured to her.

"She must have a cold. I'm sure Dominic doesn't let her get enough sleep." He grinned.

"No, Mika'il. Take a real good look at her. She's sick and I don't think it's just the flu."

The archangel stepped closer to Teresa and placed his hand on her forehead. When he closed his eyes, Danielle assumed he was sending his power through Teresa's body. He gasped as he jerked his hand away.

"There's something off balance in her body."

"Can you fix it?"

"I can't interfere." Mika'il clenched his jaw.

Danielle stared at him. "You interfere every chance you get, but you won't do anything to help her?"

Mika'il turned away from her. "It's something I can't help. Trust me, I would do whatever I could, but my hands are tied."

"What the hell good are you, then? What kind of archangel are you?" She swore at him. Touching Teresa's hand, Danielle concentrated and traced the line of illness throughout her body. "It's something from outside her. What should we do?"

"Wait until Dominic gets home and let him know. I don't think this is anything we can cure."

"What do you mean?" Danielle sat next to Teresa. "Dominic could go over the edge if he lost her."

Mika'il nodded. "I know, but I have a feeling this is a problem a mortal has to solve. I don't think our powers will help." He disappeared.

Danielle saw the surprise in Teresa's eyes when the woman woke. "Where's Dominic?"

"He had some business to take care of. He'll be back in a little bit. How do you feel?"

"I've been really tired lately. I figured it was because of Dominic." She blushed.

"He's been keeping you busy, huh?"

She nodded. "I'm not complaining." Putting a hand to her flushed cheek, she murmured, "I've been feeling weak for a couple of days."

"Tell you what. Stay in bed and keep sleeping. Maybe you'll feel better by the time he returns."

"Good idea. Thanks." She rolled over and closed her eyes.

* * * *

Dominic followed the trail of the fallen to the Fairgrounds racetrack, where he stood over the body of a young woman. He stared at Dominic through black eyes.

"Finally, you decide to grace me with your presence. Only seven had to die before you chose to end my life."

"Don't talk to me like I've inconvenienced you in some way. Why now? Why this city?" Dominic stalked toward the fallen. "You've caused countless sleepless nights and pain to a number of families. Doesn't that bother you?"

Even while he waited for the unrepentant to answer him, Dominic accepted his guilt in the whole situation. He could've ended it after the first killing if he hadn't been so concerned about protecting Teresa. For the first time, he let his own wants and wishes overrule what God wanted him to do.

"There wouldn't have been nearly as many if you had answered my call when I first got here, but I do believe you were too busy with some mortal to worry yourself about your job."

"Why should you get relief from the life you chose to live? What makes you so privileged?"

"I'll keep killing until you do it."

"I know, and that'll bring Mika'il down on me. I prefer to keep him happy, so I'm here." Dominic reached out and grabbed the fallen. Without wasting any time, he drained the power from the creature and dropped him to the ground. As he turned to go, another Enforcer appeared. "What took you so long?"

The short redhead stared at him for a moment. "If it's any of your business, Mika'il told me I wasn't to interfere until you did your job. Now, I'll punish him. Go back to your mortal and try not to let things get so out of hand next time."

"Thanks." Dominic headed home.

* * * *

He appeared beside Teresa's bed then leaned down to kiss her awake.

"Dominic." Danielle's voice broke into his head.

"What?" He brushed his hand over Teresa's forehead, frowning at the cool feel of her skin.

"I need to talk to you right now."

"Can't it wait? I'm tired and all I want is Teresa in my arms."

"I'm sure you do, but no, it can't wait."

He sighed and went to the living room. Danielle was standing, staring out of the window to the street below. The worried frown on her face set off an alarm in his mind.

"What happened?"

"Teresa's sick, Dominic."

"That's all? I'll take her to a doctor tomorrow."

She shook her head. "I don't think a doctor's going to be able to cure this."

"Why not?"

"It's an illness from outside her body, and our powers won't be able to stop it. She's wasting away. I can feel it."

Dominic stalked across the room and grabbed her arms. He shook her roughly as rage and fear coursed through his body. His only chance at a love that would make his life worth living, and Teresa could die. "Wasting away? She can't be dying."

She didn't protest his rough treatment. "How much weight has she lost in the last couple of days? Has she been more tired than usual?"

Dominic thought back. He had been so caught up in trying to find Vincent Delacourte that he hadn't been paying enough attention to Teresa. "She's lost a few pounds."

"She's lost at least ten pounds and she's losing more every day. Teresa doesn't eat, and has no energy. Take her to a doctor tomorrow and I pray he'll know how to cure her."

Dominic dropped to the couch then put his face in his hands. "I can't lose her, Danielle."

She brushed her hand over his hair and swore softly. "I know, my friend, I know."

"Mika'il can't do anything to help her?"

"If he can, he won't. He's not allowed to interfere."

He growled softly before asking, "Why not? He interferes every chance he gets."

"He interferes in the small things that push us in the right direction, but not in the big things that can change our lives. It hurts him not to be able to help.

He's not sure our powers would be able to save her, anyway." Danielle sounded worried.

"What'll we do?"

"You'll take her to the doctor tomorrow. Rule out any possible illness it can be. I'll do some research and try to find Delacourte. I think he has something to do with it. We'll stay strong and stay together. Also, we'll pray. He might not hear prayers for ourselves, but He has to hear prayers for someone as good as Teresa."

He nodded. There wasn't anything he could do at the moment. "If I lose her..." His voice cracked.

"You won't lose her. Go get some sleep. Hold her tight and dream of all the things you'll do when she's better."

He got up and went to join Teresa in bed.

* * * *

Dominic was jolted awake by the racking fit that tossed Teresa from side to side. She was having a seizure and he didn't know how to stop her. Their bed shook with the force of it. He held her tight to him and prayed. When the seizing stopped, her body relaxed and her eyes opened. He looked into their glazed depths and saw fear.

"I think I'm really sick," she whispered.

"I know, love." He saw a note on the nightstand. He leaned over to grab it. "Danielle made an appointment for you—it's in thirty minutes. I'll help you shower and get ready."

They walked slowly to the bathroom. Before he started the shower, he called Terrance and asked him to meet them outside Teresa's apartment in twenty minutes.

He let her lean on him while he washed her. Dominic wasn't sure where the first drop of blood had come from. Another drop hit and he realized Teresa was spitting it out. He panicked. There wasn't an illness he knew of that struck so quickly and seemed to do so much damage.

He shut off the water and toweled her dry. With a wave of his hand, he dressed them both—he couldn't waste time doing it the mortal way.

Teresa smiled. "I can see an advantage to being with you. I'll never have to worry about being late because of a quickie in the shower." She started coughing again.

The strength of the cough beat against her body and he was afraid she'd fall over. After sweeping her into his arms, he headed down to the car.

Terrance held open the door for him. "Is she going to be okay?"

As much as he wanted to reassure him, he couldn't. "I don't know. Just get us to the hospital. It's progressed too far for a doctor's visit." He settled in the back seat, knowing Terrance would get them to the emergency room fast.

"Certainly, sir." Terrance shut the door then climbed behind the wheel.

They got to the hospital in record time and the nurse admitted Teresa right away. The doctor came in shortly after that. He listened to their story and ordered a battery of tests. Dominic waited for several hours until the doctor returned with the results.

Dominic grabbed Teresa's hand. She was so tired, she couldn't open her eyes. The doctor shut the door then stared at them for a moment.

"Well?" Dominic asked to break the silence.

"Negative. All the results are negative. I can't find a single thing wrong with Miss Ryder."

"Of course something's wrong with her. We aren't making it up."

"I'm not saying you are. Obviously there's something wrong, but whatever it is, our tests can't find it." The doctor looked down at his feet, then back up at Dominic. He stared at the Enforcer for a minute. Something in Dominic's eyes must have convinced the doctor. "If I believed in this sort of thing—and I'm not saying I do—but I would be led to believe this might have something to do with Vodou. Is there any way she could have gotten into trouble with a Vodou priest?"

"I didn't think they did anything like curse people."

"Not the priests, but the *bòkò* or sorcerer will do it for a price. If you have connections in the community, see if you can find someone who will look at her." The doctor smiled at Dominic. "Of course, that's off the record."

Dominic nodded. "I understand. Thanks, Doctor." He gathered her in his arms and headed for the waiting room.

"Please let me know if Miss Ryder makes it."

"I'll have you over to my club for a night on the town when she's feeling better."

"I look forward to it. God's luck, Miss Ryder," the doctor said.

Terrance jumped to his feet when Dominic entered the waiting room. He led the way as Dominic carried her to the car. He held open the door as Dominic slid into the car as gently as possible.

"Go to Paisible. Then call Randy and have him meet us there." There was no break in Dominic's voice, but tears rolled down his cheeks.

"All right." Terrance didn't ask any questions. He started the car and headed out.

Dominic held Teresa tight to him, rocking her slowly as he whispered his love to her. He wasn't sure she even understood him, but he couldn't stop talking to her. It was a foolish thought that if he kept talking, she wouldn't slip away from him.

"Dominic, what did the doctor say?" Danielle contacted him.

"Off the record, the doctor said she probably got cursed by a sorcerer or Vodou priest. On the record, there's nothing wrong with her. She started throwing up blood this morning."

"I'm sorry. Are you going to talk to Randy?"

"Yes."

"Then I'll meet you at your house. Keep strong."

"I don't have a choice."

He brushed a kiss over Teresa's cheek and she smiled up at him. Raising a shaking hand, she cupped his cheek and wiped a tear away with her thumb.

"Why are you crying?"

"I'm afraid. I don't want you to leave me."

"You'll find a way to save me. I have faith in you."

"I'm not sure you should." He frowned. "I still don't know what's wrong with you."

"Oh, you'll find out and figure out a way to cure me. You're an angel, after all."

"A fallen one, so I don't know if miracles work for me."

"An angel's an angel. Even a fallen one deserves a miracle now and then. I'm sure He won't ignore you." She closed her eyes and rested her cheek against his shoulder. "I'm so tired."

"Sleep then, Teresa. We're going to Paisible to talk to Randy. If we need to know anything from you, I'll wake you up."

She nodded and fell asleep. Dominic met Terrance's eyes in the rear-view mirror. Both men recognized the determination in the other to keep Teresa alive and well. Dominic nodded to the ex-mercenary then turned his gaze to stare out of the window. His thoughts moved to the rage burning in him. He knew Vincent Delacourte had done something to Teresa, and he hoped Randy would know someone who could help them.

Chapter Ten

Terrance pulled up in front of the plantation house. Dominic handed Teresa to Terrance so he could get out of the car, then he took her back to carry her into the house. Danielle and Randy were on the front steps waiting for them. Neither one remarked about the tear tracks on his face. What could they say? They knew the situation was grave and if they didn't find a way to cure her, Teresa would die. Terrance unlocked the door and they followed Dominic to his bedroom where he put Teresa to bed. He waved them to the small office next to the bedroom. He didn't bother to shut the connecting door—he figured she wouldn't be disturbed by their conversation.

Randy waited until they were all in the other room before he asked, "What the hell is wrong with her?"

"That's what we have to find out. A doctor suggested we get someone from the Vodou community to look at her. He thinks she might have been cursed by a *bòkò*."

Dominic watched as Randy went into the other room to stare down at Teresa and he seemed deep in thought. When Randy came back to the rest, he poured them all drinks, then stood looking outside. Dominic didn't know what to do—he had never been so helpless in his life. There had never been a time when his powers couldn't solve a problem.

"What good are these powers when they can't even save the one person I love?"

"They are good for saving the rest of the world. Is one person more important than thousands of others?" Mika'il's voice danced through his head.

"Don't talk to me about importance. I love her, Mika'il. Whether you understand that or not doesn't make this any less heart-wrenching for me."

"Who said I didn't understand the pain you're going through? No one ever said I hadn't experienced loss for myself. I'm only doing what I'm told to, Dominic. Don't you think I want to be there? Don't you think I would help you if I could? Watching anyone – mortal or angel – suffer isn't my idea of a good time."

"Then why make her go through this? Is this some sort of test for me? Are you testing me to see if I'll turn to or away from God because of this?" There was outrage in Dominic's heart and mind. *"To use someone as sweet as Teresa for a simple test is cruel. Why wouldn't I turn from a God who cruelly uses His believers in silly little tests for His own ego?"*

A wave of gentle love and infinite tenderness washed over him. *"I don't use people for my own selfish purposes, Dominic. I use them to prove my mercy and love. The purpose for Teresa's sickness isn't for you to know. Don't take your anger out on Mika'il. He is my archangel and is only following the orders I give him."*

Dominic fell to his knees, holding his head in his hands. The Father didn't speak to the fallen very often, but when He chose to, the experience wasn't something they wanted to repeat. Danielle knelt and started praying. Terrance followed her lead and knelt as well. Randy put his hand on the window glass and bowed his head. Together, their prayers filled the air and a sense of peace filled the room.

"Your friends love both you and Teresa. That is a good sign. Find it in your heart to trust me and I promise love will fill your life for the rest of your days." The sense of tenderness lingered as the voice disappeared.

Sighing, Dominic stood then turned to the others and smiled. "Thank you all for being here. I've been blessed with loyal friends."

Randy shrugged. "You'd be right beside us if we needed you, so we're repaying you. I've been thinking. If it is a Vodou spell, we'll need a very powerful *oungan* to break it. I don't know any, but my priest might be able to get in touch with the right people. I'm going to go and talk to him right now. I'll let you know when I get in touch with the right person to help us."

Dominic hugged the man. "Thank you so much. I bet you didn't think fighting evil spirits was in your job description."

"Good and evil balance each other. Where one is present, you must always guard against the other. Also, if there is a *bòkò* out there selling these spells to others, he needs to be dealt with and the community needs to be informed about it." Randy nodded to the other two then left.

"I'm sure Randy will find someone." Danielle sat down at the desk and watched Dominic pace.

Terrance stood in the corner as if he didn't know where his place was in this whole thing, but he planned on hanging around until he could help in some way.

"We have to find Delacourte. He has to tell us what he did to Teresa." Dominic clenched his hands. "I'm not sure if I could be in the same room as him and not try to kill him."

Terrance moved forward. "I can find him. I'll use all my connections to hunt him down. When I do, do you want me to bring him to you or get the information from him myself?"

Dominic looked at the man and shook his head. "Bring him to me. You're trying to separate yourself from that world. Let me deal with him."

Terrance nodded. He was already dialing his phone as he walked out of the room. He ran down the steps to the front door. Dominic knew Terrance would find the bastard as quickly as possible.

"I wish I could make everything better with just a wave of my hand, but I don't have that power." Danielle spoke up.

Dominic leaned against the windowsill and looked at her. "What sort of powers do you have if you're not an Enforcer?"

She shrugged. "I have all the same powers you or any other fallen has, plus a few others that you probably have, but Mika'il hasn't seen fit to tell you about."

"Which are?"

She shook her head. "If he hasn't told you, I'm not going to. I don't need him angry at me."

"Who are the Enforcers in Chicago?"

"I don't know, and I have to say I don't want to meet them. My helping you down here has destroyed my credibility as a neutral party already. I don't want to become fast friends with any of them up there." She traced a pattern on the top of the desk. "Have you ever wanted to be mortal? To live as a normal person who will have a finite time and die?"

"I might have when we first were banished from Heaven. There didn't seem to be a reason to live forever. It was hard to watch friends and lovers age and die while I didn't have an end in sight." He glanced over to the bedroom where Teresa slept. "Now, I'm glad I lived this long. If I had died sooner, I wouldn't have met her and known what real love was."

"What is real love? I don't think I've ever known, or will ever know, what it is." Danielle sounded sad.

"For me, it's knowing there is someone I would do anything for, even die if I have to. From now on, she is the most important thing in my life. She ranks before everything else."

"Yes, you've proven that, but you might want to remember what will happen if you ignore your purpose for being on this Earth. There will be more unrepentants that will come to challenge you. Once she is feeling better, there will be times when you have to leave her alone."

"I know, but Terrance will be here to protect her while I'm gone."

"So real love is being willing to die for someone." Danielle nodded. "I can see that as being a sign of true love."

"Do you believe in soulmates?"

"You mean soulmates as in there is a person out there meant just for me and no one else?"

He nodded.

"I can't say that I do. Why would a God who couldn't forgive us love us so much as to make such a person for us?" Danielle shook her head. "I think you're one of the lucky ones, Dominic. You were able to find a woman to love in a world where relationships are a thing of the past." Changing the subject, she said, "So you trust your ex-mercenary with your most precious possession."

"Yes. He's never shown me any reason not to trust him."

"Even though at one point in his life, his loyalty could be bought?"

"We all make mistakes."

She laughed. "You're right, and I shouldn't judge him when I made the biggest mistake of all."

Sighing, Dominic turned to stare out at the bayou waters swirling behind his house. He knew Danielle was trying to keep his mind off Teresa and their problems, but his love was always in his mind. He prayed Randy would be back soon with someone who could help them. His phone rang right then.

"Hello?"

"Hey, boss man. I talked to my *oungan*. He thinks he knows someone who can help us. It'll take a little bit to get a hold of him, but we're working on it. Just hold on a while longer."

"Thanks, Randy."

"Welcome. I'll call when we're on our way over." Randy hung up.

"So we should be getting help soon?"

Dominic nodded. He rubbed the back of his neck as he sighed.

"You didn't get a lot of sleep last night and your power isn't at full strength. Go take a nap and hold Teresa. Maybe that will make both of you feel better. I'll hang out and fix lunch for us. I think it's going to be a long day."

Dominic didn't say anything as he headed into the bedroom. After shutting the door, he stripped. Sliding into bed with Teresa, he pulled her feverish body tight to his and closed his eyes. No dreams or nightmares haunted his sleep this time. Somehow a sense of peace and acceptance filled his spirit. Whatever happened would be the will of God and he believed with all his heart that God wouldn't allow Teresa to die.

* * * *

"Hey, Janet. How are you?" Danielle held her phone between her shoulder and ear as she stirred some gumbo in Dominic's kitchen.

"I'm doing good, girl. Are you home?"

"No. Business is taking a little longer than I planned down here. I've got a few odds and ends to tie up before I get back."

"Meet any good-looking men down there?"

Danielle smiled. Her best friend was always on the lookout for men. "A few, but they're all taken. Anyway, I wouldn't want to start anything long distance. Too much work."

"And you're interested in a certain archaeologist who won't give you the time of day."

"We all have to have a goal and mine is to get him to kiss me one day. I'm sure it'll be explosive."

"Are you going to get him drunk at one of those museum functions? That might be the only way you have a chance to convince him you're not trying to steal his limelight."

"The museum has been a bit dull since he's been in Peru. I wonder if he's found anything exciting down there." Danielle couldn't wait until Grant Carson came back. His rugged good looks would definitely brighten her day. "I just wanted to let you know I wouldn't be back for a few more days."

"Okay. I'll make sure your plants have water and your cat has food, even though the little princess doesn't like me."

"Princess doesn't like me on good days. I'm just the human who feeds her and adores her when she wants to be worshiped." Danielle laughed. "I'll call you with the flight information when I'm ready to come home."

"Okay. Take care and have a fling or two." Janet hung up.

Danielle set the phone down then dished out two bowls of gumbo. She set them on the table as Dominic came in. She didn't say anything as he seated himself and picked up a spoon. They ate in silence. When they were finished, he stood and cleaned up the bowls.

"Did she wake up at all?"

He shook his head. "She didn't move the whole time I was with her. I'm starting to get really scared, Danielle, and I don't like it."

"It's hard not being able to do anything when you're used to waving a hand and correcting all the problems."

He agreed with her. "Normally I can fix it and just go on with my life. Most problems don't make an impression on me because I know there isn't any that I can't fix."

"Except this."

"Yes, except for this one. Do you think He did it to teach me a lesson?"

Danielle wasn't about to guess why Teresa got sick. "I don't presume to know why He does anything He chooses to do. He can see the beginning and end of time. He sees things differently than we do. We're caught up in the here and now, so we don't see the future in any other way than abstract. Since He knows what is going to happen in the future, He plans accordingly and we can't begin to understand that."

"What do we do then?" Dominic's question held a hint of desperation.

"We accept He knows best and keep living. I'm not saying things work out for the best. I've seen some that haven't, but I'm saying we have to trust Him and believe that, in the end, He knows how much we can take before we'll break."

His phone rang, interrupting the conversation. "It's Randy. I'll put him on speaker."

Danielle nodded, and watched as Dominic hit the speaker button. "Hey, Randy, what can you tell us?"

"I'm on my way over with an *oungan*. He's one of the most powerful in New Orleans. If this is a curse, he should be able to lift it." Randy announced.

"Okay. What do we need to have ready for you when you get here?"

"Just be ready for a long night. This isn't something we'll be able to lift right away."

"Right. We'll see you when you get here." Dominic ended the call, then met Danielle's gaze. She saw the contained excitement in his eyes.

"We should probably get some candles lit," she suggested.

They headed upstairs without a word. The sun was beginning to set as they went about lighting the bedroom with candles and opening the French doors to let in the humid breeze. Danielle moved out onto the balcony. She tried to ignore the sorrow she felt coming from Dominic. She found herself longing for home and the uncomplicated life she had made for herself there. Maybe that was one reason she had never joined sides with the Enforcers. They had to deal with so many problems. She didn't like complications. She loved an easy life with good friends and excellent wine. *I guess everyone should have some adventure in their life.* She smiled slightly.

A commotion had her heading back into the room. A very tall man with café au lait skin stalked in. Power rolled off him like a tidal wave and she knew this was the *oungan* Randy had found. The man didn't look at anyone, but went right to Teresa. He held a hand over her forehead and closed his eyes. Danielle could see the power flowing from him into Teresa.

Even though he wanted to protest, Dominic managed to keep his mouth shut. He had to rely on this man to save the woman he loved. He couldn't afford to alienate him.

"It was a good thing I happened to be in the city today." The man's Creole accent gave his voice a deep, soft rhythm. "The young man here informed me what was going on. I'm afraid your woman has been cursed by a *bòkò* and he used the deadliest of spells. It is the *voye lamò* and it will take some time to lift it. She has slipped further away from us. We need to get started as soon as we can."

Dominic bowed his head in respect. While the *oungan* had been talking, Randy had been setting up a drum and lighting incense. The robes the *oungan* was pulling on were purple, black and white. Once dressed, he turned back to the fallen angels.

"The spell cast on your woman used the spirits of the dead. Also, she is standing close to the gates of the spirit world. We must petition the *lwa*, most importantly the *Gédé*. They are the spirits who deal with the dead and death. They watch over the use of black magic, so they offer protection from it. We must ask them not to allow her into the spirit world and to take the spell off of her." The *oungan* studied the others. "I don't usually allow those who aren't of our religion to watch during such an important ritual, but I think your powers might be of help to me. Usually, such rituals would take place in the *ounfò* because we wouldn't want to insult the spirits by asking them on unconsecrated ground. There is a feeling, though, that there have been other Vodou rituals held on this plantation."

Dominic nodded, but kept silent. He stayed seated next to Teresa, holding her hand.

"You stay there and keep holding her hand. You offer her a lifeline to come back to this world. Focus your energy on showing her the way back." The *oungan* pointed to Danielle. "You should stay out of the way, but don't leave the room. We need your power as well. Pray to your God."

Danielle moved to the corner of the room, kneeling down and bowing her head. Dominic closed his eyes. If he was to focus his energy, he couldn't allow the rituals to distract him. The drumming started and the power swelled in the room. The chanting soared and softened with the beating of the drum. Dominic swayed to the rhythm and he began to lose track of reality. The only solid thing he could feel was Teresa's hand in his. His power started to drain from him. He sent a silent wish that he had had time to replenish it, but he hadn't had a chance to because Teresa had been so sick. He would give all he had — even his life — to make her better. The squawk of the rooster made him open his eyes for a moment. The *oungan* was holding the dead bird over a bowl to collect its blood. Then he poured the bowl of blood over the altar. Dominic quickly shut his eyes again. He didn't like that part of the Vodou religion, but he understood it. Didn't

Christianity have its own version of sacrifice, when Jesus offered himself up on the cross?

The atmosphere of the room changed when another presence entered. The *oungan* spoke to it, offering the blood and tobacco in a black box. Dominic didn't know what they were saying. The language wasn't any he had ever heard before, but he could hear the respectful plea in the priest's voice. As the last of his power drained from him, he slowly sank to his knees on the floor. He hoped it would be enough for them to save Teresa. He offered up a prayer to God. He knew he didn't have a chance of saving her even with all his power, but the Father could do it, if He chose to. Dominic had to trust that God wasn't so unforgiving that He would cause this curse to destroy her. The world went black.

* * * *

Teresa found herself standing in a white room with no furniture except for a desk at one end. There were two windows in the walls on either side of the desk. A man was leaning on it, studying some papers. He hadn't noticed her, so Teresa cleared her throat. She couldn't help but laugh when the man jumped and the papers went flying. He stared at her with familiar silver eyes.

"Mickey O'Flynn? What are you doing in my dreams?" She approached him.

"What the hel…heck are you doing here? You're not supposed to be here." He stalked over to her. Grabbing her arm, he turned her around then started walking her back toward the other side of the room.

"Where am I?" Teresa asked as she tried to keep up with his long strides.

"This is a waiting room," he said vaguely. "They must have left it too late. I told them this test was too dangerous, but no one listens to me. I'm just a warrior angel. What do I know about spirits and the 'other' world?" he mumbled to himself.

She was puzzled and rather intrigued because she got the feeling Mickey didn't lose his cool very often. "Left what too late? What kind of test?"

Mickey opened a door in the wall that she hadn't seen. He ushered her through and she saw Dominic standing on the other side. Dominic looked shocked to see them both together. He rushed forward to take her into his arms.

"What the heck are you doing here?" Mickey demanded of Dominic.

"My power was drained and I believe I died, but why I came to Heaven, I have no idea." Dominic glared at Mickey. "What is she doing here? I thought she would be all right."

"She will be when you take her back. I can't believe you gave your life for her, Dominic." Mickey sounded surprised by Dominic's sacrifice.

"I knew He would take care of her whether she lived or died."

The two men smiled at each other for a second, ignoring the third man standing nearby. His face was white with powder and he wore a pair of sunglasses. Cotton was wrapped around his head. He grinned at her and she shivered.

"What is that?" she asked as she pointed at the man.

"That's something you weren't ever supposed to see. Take her out of here, Dominic, and remember how close you came to losing her." He waited until the couple had disappeared. He turned to the man. "You cut it too close. You promised me that she would never get this far."

The man shrugged. "Things happen, man. She's fine and will get better. Death didn't get her this time." He laughed.

Mika'il grabbed him to shake him. "It was never supposed to be like this. There was never to be a chance that she could die."

The *Gèdè* shook off Mika'il's hand. "Remember you came and asked us for help. You needed us. We do things a little differently than you. We're on a different schedule. We all work for the God, but the *lwa* interact with the mortals every day. We know how close we can cut it."

"She better not suffer any damage from your joking around. I have little patience with spirits who believe they can be excused any mischief." Mika'il glared at the *Gèdè*. "Get out of here and take care of that *bòkò* of yours."

"Don't worry. He'll be taken care of. He knows practicing black magic is against the rules." The *Gèdè* smiled up at Mika'il. "Hey, all's well that ends well, man. She's fine. Your fallen has found his soulmate. So she got a peek at Heaven before she should have. She'll forget about it." The man disappeared.

Mika'il ground his teeth in frustration. He hated dealing with the Earth spirits that inhabited the mortal world. They reacted with shocking disregard for His plans. He made a mental note to check in with Dominic and Teresa in a couple of days to make sure she had made a complete recovery.

Chapter Eleven

Dominic heard Danielle's voice calling him from out of the dark. He struggled through the fog to find her.

"Come on, Dominic. You've got to wake up."

There was a light touch to his forehead and power surged into him. He opened his eyes and saw the other fallen standing over him. He was lying on the bed entwined with Teresa. He looked over at her and his tears welled when she smiled at him. Her eyes were clear and sparkling.

"I'm glad to see you're both okay. I'm heading back to Chicago now. You know how to get hold of me if you need me." She hugged them. "Rest for a while, but first Terrance needs to talk to you."

She left as Terrance came in. "I heard the good news. I'm glad to see you awake, but I don't have good news about Delacourte."

Dominic pulled himself up to lean against the pillows and headboard. Teresa snuggled close to him, resting her head against his chest.

"I can't find him. He seems to have disappeared." Terrance shrugged. "I talked to all my contacts and no one's seen him."

A surge of anger raced through Dominic. He couldn't believe Delacourte would get away with almost killing Teresa.

"He's being punished," Mika'il said.

"How do I know? Why should I trust you? Didn't I see you with one of the lwa?*"*

Mika'il didn't answer for a moment. Then he sighed. *"That didn't work out quite the way we planned, but just focus on the fact she's alive."*

"I will, but how can I trust you about Delacourte being punished for what he's done?"

"Trust me. The Vodou community won't allow him to go unpunished. Anyone who messes in something he doesn't understand deserves what he gets. The spirits are vengeful."

Dominic gazed down at Teresa and decided he really didn't care. *"I'll believe you, Mika'il."*

He told Terrance, "Don't worry, Terrance. I have it on good authority that Delacourte is being punished."

Terrance looked puzzled for a moment before he shrugged. "Thanks, sir. I hope you're both feeling better soon."

Dominic and Teresa cuddled for a while. He couldn't find the words to tell her how scared he'd been and how much he loved her. Before he could say anything, a knock sounded on the door.

"Come in," he called.

Randy came in with a bright grin on his face. "I'm glad to see you both awake."

"How long was I out?"

"About four hours. The *oungan* said the ceremony was a success. The *Gèdè* denied Teresa entrance into the spirit world and lifted the curse. We cleaned up, then I took him home."

Dominic shook Randy's hand. "I can't ever thank you enough. When I get back to the club, we'll talk about what kind of compensation I should give to the *oungan*."

"He'll appreciate it, boss."

"Tell me what happened after I passed out."

"The *oungan* was possessed by one of the *Gèdè*. When it found out what was going on, it lifted the curse because Teresa was such a beautiful girl. The *Gèdè* like beautiful women." Randy smiled. "He went away and, about five minutes later, Teresa opened her eyes. She'll need a few weeks to recover, but she'll be fine. The *oungan* said you and Danielle passed out because the spirits took your strength to materialize."

"How did I get cursed in the first place?" Teresa asked.

"At some point, the *bòkò* must have sprinkled dirt from a grave on you, or a route you walk often."

"I think I know how it happened." She told them about the odd little man who had spilt dirt on her.

"The *bòkò* who did this to you, along with Delacourte, will be dealt with," Randy promised them. "Now, I'm the last one to bother you. Terrance is downstairs if you need anything. He's planning on staying here for a couple of days until you recover, boss."

Randy smiled at them then shut the door behind him. The French doors were open, allowing the night sounds to provide a soothing background for them. Dominic moved Teresa to her back. He leaned over her and smiled. "I'll be forever grateful to all of them for bringing you back to me."

"And I'll be grateful to them for their loyalty to you," she whispered.

"My love, you were leaving me. I don't know how I would have survived without you." Dominic buried his head against her shoulder and cried.

Teresa ran her hands up and down his back as she tried to soothe him. "Please don't. You didn't lose me. I knew you would find a way to save me. The closer I got to dying, the more faith I had in you."

"At the end, I gave up and put all my trust in God. I had done everything I could to save you, but ultimately it was God's strength that did it."

"A hard lesson to learn, my friend, and I'm sorry for that," Mika'il whispered in his mind.

"Do you think it was a test?"

He shrugged. "It doesn't matter. You've alive."

He crushed his mouth to hers. He nibbled along her lips and teased her tongue with his. With a thought, he stripped them—he didn't want to take any more time than he had to. Getting inside her warm, moist body was more essential to him than breathing. He slid his hand down between her legs and teased her hard clit with the tips of his fingers. She gasped and sighed as he inserted two fingers inside her pussy. Her inner muscles tightened when he pulled them out. He thrust in again and she arched her back. When her juices were coating his fingers, he knew she was ready.

After grabbing a pillow, he tucked it under her hips to give him a better angle for a deeper penetration. Finally, he slid home and they sighed.

"This is where I belong, love. Deep inside you and loving you. No place on Earth will ever be a paradise again unless you're with me."

She wrapped her legs around him. "Take me to Heaven, Dominic. I love you so much."

It only took a few thrusts before they were crying out together. She cradled him in her arms afterwards. As they were drifting to sleep, Dominic heard Teresa murmur, "Why was Mickey O'Flynn in Heaven?"

* * * *

Delacourte stared at the silent men and women surrounding him. The spirit inside him hissed at them. It didn't want to leave the fresh mortal body it had found. The *oungan* completed the ceremony and the spirit went howling back into the world it had come from. Crying out, Vincent fell face first to the ground and moaned.

"You've been found guilty of committing crimes against an innocent," one of the men said.

"You can't judge me. This isn't a proper court and you certainly aren't a jury of my peers."

"You profess to be a follower of Vodou. As such, you can be judged and punished by us." The man gestured to four burly men with ropes.

"Wait. I didn't know the spell would kill her. I only wanted to make her sick. The *bòkò* tricked me. You should be punishing him."

"Ignorance is no excuse in a crime like this. The *bòkò* who did the spell has already been dealt with. It's your turn."

As the men came toward Delacourte, he realized he had lost everything. There was nothing left of the world the spirit had helped him create. He would be charged with worse crimes if he was sent back to the world he considered his. His mind went black as one of the men clubbed him.

A few days later, Vincent Delacourte's body washed ashore on Lake Pontchartrain. He had been beaten to death and a small black cross was tucked into his shirt pocket.

* * * *

Two weeks after her illness, Teresa walked into The Fallen Angel club. Dominic had closed it for the private party he was throwing—he had invited everyone who had helped them. Danielle had sent a gift, but her note said that one trip to New Orleans had been filled with so much excitement, she was afraid a second trip might kill her. The old *mambo* they had talked to first had died earlier that week. Teresa said a prayer every night for that wonderful old woman.

She stood on the edge of the crowd watching Dominic before he noticed she was there. Her fallen angel had lost the weariness that had always haunted his eyes. His beautiful smile came more often and the sadness didn't plague him. She was pretty sure it was the daily glimpses of Heaven they had that were making him happier.

"There you are, love. Come here." Dominic grabbed her arm then dragged her onto the middle of the dance floor. He raised his hand and everyone went silent.

"Teresa and I would like to thank you all for coming tonight. This is our way of showing our appreciation for everything you've done the past several weeks."

He took her hand before going to one knee. Smiling up at her, he said, "Teresa Ryder, will you marry me and take me to Heaven forever?"

"Go ahead, child." The voice speaking in the back of her mind was the same raspy one she had heard in the church. *"He's your best friend and your lover. You have the best of both worlds."*

"Yes, I will." She threw her head back and laughed as Dominic picked her up and twirled her around. The crowd cheered.

Mika'il watched the commotion with a hint of envy in his heart. Dominic and Teresa had discovered the truth that Mika'il had learnt so many centuries earlier. Sometimes love comes with a heavy price.

CHICAGO

Dedication

Thank you to my awesome editor for cleaning Chicago up, and to the line editors and proofers who did their best to bring my story up to its highest level. Also, thank you to all the readers who are enjoying the continuing stories of my fallen angels.

Chapter One

Danielle stepped from her car and handed the valet her keys. It had been a long time since she had eaten at Geja's. She'd always enjoyed the fondue restaurant. Smiling at the doorman, she entered the cozy restaurant on the basement level of a town house.

"May we help you, ma'am?" the maître d' asked.

"I'm here to join the Reynolds party."

"Of course. Right this way."

Trisha's laugh rang out as Danielle followed the man around the corner, and her mood lifted when she saw her three best friends.

"Already enjoying the wine, I see," she joked as she slid into the booth next to Janet.

"It's about time you got here. It's your damn birthday party." Trisha giggled as she toasted Danielle with her glass.

Joan leaned over to hug her and whispered, "Dickhead broke up with her today. She's been crying off and on all day."

Danielle reached out and squeezed Trisha's hand. "I always said you were too good for him."

Trisha giggled again. "It's strange but you were the only one to tell me that. I thought you were jealous."

Her eyebrows shot up. "Jealous?" She saw Janet's warning glance. "Maybe, but let's forget about that and celebrate."

"You're the only woman I know who doesn't freak out about getting older." Patty shook her head as the waiter poured Danielle some wine.

"Why freak out when it's just a number?" She smiled. *When you've been alive for thousands of years, one more doesn't matter.*

* * * *

Janet and Patty were trying to fish their potatoes out of the boiling oil in their fondue pot while Trisha laughed hysterically at them. Danielle wanted to remember this moment when all her friends were happy and enjoying life. Pausing time, she tried to burn an image of them in her mind so she could remember it when they were gone.

"What are you doing?" Mika'il appeared beside her table. He glanced around at all the frozen people. "You're not supposed to be able to stop time."

"I'm not? I must have missed the meeting where you told us what we could and couldn't do. Are you here to yell at me for this or was there some other reason why you're gracing me with your presence?"

He glanced down at her. "I just wanted to say thank you again for helping Dominic. I know it goes against your beliefs."

"This is the third time you've thanked me. Let it go. It wasn't Dominic I was helping out anyway. I'll pay for it somehow, I'm sure." When the archangel didn't answer, she looked up at him. Narrowing her eyes, she said, "I'm right, aren't I? I'm going to pay for being a Good Samaritan."

"It's not my place to tell you how hard I worked on setting this up, Danielle."

"What the hell do you mean by that?"

"I can't tell you how difficult this job has been."

She snorted. "I sometimes wonder exactly what your job is, Mika'il."

"There are moments when I ask God the same thing."

Her cell phone vibrated, breaking the spell. When she reached to answer it, Mika'il disappeared. Her friends were laughing again.

"I have to answer this." She stood and went outside, since the use of cell phones was prohibited within the restaurant. "Hello?"

"Miss Weston?" A husky and angry voice came over the line.

"Yes?"

"This is Grant Carson. I need you to meet me at the museum as soon as possible."

"Why?" She could tell by the tone of his voice that whatever he had planned wasn't going to be a happy meeting.

"It's very important. I don't wish to discuss it over the phone."

"Okay. I'm in Lincoln Park. I'll be there as soon as traffic will let me."

"Fine. I'll be in my lab." He hung up.

She looked at her phone for a moment then put it away. When she went in to say goodbye, her friends protested.

"It's an emergency. I really have to go." She tossed some bills across the table to Janet, ignoring their pleas to take her money back. "That'll cover most of the meal. I'll call you later."

She rushed from the restaurant and waited impatiently for her car. There had to be something wrong, otherwise Grant would never have called her. A faint feeling of uneasiness gathered in her stomach, and suddenly she had a compelling urge to get to the museum. Danielle contemplated using some of her power to hurry the process up, but she wasn't sure if the problem was worth her wasting her power on. Since she didn't have a way to replenish her powers, she decided to drive like mortals would.

Her car arrived and she drove across town without causing an accident or using any power while going as fast as she could on the crowded Chicago streets. She rang the bell beside the employee door. The security guard opened it and nodded.

"Miss Weston, Dr Carson is waiting for you in his lab."

"Thank you." She headed toward the basement area where the labs were.

She opened the door and gasped. Grant stood in the middle of the lab, pottery shards littering the floor around his feet. His tense shoulders and fists propped on his hips spoke of his rage.

"What happened?" She looked around.

"Why don't you tell me?" He glared at her.

"What are you talking about? I didn't have anything to do with this."

"Someone broke in and destroyed all my Peruvian objects. Can you tell me what they were looking for?" He swung an arm wildly to encompass the entire room.

"How should I know?" The unclean feeling hanging over the room kept her from moving past the doorway.

"They left a note." He tossed her a piece of paper.

She caught the note and read.

Tell Danielle I'll be back.

She looked up at Grant. "They mustn't have found what they were looking for."

"I guess not if they're coming back. What were you looking for?"

"I didn't have anything to do with this. I deal in authenticating, Grant, not breaking them." While the power coming from the note told Danielle that it was written by an unrepentant, she didn't sense the same power coming from the broken pottery. Someone else had done the damage. She touched the crate where some of the artifacts had been stored. "This doesn't feel right."

"What do you mean? Of course it doesn't feel right." Grant's anger was evident in his clenched hands and narrowed brown eyes. "Some asshole came in here and destroyed priceless artifacts."

"It feels like two different crimes were committed here." Danielle waved toward the note she had placed on one of the tables. "If I'm right about who might have left the note, she would never have broken any of these pots."

"Why wouldn't she?"

"She's dancing on the edge of sanity, I'll admit, but she has a great deal of respect for antiquities." She reached out to run a finger over a gold chain, stopping herself from actually touching it. "Whoever broke your pottery was looking for something and became angry when he didn't find it."

"Wouldn't your girl do that?" Grant moved to stand in front of the door leading to the vault.

"She has all the time in the world. There's no need for her to panic. If she wanted to, she could just outwait you." She glanced around at the destruction. "No, the other vandal panicked when he couldn't find what he was looking for."

"How do you know any of this? Why should I believe you?" He stared at her with suspicion in his eyes.

She shrugged. There was no way he would accept that she could feel the energy left by the intruders. The note definitely had been left by one of her fallen brethren. More than likely it was Brittany, a forsaken angel Danielle had come across while living in Chicago, and Danielle knew Brittany was holding on to her sanity by a thread. Danielle wished she could help, but from the beginning of her banishment, she had tried to stay neutral. The trouble between the Enforcers and unrepentants wasn't her worry.

For a long time, Danielle's biggest problem had been fighting the depression threatening to drag her to the dark. Finally, she had managed to make peace with her circumstances and was living her life as normally as possible.

"Danielle?"

Blinking, she focused on Grant's face. Even though he was still angry, she saw a hint of worry in his eyes.

"It's just a hunch." Her gaze moved to the vault behind Grant. "Did you bring anything else back from Peru?"

"No," he said quickly.

He was lying, but she wasn't going to push it. "I'll call a friend of mine in the police department. He can come over to write a report up."

"What am I going to tell the Peruvian government? It took a lot of promises for me to get permission to bring the artifacts here." Grant ran his fingers through his hair.

Her hands itched to smooth the locks sticking up, but she didn't think he'd be interested in her touching him. "Put them in some boxes. I'm sure we'll at least be able to glue them back together."

"Glue?" He groaned. "You've got to be kidding."

She was, but she wasn't going to mention it to him. When everything was settled, she'd put them back together. It wouldn't use up too much of her power and he wouldn't get into trouble with any of the governments.

She got out her phone to call Nevan Largent, a detective in the Chicago police department to ask him to join her at the museum. While they waited, she and Grant stood staring at each other. Danielle wanted to know what was behind the vault doors. Whatever it was made Grant extremely nervous whenever she moved closer.

* * * *

Thirty minutes later, the security guard buzzed them. "Dr Carson, there's a Detective Largent here to see you."

"Escort him to the lab, Jeffery." Grant glanced at Danielle, trying to ignore how his body reacted to her being in the same room as him. "Your friend got here quickly."

"Nevan had a feeling something was wrong."

"Does he get those kinds of feelings often? Just like you do?"

He wasn't sure how he felt about her. Anger still boiled under the surface, but instinct told him Danielle didn't have anything to do with the destruction, though she might know who did it. And feeling that way made his attraction to her a little easier to take.

"More than I like," the detective said as he entered the lab. Nevan stood about six foot with a stocky build. His light green eyes surveyed the room, searching the dark corners.

"No more of you waiting to pop out?" Nevan asked Danielle as he moved toward them.

Nevan reminded Grant of a jaguar he had glimpsed in the jungle. The feline had glided across the ground cover without making a noise—Nevan moved with the same grace and stealth.

"It's only me right now," Danielle answered the detective.

"But there were others here earlier and they left angry. What they were looking for wasn't here." He glanced at Grant with eerily intelligent eyes then looked beyond him to the vault. "Or it was here, but they couldn't get at it. Are you going to tell me what they were looking for or do you want me to guess?"

Grant didn't say anything, not trusting the detective simply because Danielle vouched for him.

"I'm Detective Nevan Largent, Dr Carson. While I'm inclined to trust you, Danielle, I want to know what happened from the doctor's viewpoint."

Danielle ignored the detective's wish, and said, "I know who left the note, but she didn't destroy the pots and I had nothing to do with this."

Grant was shocked to see the detective nod. "Why do you believe her?"

"I've worked with her enough to trust her when she tells me she knows who did this." The look Danielle got from Nevan told Grant that the detective wouldn't take any nonsense from her. "What was she looking for, Danielle?"

She shrugged. "I don't know. There's nothing here that would set her off."

Grant shot a glance at the vault. When he looked back, both of them were watching him.

"Is there something in that vault we should know about, Carson?" Nevan asked.

"No, nothing," he stammered. The looks of disbelief he got said neither of them believed him. *I never could lie worth a damn.*

"I don't have a fingerprint kit on me, but I don't think we'd get anything off the pottery anyway." Nevan closed his notebook before turning to Danielle. "Things better not get out of hand."

"Why are you telling me? I've got nothing to do with any of this." She seemed defensive.

"You're the only one I've dealt with and if bad things start happening, I'm going to blame you."

"Thanks a lot, Nevan. I've never caused you trouble." Danielle's face was flushed, anger and disappointment sparked in her blue eyes.

Stay out of it, man. He fought a strange urge to defend her.

"You never have, but something's telling me this is the start of big trouble." Nevan scowled.

"I wish I could say you were lying, Nevan, but I'm afraid you're right. Don't worry, I'll bring people in to help."

"It's those people that worry me." The detective grimaced. "I'll take the report, but you had better fix this problem before I go over the edge."

Largent proceeded to take notes and pictures. An hour later, he was finished. "I'll file the report in a few days." He glared at Danielle again. "I meant what I said. Fix this or I will, and no one will like how I take care of it."

They were silent for a few minutes after the detective left. Grant looked over at Danielle and asked, "A scorned lover?"

She laughed bitterly. "On a good day, Nevan can barely tolerate to be around me. I would drive him to murder if we were lovers."

"Why did I get the feeling there was more being said than just the words I was hearing?"

"There was, but it wasn't anything you'd understand." She turned to sweep the lab with her gaze, pausing at the vault door before looking back at him. "Do you need me to help clean up?"

For the first time, he stopped to look at her and he instantly went hard. Her black linen pants hugged her hips and ass with a faithful touch. Her sequined halter-top was ocean blue to match her eyes. When she turned to walk towards the lab door, he spotted the tattoo on her shoulder. A butterfly decorated her pale skin, perched on a flower. Its blue and black wings were unfurled, striking him with the urge to run his fingers over them to see if they were real.

"No, you go back to whatever you were doing when I called. I hope your date isn't too mad that you left." He didn't like the surge of jealousy rushing through him.

Danielle smiled at him. "It's my birthday. I was celebrating with a few friends, and they know I'll make it up to them."

For some reason, Grant felt like a complete heel. It was her birthday and he'd been giving her shit about the note. *But she knows who left the note. Don't get sappy now just because your cock's interested in her.*

"Happy birthday," he murmured.

"Thanks. I'm going to do a little looking around tonight. Can I catch up with you tomorrow and talk about some things?" Her gaze burned into his and a willingness to agree to anything welled up in him.

"Sure. I'm going to have to talk to the director and the board about the break-in. Can you come later in the afternoon?" He wasn't looking forward to telling his superiors the Peruvian artifacts on loan had been destroyed.

"It'd be a good idea since the people who broke the artifacts had to have gotten into the museum some way and they'll need to look for a security breach."

"Your friend wouldn't have broken in as well?"

An odd smile skipped over her mouth. "There isn't any way you can keep her out and there won't be any sign of her passing through." Danielle nodded at him. "I'll see you tomorrow then."

His gaze followed her out as he told himself he was making sure she was really leaving and that he wasn't checking her ass out. Grumbling to himself, he went back to sweep up the shards of pottery from the floor.

* * * *

Danielle kept a sharp eye out as she walked down the sidewalk in the projects of Chicago. No one would be able to hurt her, even if she wasn't wary about her surroundings. Being a fallen had its advantages.

"Danielle, I'm surprised to see an uptown girl like you hanging out with the dregs of society." Brittany's sharp laugh brought her to a halt.

Turning, she saw the tall blonde woman leaning in a doorway. "I was looking for you, Brittany."

"Oh, I bet I can guess why. That archaeologist didn't like the note I left you." The fallen's smile was all teeth.

Danielle looked into the woman's eyes and saw the darkness encroaching. "No, he didn't. Why did you have to break those artifacts?"

Brittany looked confused. "Those artifacts were fine when I left. I couldn't find what I was looking for."

"What were you looking for?"

A gleam shone in those slightly mad eyes. "The brethren are saying your archaeologist uncovered something that belongs to us. I wanted to see if he really did have it." Brittany shrugged. "I couldn't find it, but I'm warning you. Others will be coming, Danielle."

She was puzzled and worried. "What's so important they'd come here and risk revealing themselves?"

"I don't know. Some say it's so important even Lucifer might come looking for it."

"Lucifer?" That was a name she never wanted to hear. There was no way she could stop Daystar if he chose to take whatever Grant had uncovered.

"Yes. The angel we all love to hate."

"If you found it, what would you do with it? Currying favor with Lucifer isn't something I thought you'd be interested in." She couldn't understand why Brittany would want to help Lucifer out.

"I don't know. Maybe I just want to know what it is." Brittany scowled. "Just know that this city will be crawling soon, if you don't discover what your archaeologist brought home and fix the problems it'll cause."

Brittany disappeared, and Danielle frowned. She wasn't sure how to get Grant to trust her enough to show her what he had discovered, and she didn't have a good feeling about this whole thing if Lucifer was involved. Shivers danced down her spine. Calling in reinforcements wasn't something she wanted to do, but she didn't know if there were any Enforcers in Chicago — it might be easier to ask Dominic to join her for a few days.

She needed to get home. Since she hadn't driven down to the projects, she gathered her power. Disappearing from the sidewalk, she reappeared in her town house and Princess meowed at her, probably annoyed that her dinner was late again.

* * * *

Mika'il stared out of the window of the John Hancock building from his seat at the bar. He sipped his drink and wondered why he'd chosen whiskey when the alcohol didn't do anything to him. He must have gotten into the habit from hanging out with William and Dominic. Both Enforcers felt it helped them to feel more normal.

He didn't understand that. They would never be normal. Even though they had fallen, they were still angels and there was no such thing as a normal angel. Maybe if there was such a thing, he wouldn't feel so helpless when the Lord tested them.

A light streaked across the sky and he found himself wishing on it. *Silly angel,* he thought. *Wishing on a falling star isn't going to change things.* He couldn't help it. His close association with mortals gave him a mixture of beliefs and a vast understanding of yearning for something out of reach.

As he looked out over the city, he noticed a darkness spreading over Chicago.

"So it begins," he said.

"Excuse me, sir, did you say something?" the bartender asked.

"Just talking to myself." He smiled politely. After paying his tab, he stood and moved out of the bar. *Why must we test them?*

A vast silence met his question and he sighed. There were times he hated his job.

Chapter Two

Grant stared at his lab assistant. No wonder there hadn't been any sign of forced entry last night. The idiot's swipe card had been stolen and he hadn't noticed until he'd got to work this morning. The man had been apologizing to him for the past hour.

"Stop it, David," he said, putting a hand up to halt the flow of words. "I know you didn't lose it on purpose and you didn't have anything to do with the break-in. Get back to work."

After going into his office, he shut the door. He hadn't slept a wink last night and wasn't in the best of moods to begin with. Now he had to deal with the grumpy detective Danielle had brought into the problem. Grant dialed the number on the card Nevan had given him.

"Largent," a voice barked into the phone.

"Hello, Detective, this is Grant Carson from the Field Museum."

"Yeah?" There wasn't a hint of friendliness in the man's voice.

"I think I know how the vandals got into the lab."

"Which set of vandals?"

"The ones who broke the pots." He stood up then moved around his office, irritated by Nevan's gruff tone.

"Really? Are you sure you haven't figured out how the note got there?" Sarcasm dripped from the man's words

"I'm taking it one step at a time, Detective. When you catch the guys who broke the pots, more than likely you'll find the person who left the note."

A burst of laughter came over the phone. "Don't count on it, Carson. Okay, I'll stop by after lunch sometime to see what you figured out." Nevan hung up on him.

Slamming the phone down, Grant swore. He had never met anyone as abrasive as the detective. The sound of a throat being cleared brought his attention back to his office. Turning, he saw Danielle standing in the doorway. She was dressed in a black business suit. The straight skirt stopped mid-thigh and her fitted jacket hugged her breasts with mouthwatering precision. The camisole she wore under it was the blue of her eyes. He had noticed she always wore blue in some fashion.

He shifted slightly, uncomfortable with how hard his cock had gotten at the sight of her. It had always been like that, but for some reason, it seemed to be happening more since he had returned from Peru.

"Why do you wear blue?" He blinked. He hadn't meant to ask that—he'd meant to yell at her for bringing that asshole of a detective around.

Her eyes held a weary look tinged with a hint of sadness. "Blue reminds me of home."

"Where is home for you, Ms Weston?" Grant gestured to the chairs in front of his desk and tried not to stare as she made her way over to them before sitting.

Smiling, Danielle pushed her hair back over her shoulder. "You wouldn't have heard of it."

"Do you miss it?" He could have kicked himself. Why was he asking her all these questions? He had managed to go several years without ever talking to her about anything personal, even though he had thought about her in ways as far removed from business as possible.

The look she gave him said that she wasn't sure he really wanted to hear what she had to say. And maybe she was right. He had always been uneasy around her, mostly because of how much he fought his attraction to her. He understood there was something about her that could change him deep inside if he let her close.

"I've missed it since the day I left. The memories of my home haunt me."

"Then why don't you go back there?" He started to reach out and touch her hand. *Don't. You could live to regret reaching out to her.*

After standing, Danielle went to look out of the door into the lab where his assistants were working on several different artifacts. "I'm not allowed to return. I was thrown out long ago for a foolish act and I'm forced to live here among you."

"Live among us? That makes you sound like an alien. Are you from outer space?" He laughed.

She turned back to him. "I talked with some people last night. What else did you uncover at your dig site, Grant?"

The abrupt change in subject startled him for a moment. Blinking, he switched gears. "Nothing."

"I suggest you don't ever try to lie. You're terrible at it. Whatever they were looking for is in that room."

She pointed at the vault door. "And if you don't tell me what it is, we're going to be in some serious trouble."

"What did they tell you?" He wasn't about to expose his secret. It could make or break his career and he wasn't going to say anything until he could prove if it was real or not.

"It's something my associates will come looking for and one of them in particular isn't a man you want to mess with."

"How do I know you're not just trying to find out what it is so that you can tell them about it?" He grimaced—he had as good as told her there was something.

A small smile graced her lips, but she didn't say anything about his slip. "We had a falling out—so to speak—a long time ago, and we try very hard not to have anything to do with each other." A serious expression came over her face. "Trust me, you don't want to get involved with them or the man who leads them. He has no conscience and no compassion. What he wants, he takes and to hell with anyone who might be in his way."

"You make him sound like a devil."

Danielle's harsh laugh broke into the room. "A devil? I guess he could be considered the Devil. He isn't someone you want to deal with either way. I need to know what you have, Grant, before things get worse."

"Why are you and Detective Largent so insistent that things are going to get worse? I'm not thrilled with the fact that someone broke all my pottery, but that doesn't mean the end of the world is coming." He smiled at Danielle. "Couldn't you have found a friendlier detective?"

"Not if I wanted one who will look beyond the obvious to the possibilities. Largent is a pain in the ass, I know, but he's a good detective and he'll do what needs to be done. He's seen a lot in his life and it has left his mind open, much to his anger." She leaned on the desk beside him then stared down at Grant.

"Beyond the obvious?" His gaze was caught by the expanse of creamy thigh exposed by her short skirt. He itched to run his fingers over her skin and see if it was as silky as it looked. Her faint floral scent surrounded him and he took a deep breath to store it in his memory. He realized she was talking. "Excuse me?"

A smirk tipped those full lips and he knew she'd caught the fact he couldn't keep his eyes off her legs.

"There is more than one perpetrator here. Nevan won't have trouble catching the one who broke the pots. The one who left the note, he'll leave to me."

"Why would he be angry about doing that? Seems to me he would be happy to have one less thing to do."

Grant shifted closer to her and his hand brushed against her knee. They both took a sharp breath. She was soft and warm, and he fought the irrational urge to lick the tender area behind her knee. *What the hell has gotten into me?*

He pushed his chair back before standing to move away. If he didn't get away from her, he would do something stupid…like kiss her. That would totally be the wrong thing to do because he still wasn't sure he even liked her.

"Nevan would prefer to be like you. Eyes open to what can only be proven. In his world, there are things that can be seen and touched that can't be proven. Things that must be seen to be believed." Straightening, Danielle headed to the door.

"What things?" He wanted to kick himself. He didn't want her to stick around, but it was obvious his body was ruling his mouth today, not his mind.

"Angels, for one thing."

"Detective Largent sees angels? He doesn't strike me as a particularly religious person." He sounded skeptical, he knew, but he didn't believe in angels any more than he believed in Big Foot.

"It has nothing to do with religion. Angels don't need a mortal's belief in God for them to exist. They were around before mortals came into being. In fact, many would say it was the existence of mortals that caused the downfall of the angels." A dark look showed in her eyes.

What thoughts are racing around her head?

"Legends and myths of ancient people help us form an idea of how they lived. It's interesting that the ancient Jews believed that the evil people did to each other had a spiritual reason behind it," Grant pointed out.

Smiling, Danielle nodded. "All myths and legends hold a bit of truth in them. Why do most cultures in the world have stories of guardians, spirit beings or angels? As a scientist, you don't believe in anything 'otherworldly' or supernatural? Does that include God?"

He wasn't thrilled with the direction the conversation was going. He didn't want to discuss his religious leanings, or lack thereof. "So what do you think is going to happen now?"

She didn't say anything for a moment, just stood there, staring at him. "I'm not sure. The people who vandalized the lab might be regrouping and trying to think of another way to get in here. I don't know what they were looking for, so I can't tell you how determined they are. As I told you about the person who left the note, she has all the time in the world and can outlast you. She might not come back tonight or next week, but she'll be back and there's no way you'll be able to keep what she's looking for away from her."

"Unless I tell you what I brought back." He wasn't going to be scared into doing anything.

"I could make you tell me."

"Yeah, right." He snorted.

The blue of her eyes darkened to black and anger flashed in them. Was Danielle angry because he didn't believe her or because he wasn't scared of her? The walls in the room seemed to close in around them and he couldn't tear his eyes away from hers. When Danielle finally blinked, he found himself standing right in front of her, his lips almost touching hers.

"What the hell?" Grant scrambled away from her.

"I could make you do whatever I wanted you to do, Grant. Lucky for you, I swore never to use my powers against people like you." She glanced down at her watch. "I've got to go. When you decide to get that stick out of your ass, call me and we'll see what we can to do to protect your precious discovery."

She whirled around then stalked out.

Standing there, he watched her leave. He'd almost kissed her. What had short-circuited his mind to cause him to make that mistake? He shook his head while going back into the lab. Maybe some mindless washing of some fire-cracked rock would keep his mind from wondering just how soft her mouth would feel under his. His cock wanted to know how Danielle felt crushed up against it.

Down, boy. There was no way Grant was going to get involved with that woman. His body might think she was the best kind of sex he'd ever seen, but his mind

said there was something else going on behind her
beautiful face.

Chapter Three

"Okay, I'm here now. What did you have to tell me?" Detective Largent strolled into the lab with a glare.

Sighing, Grant set down his tweezers. Taking off his gloves, he told his lab assistants, "You guys can leave for the day."

Nevan stood staring at the graduate students as they made their way out of the lab. When the last one left, shutting the door behind him, Nevan said, "What news have you got for me?"

"I hoped your rude attitude had to do with Danielle and wasn't just part of your everyday personality." Grant gestured for Nevan to sit at one of the tables.

The detective shrugged. "I don't like it around here. Too many old things with too many ghosts attached."

He frowned. "Danielle said your mind was open to the possibilities existing in this world. She said angels were one of them. Are ghosts another?"

Nevan's gaze pinned him with pale green intensity. "She's been talking out of turn, I see. My attitude generally reflects just how bad a day I've been having,

Doctor. Trust me when I tell you that everyone gets treated the same by me."

"Do you believe in angels?"

Those green eyes darkened as the detective snarled at him. "I believe in angels, demons and ghosts, Doctor. You can believe that I'm crazy if you want, but when you've seen them all your life, you tend to believe in them."

He wasn't sure what to say. Grant hadn't been ready for Nevan to confirm what Danielle had told him. "Umm…one of my lab assistants discovered his swipe card was missing when he came to work this morning. I assume that's how the vandals got in."

Nevan was quiet for another moment, just studying him. "You're in for a rude awakening if you hang out with Danielle long enough." The detective pulled out a notebook. "What's the man's name and address? I'll go and talk to him. You're right—one of the criminals who broke in here probably used the swipe card. Locked doors and security systems wouldn't keep the other out. Just keep that in mind."

Grant pulled the information for Nevan out of a pile on the table. He watched the detective fold the paper, then tuck it in his suit pocket. "What do you have against Danielle, Detective?"

Nevan shrugged again before moving aimlessly around the lab. "Nothing except that her kind causes trouble wherever they go. She's been good so far, but I don't trust her not to start something."

"Her kind?" Grant turned on his stool to keep his eyes on Nevan.

"She's a fallen angel." The announcement didn't seem ridiculous coming from the stern detective's mouth.

Grant laughed. "A fallen angel? Like one of those who rebelled against God?"

"Yeah, one of those angels." Nevan held a hand over one of the ropes of gold they'd found in Peru. A frown flitted over his face along with a hint of sadness.

"That's just a legend to explain why evil exists. It's to give people excuses to explain away their own bad behavior. You know, 'the Devil made me do it' sort of thing." He fought the urge to cringe when Nevan turned a cruel smile his way.

"I can see why Lucifer thought he was better than us. We bury our heads in the sand when things aren't the way we think they should be. We deny anything that doesn't make sense to us. Trust me, Doctor, fallen angels exist and they've lived in the world far longer than any civilization of man. They are the superior beings on Earth and we should be happy that the Father hasn't allowed them free rein to do with us as they want."

"But—"

"You can think I'm crazy if you want. It makes no difference to me. I've seen the truth and it hasn't set me free. It's chained me to a world populated by things no normal human should have to see. Other people's belief in my sanity doesn't matter to me. I'll find the person who broke your pots. Danielle will find the fallen who wants the skeleton you're hiding in the vault."

"What?" Grant looked up to see Nevan standing in front of the vault, hand pressed tightly to the door. He wanted to order the detective away from it, but he knew Nevan wouldn't listen. "How did you know?"

"I can feel the spirit that belonged to the skeleton. It's calling to me and if Danielle had gotten closer to the vault, she would have felt it as well." Nevan pulled away to look at Grant with glowing eyes. "I want to see it."

His tone brooked no argument. Sighing, he opened the vault, then pulled out a stainless steel, sheet-covered cart. He lifted the sheet to reveal a pile of bones. A grunt was the only reaction Nevan gave while holding his hand over the skull, his face pale.

"Shit, is this all of it?" Nevan gestured for him to put it away.

"No, there's still one more crate coming. It got lost in the trip up here." Grant grimaced at Nevan's disbelieving look. "I know. I should have made sure all the crates got on the planes at each connection or I should have flown them back here myself."

"I can't believe you let these bones out of your sight. Do you know what kind of trouble could ensue if the wrong people got hold of them?" Nevan shuddered.

"I'm still not sure they're real, so it doesn't matter. I have enough here to test and authenticate."

"Not real? Do you really think someone took the time to make this skeleton and hide it in your dig site just for shits and giggles?" Nevan headed toward the lab door.

"Have you ever heard of a species of men with wings before, Detective?" Grant asked.

"Yes, angels. You need to talk to Danielle, then get this taken care of. Things are a lot more complicated than you think." With that ambiguous parting shot, Nevan disappeared out of the door.

* * * *

"Talk to Danielle. Everyone is conspiring to make sure I talk to her, but it isn't talking I want to do with her," Grant muttered to himself as he sat at the bar.

He had headed there after locking up at the museum. He knew it was stupid, but he was feeling cranky and several stiff drinks might help. He slammed back his shot of whiskey and gestured to the bartender for another.

"What would you like to do with her?" someone asked from beside him.

He turned to see a man take the stool next to him and order a whiskey as well. The stranger was dressed in a tailored three-piece suit. The coat and vest were unbuttoned and the silk tie had been loosened. The man's dark hair gleamed in the low light of the bar. Grant had never seen a man more beautiful. It sounded weird, but that was the only way he could describe him.

"My name is Meical." The man held out his hand.

Grant shook it, trying to rid himself of the feeling that the man knew all his secret thoughts and desires. "I'm Grant."

"I couldn't help but eavesdrop on your ramblings. I was just wondering what you wanted to do to this Danielle if it isn't talking." Meical gripped his shot glass and winked like he knew what Grant was thinking.

"It doesn't involve that, that's for sure. See, the thing is, I'm just not sure I like her. I know my body wants her. It has from the moment I saw her, but there's something about her that makes me uneasy. It's like she knows everything there is to know about me and I don't know a thing about her." Grant listened to his mouth run, wondering why he was telling a stranger all this shit.

"I'm less of a stranger than you think, Grant. So this Danielle is a woman of mystery, huh? Do you think she's going to murder you or something like that?" Meical ordered another shot.

"No. I'm not physically scared of her." Grant met Meical's intriguing silver gaze.

"Then why are you scared of her? She won't hurt you. Heck, she can't hurt you. It's against promises she made herself long ago."

"Do you know Danielle?" Grant looked around the bar. The other patrons were going about their business, but it was like he and Meical were in a bubble and no noise or people intruded.

"I might, but tell me why you're scared of her."

Shrugging, he said, "I guess I'm afraid I might fall in love with her."

"Why is that bad?" Meical frowned.

"Because she could break my heart and I don't want that to happen." Scrubbing his face with his hands, Grant couldn't believe he was turning into such a sap.

"A broken heart is a terrible thing for a man to suffer." There was knowledge and deep understanding in the melodic voice. Meical reached out to tap the bar next to Grant's hand, drawing his gaze back to Meical's face. "But not being willing to risk getting that heart broken is the worst thing to happen to a man."

Shaking his head, he protested, "I don't think so. I had my heart broken once already. I don't plan on going through that pain again. Besides, the lady might be crazy."

"Crazy? What makes you say that?" A puzzled look came then quickly went on the man's face.

"She thinks she has powers and the detective I talked to thinks she's a fallen angel. Of course, he thinks he can see ghosts, spirits and demons so maybe listening to him isn't the best thing to do."

Those silver eyes studied him for a second. "Does it really matter what she might think? She's a beautiful woman. I mean, if you aren't scared of her, then why not see where your interest in her runs?"

"Because I might regret what happens."

"True, but don't you think you might regret never knowing what might have been? I've learned that living with regret is hard, but having regret about not loving is worse. Don't let fear blind you to the chance of a lifetime. Who knows? She might just be your soul mate."

Turning to flag down the bartender and pay his tab, he said, "Soul mate? Man, where are you from?" He turned back to find Meical was gone. If it wasn't for the empty whiskey glass on the bar next to him, Meical might not have even been there.

As he walked out of the bar, he pulled out his cell phone and dialed Danielle's number. Maybe it was the liquid courage or maybe it was Meical's words about regret, but he was going to do something about his attraction. If it all blew up in his face tomorrow, at least he'd have tonight.

* * * *

Danielle hung up the phone and stared at it for a minute.

What would possess Grant to come see her if he couldn't stand her? After their conversation earlier in his office, she figured he'd think she was crazy. *Maybe crazy women turn him on.* That thought made her laugh.

When she had gotten home, she had literally hit her head on the wall. What had she been thinking? Admittedly she was only taking advantage of an urge he'd already had, but to take over his mind and have him almost kiss her? Thank God she had come to her senses before he did. Kissing her would have pushed him over the edge, she imagined.

The phone rang at the same time as the doorbell. After grabbing the cordless phone, she went to answer the door.

"Hello," she said while opening the door to allow Grant in.

Nevan's harsh, "Largent here," drowned Grant's greeting out.

She waved Grant in as she acknowledged the detective. "Nevan, to what do I owe this dubious honor?"

Grant stiffened, glaring at the phone. She couldn't help but smile. Nevan had that effect on a lot of people. Covering the phone, she told Grant, "Why don't you make us some drinks? The liquor and glasses are in the living room."

Turning away, she uncovered the receiver to hear Nevan ask, "Who's there with you?"

She laughed. "It's none of your business."

"Tell Dr Carson he had better tell you the truth or I will," Nevan ordered.

Danielle couldn't stop the twinge of jealousy racing through her. "I'm not going to make him tell me anything. He told you — that should be enough."

"Not remotely. What he's got in his vault is a time bomb waiting to explode and I don't want it going off in my jurisdiction." The detective's annoyance was obvious.

"Then you better work your magic, Detective Largent. I'm staying out of it until I'm asked." After hanging up, Danielle tossed the phone onto the counter. Rubbing her neck for a second, she wondered why everyone was looking to her to solve whatever the problem was. Hell, she didn't even know what was wrong.

"Are you done chatting with our friendly detective?" Grant asked as she made her way into the living room where he sat.

"Yes," she said, sitting next to him on the couch, then took the drink he handed her. "Thank you."

Nodding, he looked around the room. "You have some very nice antiques. I noticed that great sketch of an angel in your hallway. It looks pretty old."

"Of course, it's what I do. Each piece is the perfect example of its style and the period it was created in. Each was chosen for the story that came with it." Danielle was in love with everything in her house.

"What kind of stories?" Grant visibly relaxed, leaning back into the cushions before turning to face her.

There was no way she was going to tell him the true stories. The stories of how she had each piece made by the greatest craftsmen of their time. How she remembered sitting at the Colonial roll top desk listening to the cannons and guns of the Revolutionary War. Grant would never believe that Michelangelo had sculpted the statue of the young Greek boy on her end table or that the sketch hanging in her entryway was a Da Vinci, drawn for her by the master himself.

He'd never understand the importance of the beat-up trunk in her bedroom. She tried to imagine what he would do if she told him she had hidden a runaway slave in it during the Civil War. Each piece was a chapter of her life and told her story throughout the centuries.

"Stories of the families that used to own them." Maybe if his mind were open to the possibility of a supernatural world existing, she would have told him.

"Do you ever imagine what they might have been like?" He studied his glass.

Danielle didn't have to imagine. She knew. "Yeah, it's hard not to. Some of these pieces are hundreds of years old. Think of what they saw. Do you try to create the world and people that made your artifacts?"

"Sure, who wouldn't? It's hard to hold a pot in your hand and not wonder who made it." He sipped his whiskey.

"Grant, why are you here?" She didn't want to destroy the truce they seemed to have, but she couldn't help being curious.

Taking a deep breath, Grant set his glass down then reached for hers. She didn't argue, letting him take it. Her pulse jumped when he ran his callused fingertips over her cheek. She touched her tongue to her lips and licked his finger instead. Grant gasped. Opening her mouth, Danielle sucked his finger in and tasted the salt of his sweat and a little spice. Biting gently, she teased him with her tongue.

Groaning, Grant jerked his finger from her mouth before pulling her to him. Their lips met in a bruising kiss and she melted into him. She wrapped her arms around his neck, deepening the kiss. Danielle's mind yelled at her to think about what she was doing. Her body just begged her to keep doing it. She decided to listen to her body tonight and worry about the consequences in the morning.

They slid their tongues against each other. She ran her fingers through his dark hair. When they pulled away to get a breath, she found herself lying back on the couch. Grant was braced over her with his hips settled between her thighs. He rocked, grinding his erection against her mound. Feeling his hardness, she thrust her hips up to meet him.

She put her hands on his chest and pushed. "Off."

The look of surprise on his face made her giggle.

"Our clothes. I want us naked," she begged.

"Right. Naked is good." Grant jumped to his feet then stripped.

She found buttons and zippers. Her clothes flew off and landed in a heap with his. She had a feeling their first time wasn't going to be slow and gentle. They had been denying their attraction to each other for so long that now the dam had burst, the lust was like a flash flood washing over them with a crash.

Grant pulled her nipple into his warm mouth, causing her to cry out. He combed his fingers through the curls covering her mound. She couldn't believe how wet she was already — of course, she was always wet when Grant was around.

Danielle arched off the couch when Grant found her clit, tugging, rubbing and tapping it until she begged.

"Please, Grant," she pleaded. Danielle wanted his cock buried as deep as possible inside her.

A chuckle vibrated against her nipple as he slid a finger down to her wet entrance. She urged him on with the tilt of her hips. Just the tip of one finger slid inside and she moaned. He pulled it out to run it up and down the sides of her pussy without touching her clit. He kept teasing her until she was wriggling beneath him. Then he pulled away from her breasts and her pussy.

Staring down at her, he grinned. "What do you want, Danielle?"

She wasn't sure she could talk, but if he didn't fuck her soon, she was going to kill him. "Fuck me, Grant. Quit teasing."

"I don't have protection with me. I wasn't planning on coming here."

Danielle shook her head. "You don't need it."

"Are you sure?" He didn't look convinced.

"Yes. It's taken care of." She gripped his hips.

"All right."

She almost came when he took his shaft in his hand to run the head over her clit. He pushed into her, and she spread her legs as far as she could.

Thrusting deep into her, he leaned over and whispered, "I've dreamed of you spread like this, taking my cock hard and fast."

When he was in, she wrapped her legs around his waist and said, "Let's give you what you want."

He took her hard. The sounds of their flesh slapping together blended with their moans. He cupped her ass, bringing her hips up at an angle so his cock rubbed against her sweet spot with each thrust and retreat. Pleasure built and she knew she would be coming soon. Grant's climax would hit as well, she could tell from the way he lost his rhythm.

One more quick thrust exploded her world. Pleasure shot through her, trying to short-circuit her brain. She cried out as he jerked once and filled her with heat. Some small part of her mind was still working and she gathered the power their mutual orgasms released. Danielle didn't normally do that when she had sex — since she wasn't an Enforcer or an unrepentant, she didn't use up her supply of power very often, but something was telling her she was going to need a large store to deal with what was coming.

Panting, Grant collapsed on her. She ran her hands up and down his back, soothing him. He laid his head on her breast and she sighed. It had been a long time since she had shared space with a man she really liked. Her heart wanted to keep him right where he was, but she knew it wasn't the most comfortable place to sleep. When his breathing deepened, she shifted slightly to keep him awake.

"Grant, don't fall asleep yet. Let's get to the bedroom. You can sleep there."

"Oh, okay." His voice was low and satisfied.

A smile broke on her face and smugness reigned for a moment. She had put that satisfaction there. He heaved himself off the couch before reaching down to help her up. Admiring the lean, hard lines of the man standing over her, she took his hand, letting him lift her. She pushed against him, then wrapped her arms around his neck. Pressing her lips to his, Danielle thanked Grant silently.

They made their way to her bedroom then crawled under her blankets. Soon he was sleeping and she lay staring at him. She had a feeling the regrets would arrive tomorrow. She couldn't help being happy that he had come to her place. Now she knew what he tasted and felt like. It was a taste she could easily get addicted to.

Shrugging, she brushed back the hair falling over his forehead. If he turned away and didn't want to continue what they'd started, she'd move on. All the long years of her life had taught her how to deal with disappointment.

Resting her head on his chest, she went to sleep, content for the first time in a long while.

Chapter Four

Danielle snuggled closer to the warm body sharing her bed. She could get used to it if the same mind-blowing night of sex went with it. She was drifting back to sleep when Grant cried out in obvious pain. Shooting out of bed, she looked around, trying to figure out where the trouble was.

"God damn, get this fucking cat off me." Grant's voice was rough from sleep.

Looking at the bed, she burst into laughter at the sight of Princess crouched on top of Grant's groin. His erection had tented the sheet and given the cat something to play with. "Danielle, this isn't funny." Grant's teeth were clenched together and his hands fisted in the sheets.

Drying her cheeks, she stifled the giggles. She went over and picked up her cat. "Princess, he didn't come to play with you."

Danielle dropped the animal on the floor before making her way to her bathroom. Stopping in the doorway, she looked back. Awareness was dawning on his face as he noticed her lack of clothing. "I'm taking a shower," she announced as she shut the door.

Leaning back on it, she called herself a fool. He hadn't really wanted her. It had been the alcohol. Sighing, she pushed away from the door. She'd take a shower then when she got out and found he had left, she would cherish the memory for the marvelous experience it had been and try to forget him.

Danielle managed to conceal her surprise when she stepped from the bathroom and Grant was still there. She thought she had given him the perfect chance to leave, but for some strange reason he hadn't.

Pulling her hair into a ponytail, she went to her closet to grab some clothes. She could feel him staring at her, but she wasn't ready to acknowledge him. She threw on her favorite pair of jeans and a Chicago Bears T-shirt. After heading out to the living room, she picked Grant's clothes up, then took them to him.

"Here, get dressed and we'll talk. Do you want breakfast?" she asked.

Why the hell are you offering him breakfast?

"Yes. That'd be great."

Nodding, she walked to the kitchen. She didn't want to watch him cover up that fine ass. All she wanted was for them to crawl back in bed and have sex for the rest of the day, but she knew that wasn't happening.

After joining her in the kitchen, he looked at her with a confused glance. He seemed to be having trouble deciding what to say to her. She cracked the eggs for the omelets and said, "I know you're wishing we'd never done this, but it happened and we can't go back."

Nodding, he filled two glasses with orange juice. "I know."

"Well, I was surprised you acted on the attraction we feel. I thought you didn't like me." She handed him a plate with an omelet and some toast on it.

He smiled. "I like you, but I'm still not sure I can trust you."

"You don't have to trust someone to sleep with them, I guess." She gestured for him to sit at the table in her breakfast nook.

"True, but if we're going to have any kind of relationship besides the occasional fuck, I need to trust you." He pushed his eggs around his plate.

"I didn't poison them. You can eat it." She took a bite then studied him. "What made you decide to come here then?"

"A conversation I had with a stranger about regret. He acted like he knew you." He lifted his fork to his mouth. "This is pretty good. I didn't think you liked to cook."

"How would you know? I've never had a personal conversation with you before. I'm surprised you knew where I lived." Raising an eyebrow, she made her point.

He flushed. "You're right. I wouldn't know. You're a good chef."

"I've had years of practice. This guy who seemed to know me. What was his name?"

He narrowed his eyes, obviously trying to remember what it was. "Meical."

"Meical? What did he look like?" Danielle had a sneaking suspicion she knew who the stranger at the bar was.

"He was beautiful." Flushing, Grant ducked his head. "I know it sounds weird, but that's the best way to describe him. He had the most unusual silver eyes."

Mika'il, what the hell are you doing?

She stared at Grant. "What did this Meical tell you?"

"As long as I wasn't scared of you, it shouldn't matter if you were crazy or not." Grant frowned.

She laughed at him. "You didn't mean to say that, did you?"

He shook his head. "Not really, but you have to admit those comments you made in my office did make me wonder."

"The ones about making you do whatever I wanted you to do?" She finished then took her empty plate to the sink.

"Yes, those comments. No one has mind control except comic book heroes."

"I know you don't believe in the supernatural. I can accept that, but you have to give me the same respect and accept that I do."

"I'm amazed at how calm you are about everything." Grant really did seem surprised.

She smiled at him. "Did you think I'd pitch a fit and make you pay for sleeping with me when you were drunk?"

He nodded with a sheepish grin. "Yeah, I did."

"You must know some very insecure women then. You didn't decide to sleep with me because I was convenient, but because you were attracted to me and have been for a while. I'm going to look at it that way and enjoy what we did. Maybe I'm hoping we'll be able to do it again. I've been around long enough to know hate is closer to love than most people think. You've never said you hated me, so I figure I have a chance to get some more action from you." She winked at him.

Blushing, he pushed away from the table before taking his plate to the sink. "I should really be going. I have to stop by my apartment, then get back to the lab."

"I'll let you run away for now, but don't think I'm giving up on getting you back into my bed." Laughter bubbled up when he got a panicked look on his face and edged toward the front door. She reached out to touch his arm.

"I'm kidding, Grant. I'm not going to turn into a stalker on you. You know my number and where I live. Also, you might want to consider telling me what you have hidden behind the vault door."

The thoughts racing through his eyes made Danielle wonder, but she wasn't going to push him. It was enough for now that Nevan knew and she could count on the detective clueing her in when the time came. She pressed tight to Grant then wrapped her arms around his neck, bringing his mouth down to hers. Taking her time, she nibbled his lips, making sure he knew she wanted him. When she felt the bulge in his pants grow, she rubbed her hips hard against him.

"Danielle, you aren't making it easy to leave," he whispered, pulling away to rest his forehead against hers.

She grinned at him. "Good. I want you hard and thinking about me all day. I'll be wet thinking about what we did last night."

After giving her another kiss, he turned and headed out of the door. "Have a great day and thanks for last night."

"You too, Grant." She waited to hear the door shut before she said, "I'm sure we'll be repeating it again and again."

Power hummed through her. She'd never been this charged up. She wondered if this was how the Enforcers felt whenever they replenished their strength. Maybe she'd go for a run then head to the office for a while.

* * * *

Grant had been so caught up in remembering the night before, he hadn't noticed the open door of his apartment until he pulled his key out to unlock it. It was opened a crack, but the feeling of danger made him pull out his phone. Dialing Detective Largent's number, he stood there and stared at his door.

He couldn't help but wonder if Danielle had anything to do with the break-in. She could have called her accomplice and told them he would be staying with her, but she hadn't moved all night except for the time she woke him up for sex.

"Largent," the detective answered.

"Detective Largent, it's Grant Carson."

A weary sigh came over the receiver. "Where?"

"My apartment." He gave Nevan his address.

"I'll be there within thirty minutes. I'll bring a crime unit with me. Have you been inside yet?"

"No. I went to unlock the door and noticed it was ajar. I thought it would be wiser to call you and have you deal with it."

"Thanks a lot."

Grant couldn't help but smile to hear the sarcasm in Nevan's voice. It was kind of fun irritating Nevan. It might have been wrong to feel that way, but Nevan struck him as a man too intent on making himself miserable. "Well, you are the main guy on this. I just thought you should get the information from me before someone else jumps your case."

"I can't begin to tell you how much I'd love to have someone else take this. Don't go in there." The detective hung up on him.

Chuckling a bit, Grant put his phone in his pocket. He hoped there wasn't too much damage done. Whoever had broken in was a complete idiot if he thought Grant brought artifacts home from the museum with him. Those items were priceless and irreplaceable—he wouldn't risk breaking one by taking them to an unsecured area.

While he waited for Nevan to arrive, he called Danielle, wondering how strange it was that he had memorized Danielle's number within minutes of getting it from her all those months ago. He tried to calm his emotions, knowing that his reaction to Nevan's irritation was strange when he should be worried about his apartment.

"Hello?" Her voice was breathless.

He felt his cock harden. Maybe calling her so soon after last night wasn't a good idea. "Danielle, it's Grant."

"You couldn't even wait an entire day before you called. I must be better than I thought." She laughed.

"I wish I could say it was your body that made me call."

"What's wrong?" There wasn't any teasing in her voice anymore.

"Someone broke into my apartment last night. How did they know I wasn't there?" He shouldn't be accusing her without knowing all the information first, but she was the only one who knew where he'd been.

"Are you asking me or accusing me of calling someone?"

Grant had the silly urge to apologize. "I'm sorry, but I think I'm accusing you."

"Then would you believe me if I said that I didn't call anyone and I don't know why anyone would want to break into your place?" There was no inflection in her voice to tell him what she was thinking or feeling.

He kept silent for a moment, thinking about her question. If he disregarded the comments about being able to control his mind, she had never lied to him, as far as he knew. Maybe he should take her at face value, for now. "I think I would."

"You're lying, but that's okay. I didn't have anything to do with the break-in because I don't know what those people are looking for." Danielle changed the subject. "Do you need me to come over?"

"No, Largent is on his way." He thrust his hand through his hair. "I'm sorry, Danielle. I wish I could believe you."

He could hear the shrug in her voice. "You'll trust me sooner or later, Grant. I'm just hoping something worse doesn't happen before you do. Nevan will take care of you. Call me if you need me for anything." She hung up.

"Called her to accuse her of sending someone to trash your place?" Nevan asked from behind him.

He jumped, then whirled around. Nevan stood there in worn jeans and a black T-shirt with a windbreaker pulled over it. The man's badge hung from his belt and his gun was stuck in a shoulder holster.

"I didn't know detectives could wear jeans."

Nevan scowled. "I happened to be off duty today, asshole."

Grant felt a twinge of remorse. "You should have told me to call someone else." He saw the dark circles under Nevan's green eyes. "Have you been sleeping all right?"

Snorting, Nevan drew his gun before cautiously pushing the apartment door open.

"I don't think anyone's still in there. I've been standing out here for thirty minutes talking on the phone. Do you really think they'd have waited that long for me?" Grant pointed out.

"Shut up and stay out in the hall until I tell you to come in," Nevan ordered.

Leaning against the wall across from his doorway, Grant shut his eyes and tried to stop thinking for a minute. He was starting to get a headache.

"Okay, you can come in. Just look around, but don't touch anything. The crime unit will check for fingerprints, but I don't think we'll find any. This guy is a professional, though he tends to lose his temper when he can't find something." Nevan pushed the door open wider, gesturing for Grant to come in. "Don't worry. It isn't that bad."

Grant braced himself for the destruction of his home. His desk drawers were pulled out and papers strewn around the floor. As he walked through the apartment, he saw clothes thrown all over, empty closets and drawers. His computer had been destroyed. After making his way back to the living room, he stood in the middle of the mess. His shoulders slumped and Nevan moved to stand next to him.

"He knows what he's looking for and when he doesn't find it, he gets mad. That's his failing and the way for us to catch him." Nevan sounded sure, but exhaustion was evident in his face.

"You ignored the question the first time, so I'll ask it again. Are you not getting any sleep?"

Indecision warred with anger in Nevan's eyes. "It's hard to rest with spirits talking to you. When I sleep, they can come into my dreams and touch me." A shudder raced over the man's body.

"So a spirit touching you is bad?" Grant remembered what Danielle had said about respecting what other people believed, even if he didn't believe.

"I don't know if a spirit can do anything to you, but with someone like me, they could suck my essence dry if I let them. In sleep, there's no way I could stop them. So I tend not to sleep until my body can't take it anymore. Then I go and hide." Nevan slid his gun back in the holster.

"Where can you hide from a spirit?" Grant watched the crime unit come in to start fingerprinting things.

"My condo is built on what was once hallowed ground. I have a room close to the earth that protects me. I don't use it very often because I'm afraid someone will find out about it and destroy it." Nevan looked uncomfortable, so Grant decided to let him off the hook.

"So you think it was the same guy who broke into the lab?"

Nevan nodded. "Sure do. Same MO and everything." Those tired green eyes pinned him and Nevan said, "You're not thinking that Danielle had anything to do with this, are you?"

Grant didn't know why he felt ashamed, but the look in Nevan's eyes said the detective thought he was an idiot for believing that. "I basically accused her of it."

Nevan whopped him in the back of the head. "You're an idiot. What did she say?"

"She said she didn't know who broke into my apartment. Since she doesn't know what they're looking for, she can't help them." Grant shrugged. "I can't help it. I don't trust her yet."

"God, save me from stupid people. I hope you get your head out of your ass before it's too late. I don't want to have to attend your funeral. Something's telling me these men play for keeps." Nevan looked at his watch. "Are you going to be okay here?"

"Sure, I'll start cleaning up as soon as these people leave. I'll have to check what can be salvaged and what needs to be thrown away."

"Okay. I'm going to go home and try to get some sleep. Spirits aren't as active during the day." Nevan turned to walk away. "Don't call me unless you're dying."

"Thanks," Grant said as he followed him to the door.

"Don't thank me, man. Thank Danielle. She's the only reason I'm standing in this doorway. I would have gotten a uniformed officer to take the incident report if she hadn't called me personally."

"I thought you didn't like her or what she was."

"Some of her other brethren, I have a problem with. Danielle herself doesn't bother me. She's kept her nose clean, plus has helped me out when I've gotten into tight spots. I'm just tense because I know bad things are coming and I'm not sure how to stop it."

"Bad things? It's not the end of the world, Detective." Grant laughed.

Nevan shot him a glance. "You're right. It's not the end of the world. I've got to stop taking all this shit so seriously. It's just so hard sometimes when you have spirits trying to drain you, ghosts dancing in the shadows and fallen angels hanging around. I'll try not to worry you with my problems."

Jesus, how was it possible for him to feel bad about a silly comment? Yet he did and he wanted to apologize again, but Nevan disappeared before he could say anything. This day had gone straight down the tubes and it wasn't even noon yet. He'd clean up, then maybe get drunk, because that seemed to be something he could do without upsetting anyone.

Chapter Five

"Please tell me you didn't sleep with that bastard," Nevan's voice came over her phone.

Danielle pulled it away from her ear to stare at it for a second. Putting it back, she said, "Did you just call him a bastard?"

"Yes, I did. I hate people who hide their head in the sand, Danielle, and this guy is going to suffocate if he doesn't pull it out."

The exhaustion coming from Nevan was overwhelming. "Nevan, I think you need to get some sleep. Grant isn't that bad. He doesn't understand what's happening."

"If he'd let you talk to him, he'd understand why we need to take care of things right away." Nevan groaned.

"He's a scientist. He understands proof and things he can touch."

"I think he touched you last night, so why wouldn't he believe you?"

"Why are you so caught up in the fact that we slept together? I never thought you cared that much about me." She shuffled through some of the papers on her desk. An email her secretary had printed out caught her eye.

"It's never been you, darling. I don't really like most people I deal with." He sighed.

"I know, Nevan. It's hard to deal with people when you can see the ghosts surrounding them." She read the email, then read again slower. "Nevan, a friend of mine sent me an email. There was a jewelry store robbed in Peru."

"What does that have to do with us or you for that matter?"

"Ten million dollars' worth of emeralds was stolen two nights before Grant's artifacts were flown home." She turned to her computer then pulled up the email. "I'm forwarding it to you right now."

"Do you think Grant stole the emeralds and smuggled them into the country?" Nevan sounded skeptical.

"No. I think someone else stole them, then stashed them in some of Grant's artifacts to get them into the country. Then someone else was supposed to come and get them. Unfortunately, something must have happened along the way. Either someone else found them or they've been misplaced."

"Shit. I was really looking forward to getting some sleep today."

"Why don't you grab a nap? I'll run over to see Grant and talk to him about this."

"You just want to see him again, but I'll let you do it. I'm dead on my feet." Nevan chuckled. "I call you later when I get up."

She hung up, then called the museum—it wouldn't have taken Grant long to clean up his apartment, so she thought he would have headed to the lab.

"Archaeology lab." The young voice on the other end of the phone had to belong to one of the graduate students.

"May I speak to Dr Carson, please?"

"Sure, just a second." She heard the girl call out to Grant, "Dr Carson, you've got a phone call."

"Who is it?" Grant yelled back.

Before the girl could ask, she said, "Tell him it's Danielle and I really need to talk to him."

The message was relayed and Grant said, "I don't have time to meet with her now. I'm behind."

"I'll be by after the lab closes to see him. If he's not there, I'll track him down."

"Um…okay, I'll let him know." Hesitation sounded in the girl's voice.

"He won't kill you. Thanks." After hanging up, she turned to the computer to start her own search.

* * * *

Grant looked up when someone cleared their throat. Danielle stood in the doorway, smiling at him.

"Happiness looks good on you." He snapped his mouth shut. He hadn't meant to say that out loud to her.

"What are you talking about?" She looked puzzled.

"I was thinking early this morning how happy you looked. Then I realized I've never seen happiness in your eyes. You smile and laugh, but your eyes are always sad."

Her face was serious for a moment, then the sadness returned. "When you've lived as long as I have, there isn't much to make you happy anymore. Also, the reason for my banishment caused heartache and pain for a lot of us. I remember it every second of my life."

She turned away from him to look at some potsherds on the counter. Her red tank top revealed the butterfly tattoo he had seen before. The colorful picture inked on her shoulder drew him out of his seat and over to her. Reaching out, he traced the delicate lines of the wings.

"Why a butterfly?" Grant asked quietly.

"Why not?" She seemed reluctant to talk to him about it.

"It must mean something to you. All of the furniture in your house has some story behind it. You wouldn't put a butterfly on your body permanently if it didn't mean something to you." He pressed his lips to the tattoo, feeling her shudder.

"Some people see the butterfly as a symbol of rebirth."

"Do you?"

Sliding his arms around her waist, he pulled her close. He looked over her shoulder to see what she was staring at. On the table in front of them were two armbands. He remembered how excited the team had been when one of the grad students had uncovered them. He glanced from the armbands to the vault where the skeleton was. They had been found *in situ* in the skeleton's burial place.

"Where did you find these?" Danielle reached out a trembling hand, but didn't touch them.

"They're beautiful, aren't they? We found them at the dig site in Peru. They're the most intricate examples we've ever found. I figure the etchings must represent a mythological creature. This is the first one we were able to clean." He traced the details of a winged man kneeling like he was praying.

"Was there anything else found with them?"

"Ah, nothing worth talking about."

"You must have been a good kid when you were younger, because you couldn't lie if your life depended on it. I chose the butterfly for what it represents to me." She pushed away from him then wandered around the lab. She looked at the artifacts on the various tables, but didn't try to touch any of them.

Grant paused at the change of subject, but let it go. "Does it symbolize rebirth to you as well?"

"Not necessarily rebirth as much as it is a wish to go back to where I came from. A need to be remade into what I once was."

"What were you once? Why aren't you the same person you were before you left your home?"

Danielle made her way closer to the vault. He remembered Nevan saying that Danielle would know what was in the vault if she got close enough to it. Stiffening, he wanted to run and herd her away from the door.

She stopped then turned toward him. Melancholy had entered into her eyes. He couldn't help but go to her and wrap his arms around her. Brushing her hair with his lips, Grant ran his hands up and down her back. He wasn't sure why he needed to comfort her, just that he did, and she relaxed into him.

"I was innocent and trusting. That's where I went wrong. I trusted the wrong person and he led me astray." Leaning back, she stared up at him.

"Did he hurt you?" A rush of anger burned through him. No one would hurt this woman if he could help it. Why was he so protective of her when he didn't know who she really was?

"There was no one to blame for my banishment except myself. I won't lay my misfortunes at the feet of others. There's no point in whining about it though.

Nothing will change, so I've learned to live with it." She wound her hands into his hair, then pulled his lips down to hers.

This isn't the place for this, his prudish mind thought, but his body overruled it and threw itself into the kiss. He learned the nuances of her mouth and the smoothness of her tongue. Stroking the roof of her mouth made her shiver and nipping at her bottom lip made her moan. He pressed her back against the lab table to wedge his hips between her thighs. Lifting her up so her ass rested on the edge, he rubbed his erection against her mound.

Her head fell back and Danielle moaned, offering him unfettered access to her throat. He sucked on the pulse beating at the base of her neck. Licking her sweat from her skin, he feasted on the sensitive spot right behind her ear. One nip and all the tension melted out of her.

"Oh, Grant, that's perfect."

Pushing the short skirt she wore up to her waist, he discovered she wasn't wearing panties, leaving her pussy uncovered for him. "We rushed the first time and I was still waking up for the second. I think we'll need to take some extra time to see if you taste good."

Kneeling on the floor, he placed her legs over his shoulders and sent a puff of warm air over her clit. Her hips arched and he leaned closer to flick her with the tip of his tongue. Bracing her hands on the table, she pushed her pussy toward him, silently begging for more. Since she was enjoying it, he gave her what she wanted. He took a long swipe with his tongue from her entrance to where her button pulsed. Reaching up, he grasped her hips and held her down while he bathed her with his tongue. With long slow strokes then hard fast licks, he drove her toward her peak.

"More," she pleaded.

He pushed his tongue into her and she cried out. Grant slid his finger in along with his tongue on the second thrust. Moving his mouth back up to her clit, he sucked her in while he fucked her with two fingers, making sure to scrape her sweet spot each time he pulled out.

Danielle rode his fingers with abandon, her moans and sighs filling the lab. Grant's cock was so hard that he hurt. He couldn't wait to ride her again, but he wanted her to come first. Her inner muscles clenched around his fingers and her juices dampened his hand as her orgasm overtook her.

"Grant," she cried, thrashing her head from side to side.

He used soft licks to bring her down as the aftershocks rippled through her. When she was petting his hair instead of gripping it, he placed one last kiss on her pussy then stood up.

Chapter Six

"Well, I didn't think you had it in you, Dr Carson." Danielle laughed softly.

She didn't feel like moving either, but there was something digging into her back. She pushed at his shoulder.

"You need to get up. I'm lying on something."

After shooting to his feet, Grant yanked her to hers. "Shit, did we break anything?"

She was a little miffed that he seemed more concerned for his artifacts than her. Straightening her clothes, she made her way to the lab door. "I wouldn't have let you fuck me on a lab table if there were artifacts on it, Grant."

She found her briefcase where she had set it down when she arrived. Pulling the papers out, she tossed the folder on the nearest table. "I think these are what they were looking for. Maybe you know where they are. Maybe you don't, but you better figure something out. Next time they might come after you or one of your assistants. Have a good night."

As Danielle stalked out, she didn't know why she was so mad. Grant might be coming to like her, but he wasn't going to suddenly declare his undying love for her.

"Danielle, wait."

She turned to see Grant walking up to her. He had collected himself and held out a folder to her.

"What is this?"

"It could be the reason why the lab and your apartment were broken into." She shrugged. "Nevan's looking into it as well."

"Looking into what?" Grant matched her stride as they headed toward the exit.

"A jewelry store was robbed in Lima two days before your artifacts were flown out of the Jorge Chavez Airport. I think the thief put them in your crates. His partner was probably supposed to get them, but something went wrong and the guy didn't find them where he thought they would be. Now he's panicking and I think you might be in danger until he finds them."

They waved to the security guard as they slid their identity cards through the reader. Night had fallen while they'd been inside. She took a deep breath of the moist air coming off Lake Michigan. She became lost in the memories of walking in Jackson Park with hundreds of other people.

A touch to her arm brought her back. Grant was staring at her with a puzzled look on his face.

"Sorry, I was thinking about something else." Danielle shook off the lingering memories. "What were you saying?"

"Do you really think I could be in danger? Why would they come after me?"

"Yes, I do. There's ten million dollars' worth of emeralds somewhere. Right now they think you know where they are."

"But I don't," he protested.

"Wrong answer." A man dressed in dark clothing stepped from the shadows. He grabbed Grant, driving his fist into his stomach.

"Danielle, run. Go get security," Grant gasped as the man hit him again.

"Where are the emeralds?" The attacker drove another fist into Grant's face.

Damn. This couldn't be happening. Danielle froze in a moment when she needed to make a decision. She could stop the attacker without a problem, but she had never used her powers against a mortal, having made a promise to herself that she wouldn't do that.

She heard Grant groan and realized she needed to do something before he got seriously injured. Since she had never done anything like this before, she wasn't sure what to do. She'd have to wing it.

She grabbed the man's arm as he pulled it back to throw another punch. She sent a surge through the man's body, overloading his brain and causing his muscles to tighten. She wasn't sure how long he'd be immobile, but she managed to pry Grant from the man's hand.

"What happened?" Blood dripped from Grant's nose and split lip.

"I overloaded his brain with a burst of energy. I don't know how long it'll last so we've got to get out of here."

The level of confusion Grant was feeling was obvious when he didn't question or argue with her. She grabbed the folder he had dropped when the man attacked him. When they got farther away, she used a little power to draw a cab to them.

"Is he okay?" the cabbie asked as she stuffed Grant into the taxi.

"Yeah, he fell." She gave the driver her address and called Nevan, letting Grant lean on her.

"What now?" Nevan barked into the phone.

She didn't question how the detective knew it was her. "Get over to my place. We had an incident."

"An incident? Shit, Danielle, can't your people stay out of trouble?"

"Since it was an attack by a mortal, I don't think you should be pitching rocks at my glass house."

"What?"

"Nothing. We'll be there in ten minutes."

"I'm twenty minutes behind you."

Hanging up, she checked Grant. He leaned against her with his head on her shoulder. Digging through her pockets, she came up with a tissue and dabbed at the split lip. He drew in a deep breath.

"Sorry. I know it hurts, but you're getting blood on everything," she murmured, pressing the tissue to Grant's lip while they headed to her place.

* * * *

Nevan arrived as Danielle finished settling Grant on her couch.

"Why didn't you run like I told you to?" Grant demanded.

Sighing, Danielle gave Nevan a long-suffering look. "I wasn't going to leave you at the mercy of that man."

"You could've been hurt."

Nevan snorted. "You don't have to worry about Danielle getting hurt. She's tougher than crocodile skin."

"Thanks for the vote of confidence, Nevan."

"Hey, it was a compliment." Nevan winked at Grant, then sat in one of the chairs.

"You date some weird women if they take being compared to a crocodile as a compliment." Danielle pushed Grant's legs over before sitting on the couch, leaning against him.

"I really don't want to discuss Largent's dating." Grant realized he sounded grumpy, but damn it, he hurt. All he wanted to do was to curl up and sleep for several hours or until his face stopped throbbing at least.

She rested her hand on his thigh and a tingling radiated from that area. He didn't think he had enough energy to feel desire, but as the tingling spread, he started to feel better. Shutting his eyes, he tried to focus on the conversation instead of her hand.

"I'd given Grant the folder about the emerald theft. We were leaving the museum when this man attacked." Danielle's voice trembled a little.

In his pain, he had forgotten that she had probably been scared as well. He heard the rustle of paper and figured Nevan had pulled out his little notebook.

"What did he look like?"

He tried to recreate the man in the darkness behind his eyelids, but nothing happened. "It was too dark. He jumped us in a section of the parking lot that had hardly any lights in it."

Nevan grunted. "Why didn't you notice him, Danielle?"

The tone in his voice seemed to be blaming her for not seeing the man. Grant struggled to sit up. "Now listen here. She couldn't see him because it was dark out. He was dressed in black as well. This guy was a professional."

She pushed him back down on the couch gently. "I wasn't paying attention. I got caught up in memories."

"You can't do that, especially if these men are dangerous. Which obviously they are," Nevan pointed out.

"I know, but the museum and the area around it has a lot of memories for me." She shrugged.

Grant made a mental note to ask her what kind of memories could hold her attention that much. He stroked his palm over her hand and she smiled at him.

"I know. How did you take care of him? Should I go looking at hospitals in the city?"

She shook her head. "I hit him with a surge of energy. His muscles froze up while I managed to get Grant away without another altercation."

"A surge of energy?" Nevan glanced at her. "I didn't know you could do that."

"Sure, I can do anything I need to save myself. I've just chosen never to harm a mortal with my powers."

"A mortal?" Grant asked, not sure he was hearing them right.

Reaching out, she stroked his forehead. The tingling moved from his thigh to his face. The throbbing began to ease and his eyelids drooped.

"If you've never done anything like that before, how do you know if you used the right amount and didn't destroy that man's brain? He might be the scum of the earth, Danielle, but he doesn't deserve to get his brain fried."

"I know, but what was I supposed to do, Nevan? If I took off for a security guard, Grant could have been hurt far worse than he was. I've been granted a power that I have to use. Even if I didn't sign on to protect mortals, I can't let them get hurt."

Danielle continued to stroke his forehead, but the trembling seemed to be worse. He wanted to tell Nevan to stop berating her for trying to save him. Nothing came out and he allowed his senses to become submerged in the sensations he was feeling.

"Are you healing him?" Nevan asked Danielle as he sat watching her.

"Just a bit."

When she lifted her hand, the cuts had healed to look like they were days old instead of hours. She brushed a lock of hair off Grant's forehead, then leaned down to kiss his cheek. Standing up, she gestured for Nevan to follow her.

"Let's have something to drink. This has been a long night."

She made her way to the kitchen before making tea. While she waited for the water to boil, she studied Nevan. The dark circles under his eyes didn't seem so bad and there wasn't a feel of utter exhaustion rolling off him either.

"You were able to get some sleep."

Nevan nodded. "Enough so that I'm not in danger of killing myself if I drive a car."

"What's going on, Nevan?"

Nevan shifted his gaze away from hers. "What are you talking about?"

"Don't treat me like I'm stupid. We both know the emeralds aren't what the fallen are looking for. You know what he has. Tell me." She poured out the tea then handed a cup to him.

Nevan stared into the liquid. She wondered if he could read tea leaves as well. She was sure there were depths to Nevan she didn't even know existed. Sighing, he took a sip.

"I can't do that, Danielle. He told me believing I'd keep it a secret from you. I'm not sure why he doesn't want you to know. If he knew what he had and what you were, it would be different, but he doesn't realize what he has. All I can say is get close to that vault. Don't let him keep you away." Largent drank his tea before setting the cup on the counter. Reaching out, he surprised Danielle by hugging her. "I know he's special to you, but be sure you know what you want when you allow him close to you. You endanger him even by being friends with him."

Stunned, she stood in the kitchen while Nevan let himself out. Was Nevan able to see the future? Had he seen a time when Grant might love her? She shook her head. It wasn't important at the moment. She had to get Grant to bed and let him sleep to heal.

She managed to get Grant stripped and into her bed without disturbing him too much. Climbing in with him, she prayed that he wouldn't be hurt again. God didn't listen to prayers for herself, but He wouldn't be so cruel as to ignore her pleas for a mortal He loved.

Chapter Seven

"Wake up, Grant."

Turning over, Grant groaned. "Did you get the number of the bus that hit me?"

"If you can joke, you can get up."

Popping his eyes open, he frowned at Danielle who leaned over him. "Why are you here?"

She glanced around, then back at him. "Excuse me? This is my bedroom. Why wouldn't I be here?"

He pushed himself up to lean against her headboard. "What happened last night? I feel like someone kicked my ass."

Standing, she moved to the door. "Imagine that. Someone tried to do exactly that." She disappeared down the hall.

"What? Wait a moment," Grant called out as he scrambled to get out of bed. Ignoring the fact he was naked, he raced into the kitchen to find Danielle sipping on a cup of coffee, reading the newspaper. "Did you say someone tried to kick my ass?"

"Look at your face." She pointed to the mirror in the hallway.

He winced as he checked his reflection.

"If it happened last night, why does it look like it was a while ago?" He got back to the kitchen to catch her shrugging.

"You must be a quick healer. You've still got quite a few bruises on you."

He stared at her. "I've never healed that quickly. Didn't he want to know where the emeralds were?"

"I warned you something would happen. These men play for keeps. I just hope they don't kill anyone."

He hunched his shoulders. "Shit, Danielle, it's not my fault. I can't give them what I don't have."

She walked over, then wrapped her arms around his waist. Leaning against him, she kissed his cheek. "I know it's not your fault. I'm angry and I'm taking it out on you."

He hugged her close.

"I'm mad that these psychos are targeting you when you have nothing to do with it. To think they'd try to hurt you makes me furious."

He laughed. "How are you going to protect me? I'm worried they'll come after you. That guy doesn't know you don't have the emeralds either. What's to stop him from hurting you?"

She started giggling. He pushed her back and stared as she doubled over in laughter.

"What's so funny?"

When she caught her breath, she said, "Grant, there's no way they can hurt me."

Shaking his head, anger welled up. He grabbed her arms and forced her to look at him. "This isn't funny, Danielle."

Cupping his cheek, she smiled. "I know and I understand the danger, but until we or they find the jewels, there's nothing we can do except keep our eyes open."

Their lips met in a soft kiss. Grant didn't feel any overwhelming passion, just tender emotion. The thought he might lose her scared him in a way he'd never been scared before.

The phone rang. Sighing, she stepped back to answer it. Grant decided to take a shower, then go to his office where he had a set of clothes. He couldn't allow all the outside problems to put him behind schedule. The artifacts from the Peruvian site needed to be cataloged, cleaned, photographed and numbered. He also had to figure out a way to put the pots back together.

* * * *

Danielle waited for Grant to get out of the shower. As much as she would have loved to stay home and have sex all day, she would send him to the museum. Brittany had called and wanted to meet. The unrepentant said she had information about what her brethren were looking for. She wasn't sure if she believed Brittany or not, but she had to go. She had to find out the truth, since Grant didn't seem inclined to trust her.

She was thinking about the situation when Grant came into her bedroom. Her heart skipped a beat at the sight of him in a towel. Before she lost control and jumped him, she waved toward a pile of clothes.

"I got the blood out of them. Get dressed and I'll share a taxi with you."

"Trying to get rid of me?" Winking, he dropped the towel then teased her with the sight of his firm ass as he bent over to grab his pants.

"You have no clue how much I'd love to keep you here with me, but I've got a meeting to get to."

"An emergency meeting?" He tucked his shirt in then sat to put his shoes on.

"I guess you could call it that. I'll stop by and we can grab lunch at the museum café. I'll tell you about it then."

She led the way out of the apartment to where the taxi she'd called was waiting. She told the driver where to take them. Settling next to her, Grant took her hand.

"This isn't about the emeralds, is it? It's too dangerous for you to go looking into it on your own. Let Largent take care of it."

She was pleased he was worried about her, even though she would be perfectly safe. "No, this is about something different. Don't worry. I'll be fine and Nevan knows where I'll be."

"Why does Largent know and you won't tell me anything until afterwards?" He frowned.

Was that jealousy in his voice? Danielle shook her head. There wasn't any way he'd be jealous. They were becoming friends as well as lovers. He hadn't tried to stake any kind of claim yet, but her heart was hoping he would.

"He knows because he's the only one who can help me if something goes wrong. You wouldn't be any help to me."

He started to protest and she stopped him with an upraised hand. "Don't argue with me, Grant. I know more about the person I'm meeting than you do and this is the best way. As soon as I'm done, I'll come and tell you what I know. That's the best you'll get from me."

He sighed and sat back in the seat to pout.

Lord, save me from overprotective nosy men.

"I'll see you when you're done with your meeting, right?" Grant brushed a kiss over her lips when they pulled up to the curb at the museum.

"Yes, I'll be back for lunch. Don't worry. Nevan will be there to back me up."

"I can't say that fills me with confidence, but I'll trust you to keep yourself safe."

"Thanks. Now get out of here and go clean some artifacts." She waited until Grant was out of the cab before she told the driver, "Take me to Cabrini-Green."

The driver's eyes widened and he said, "You don't really want to go there, do you, miss?"

"Yes, I do. I have a meeting and a police officer is coming to assist me. I'll be fine."

"Okay, miss. You're not expecting me to wait around, are you?"

"No. You can leave. I'll catch a ride back with the detective." She looked out of the window as they drove into the most notorious area of Chicago. She knew why Brittany had picked Cabrini-Green for their meeting. A lot of things happened there that got overlooked by the police. The authorities did their best to curb the crime, but there were only so many officers and so much of the city elsewhere needed them, so some things got shuffled to the side. She figured Brittany was going to use that fact to her advantage. People tended not to see things at Cabrini-Green.

"Here we are, lady. You take care." The driver pulled to the curb and looked back at her.

Danielle could tell he really wanted to stop her, but she climbed out and handed him his money. "Don't worry. I'll be fine."

He looked skeptical, but didn't protest as she moved off. Danielle ignored the stares she received from the people sitting on the front steps of the houses and apartments. She wasn't supposed to be in their world, and should be glad Brittany had chosen to have the meeting during the day and not at night—it was even more dangerous after dark when the predators came out to hunt.

A whimper came from the alley she was passing. Stopping to glance down the alleyway, she saw a small bundle moving. It looked like a puppy. A lot of dog fighting went on in the area, so she headed over to check the animal. Kneeling, she unwrapped the blanket from around a small brown dog. Strips had been peeled from its skin and it was bleeding from several cuts. An attack from another dog wouldn't have caused those types of injuries. Before she could drop the dog and move away, two hands clamped down on her shoulder and she cried out at the pain.

"I knew you wouldn't be able to resist a helpless dog," Brittany snarled in her ear. "Your weakness is my gain."

Danielle tried to force words from her throat, but she felt her lungs closing. Brittany was pulling all her power from her. There was nothing she could do to counter it. The unrepentant was like a vacuum, sucking the very essence that made her not just a fallen, but an angel as well. Her body arched and she threw her head back as the pain built. It was almost as bad as when Mika'il had taken her wings.

Dear God, help me, she cried out in silent anguish.

* * * *

Mika'il looked up at the clear blue sky from where he stood at the top of the Sears Tower. "She's trying, Father. I do believe there's goodness in some of them. When will the testing be over and forgiveness given?"

A breeze blew over his cheeks and he felt a slight sting. Bowing his head, he acknowledged the rebuke. It wasn't his place to question the Father. He could only do as God demanded, even if it broke his heart to do so.

Chapter Eight

"Danielle's not going to be meeting you for lunch like she planned," Nevan told Grant on the phone.

"Why? Did her meeting run long?" Grant finished cleaning the dirt off one of the elaborate armbands with a small brush.

"She's not feeling good." Nevan sounded tired.

"Is she okay? You don't sound very good either." Grant set the tool down then walked into his office. After shutting the door, he shrugged off the lab coat he was wearing.

"I'm fine, just tired. I'm sure after a long nap and some tender care from you, she'll be fine."

"I'm ready for lunch now. Maybe I'll take a ride over and check on her." He headed back out of the lab, waving at his students.

"She might already be sleeping, so you can find her key under the red planter on her front steps."

"Why do you know where it is?" Grant wasn't jealous. At least that was what he was trying to tell himself.

"I had to feed that bitch cat of hers while she was on vacation before. There's no need to be jealous. Go check up on her and if you need me, you've got my number." Nevan hung up.

Grant went outside to flag down a cab. He couldn't help but worry that something had gone wrong at Danielle's meeting.

* * * *

The key had been right where Nevan had told him it would be. He felt strange going into her house without her permission, but he had tried knocking. When there hadn't been an answer or any sound of movement whatsoever, he had gotten worried and gone in. The cat met him in the hallway then led him to her bedroom.

Danielle lay sprawled across the bed, her brunette hair waved across her pillows. Her normally pale skin was sallow and she had lines of exhaustion across her forehead. He touched her cheek to see if she was sick, then tugging at the blankets, he managed to get them pulled over her without waking her up. He fought the urge to climb in bed with her — if he did, he'd end up spending the entire day curled around her. Grant's stomach rumbled, reminding him he was on his lunch break. *Might as well eat here.* The doorbell rang as he was making his way to the kitchen.

He opened the door just as the woman was about to ring the bell again. They stood staring at each other for a second.

"Who the hell are you?" the redhead asked suspiciously.

"I'm Grant Carson. I work with Danielle at the museum. Who are you?" Blocking the doorway, he didn't let her in.

"Janet. I'm Danielle's best friend. Hell, you're the archaeologist she's been drooling over since you started working at the Field." She looked over his shoulder. "Where is she?"

"She wasn't feeling good. She's taking a nap." He stepped back to allow her to come inside.

"You're kidding. Danielle's never sick." Janet made her way to the bedroom before peeking in on her friend. "Shit, man. She doesn't look good. What's wrong with her?"

"I don't know. Detective Largent called me to let me know she wasn't going to meet me for lunch."

Grimacing, she headed to the kitchen. "Detective Hard Ass called you? I find that unbelievable. He scares me."

Janet opened the fridge to pull out sandwich makings. After sitting at the table, he watched her and asked, "How long have you and Danielle been friends?"

"I moved here about ten years ago and I met her shortly after that. I thought she was a bitch at first." Smiling, Janet sat across from him.

"Really? Why?" He was enjoying the chance to learn more about Danielle.

"She's so beautiful and distant. If I didn't know her, I'd figure she wasn't very friendly. I know a lot of her secrets, but I still get the feeling there's a ton of stuff she isn't telling me. I think something happened in her past that she hasn't forgotten and it haunts her to this day."

He nodded. "Does she seem delusional to you?"

Frowning, Janet glared at him. "Delusional? What the hell are you talking about?"

Shifting uncomfortably, he shrugged. "Just some conversations I've had with her make me wonder if she's in her right mind."

"And what kind of sick fuck are you that you'll sleep with her even though you think she's crazy?" Shaking her head, she got up, then took his plate from him. "It truly takes all kinds. Tell you what, get the hell out of here and I won't tell her anything of what we said."

Flushing, he moved toward the door. "Who says I'm sleeping with her?"

She shot him a glance. "Danielle always gets what she wants and she's wanted you for a long time now."

"I see. How do I know she didn't make a suggestion that made me sleep with her? What am I supposed to think when she tells me she can control me with her mind? She puts her hands on me and my wounds look like the fight happened weeks ago. The detective should be rational and tell me I'm imagining things. Instead he tells me he can see spirits and I shouldn't judge people."

Janet stopped for a moment and considered him. "Nevan can see spirits? Well that would explain his problems. As for you, did you ever consider that maybe you should believe her? I've seen her do things I couldn't explain, but I chose to accept them instead of thinking she was crazy." After flinging open the door, she pushed him out. "Don't worry about the crazy woman. I'll take care of her."

The door slammed shut in his face and he wondered what he'd said wrong. Was Janet right? Was he sick for wanting to sleep with Danielle, even if he wasn't sure she was totally sane? Shaking his head, he checked his watch and swore. He was going to be late getting back to the lab.

* * * *

Danielle dragged her eyes open and stared at the ceiling for a few minutes. She was trying to decide whether she really needed to go to the bathroom or if she should just roll over and go back to sleep. Finally the urgency made the decision easy. She groaned as she climbed out of bed. She felt like she was a hundred years old. A giggle snuck out—technically she was thousands of years old. She tried to think of the exact number and if there was even a word to describe how old she was. *Ancient,* her mind supplied. Nodding, she crept to the bathroom. That word pretty much summed up not only how old she was, but also how old she felt at that moment.

After using the toilet and washing her hands, she opened the door to go back to bed, and squeaked when she saw Janet leaning against the wall. She tried to remember if they were supposed to meet today. Her friend helped her back to her room. After tucking her in as if she were a child, Janet sat next to her, brushing her hair off her face.

"You look better than you did when I got here."

"How long have I been asleep?" She snuggled into the pillows. One of them still smelled like Grant and his scent soothed her.

"I don't know. You were asleep when I got here about six hours ago. What happened, Danielle?" Her friend looked concerned.

"I'm fine and I'll be better tomorrow. Resting is the best thing for me."

Janet smirked. "I can think of one thing that would be better than sleeping for you. I met your newest boyfriend. The man is yummy. I can see why you wouldn't introduce me to him."

There wasn't any point in pretending not to know what Janet was talking about. "Grant was here. When was that?"

"He hadn't been here long before I showed up and he didn't stay long. He's a hottie, Danielle, but I'm not sure he's the right one for you." Janet seemed unsure.

"Did he say something about me being crazy?" She laughed at Janet's nod. "Don't worry. It'll take a while for him to get used to me. I don't plan on giving up on him though. He's the best lover I've ever had and I don't want to go back to a lonely bed."

"Hey, that's all I need to hear. Now do you think you can take care of yourself? I have a date, but I'm willing to break it if you need me to stay." Janet stood to move toward the hallway.

Shooing her out, Danielle said, "I'll be fine. Food is sounding really good. I think I'll order delivery and just laze around tonight. Have a good time. I want a full report on this guy when we get together on Sunday."

Janet blew her a kiss and Danielle listened to hear the front door shut. Grant had come to check up on her. She couldn't help the happy feeling racing through her. *Don't be foolish,* she told herself. *Just because he came doesn't mean he cares for you. It just means he's nice.* Those thoughts didn't stop her from reaching for the phone.

"Hello?"

"Hi," she said.

"Danielle, how are you doing?"

The concern in his voice made her smile. "I'm doing better. Still a little tired, but I'll be fine by tomorrow."

"Are you sure? You didn't look good when I stopped by earlier today." He sounded hesitant. "Janet did tell you that I stopped by, didn't she?"

Laughing, she rolled to her back and said, "Yes, she mentioned you were here when she came by. That's why I was calling. Thank you for checking in on me."

"You're welcome. When Largent called, he didn't sound very good, so I was worried about you." He paused. "What happened at your meeting, Danielle?"

She told him the truth. "Someone wanted to take my power and there was a bit of a struggle. Nevan got there before anything worse could happen."

"Who was it?"

"The woman who left the note. She was going to tell me what they were looking for and since you wouldn't tell me, I had to take matters into my own hands. It was silly to think she was trying to help, but there you go. I'm not always the smartest person in the world."

"You got hurt because of me?"

"No, I got hurt because I'm too trusting for my own good. I should have waited until Nevan got there before I went anywhere near the meeting place." She pushed herself up to lean against the headboard. "Again, my arrogance got me into trouble."

"Are you feeling well enough for me to stop by and see you tonight?"

She had been hoping he'd ask. "Sure, you're more than welcome to stop over. Maybe you could pick up some take-out. I haven't eaten all day and I'm really hungry."

"I'll get Chinese."

"Great. I'm going to hop in the shower, so just use the spare key to let yourself in."

"Okay. I'll be there in about thirty minutes, depending on traffic."

"I'll be waiting. Thanks."

"I'll see you later then." He hung up.

She put her phone down then set her alarm clock to go off in twenty minutes. She had enough time to take a nap before she hopped in the shower. After pulling the blanket over her head, she fell asleep to dream about Grant.

* * * *

Grant heard the shower running as he let himself in. After setting their food on the counter, he headed to the bathroom as he unbuttoned his shirt.

"Did you leave enough hot water for me?" Tugging back the curtain, he took in the breathtaking sight Danielle made wet and slick.

"You'll have to share with me. I'm not ready to get out."

When he was naked, he slipped under the pounding stream. She soaped her hands then rubbed his chest. He leaned back against the wall, letting her take care of him. His muscles relaxed and pleasure built. She played with his nipples, teasing and tugging, and he moaned.

"That feels great."

Smiling, she nodded as she knelt on the floor of the shower. "I thought it would."

She slid her hands down to massage his thighs. His stance widened as she made her way to his feet. When she trailed her fingers over his arches, he couldn't help but laugh.

"Someone's ticklish," Danielle murmured as she sucked his cock in.

"Shit," he cried out as his cock hit the back of her throat. He'd never had a woman take him in that deep.

She hummed and the vibrations traveled from his shaft throughout his body, warning every nerve ending of the climax to come. His legs shook as she swirled her tongue over the head of his cock, teasing the slit leaking pre-cum. A wave of lust washed over him like the water sheeting down his body. He threw his head back and hit the wall, causing him to see stars, but it didn't stop his hips from arching. He wound his hands in her wet hair. He wanted to start thrusting, but he didn't know if she was ready for that.

She slipped her hand between his thighs and cupped his balls. They tightened and he could feel his climax building in his groin. She nibbled up and down the throbbing vein on the underside of his shaft. He whimpered when she let him slip out before looking up.

"Go ahead, Grant. I'll be fine." Her voice was husky.

She took him deep again and he couldn't stop from thrusting. Holding her head still, he plunged in and out of her hot mouth, moaning with each hard suck she gave him. He banged his head against the wall again. *Shit.* That one would leave a lump, but he didn't worry about it.

"I'm going to come, Danielle."

She hummed and sucked until his climax burst from him in a low keen. He jerked and poured his seed into her. His mind blanked and every atom in him exploded into passion. He closed his eyes and instead of darkness, a bright light bathed him in a loving touch. When his hips stopped jerking, he managed to open his eyes to see Danielle licking him clean.

Danielle stood then kissed him and he could taste his own essence on her lips.

"We need to get out of the shower before we turn into wrinkles, love." She turned off the water before helping him out onto the bath mat.

He watched her as she toweled herself briskly then turned to him. Danielle took care drying him off and by the time she was finished, he was hard again. He'd never recovered this fast before, but he wasn't going to argue. He remembered what it felt like to fuck her and he wanted a repeat performance of that.

* * * *

Later, after another episode of love making, Danielle reheated all the food then filled her plate before sitting at the table. Grant got his meal then joined her.

She didn't want to ask, but she needed to know. "Where are we going with this relationship, Grant?"

He reached over to take her hand. "I'm still not sure about where we're heading, Danielle. There're so many mysteries surrounding you and I'm not convinced I'll understand them when you finally tell me. I do know that I could get addicted to you very easily."

"Really?" She turned her hand over to entwine her fingers with his.

"Yeah and something's telling me that I'm going to reach the point where I don't care what your story is. There's a voice in my head telling me that we were meant to be together." He shook his head.

"Is that voice male with a slight accent?"

A strange light came into his eyes. "How did you know?"

Laughing, she brought his knuckles up to her mouth and kissed them. "It's a voice I'm very familiar with."

"Why would I be hearing the same voices you are?" His eyes widened. "I can't believe I'm even considering the fact that I might be hearing voices in my head."

"Hang out with me much longer and you'll see things you never thought existed. I've heard that voice most of my life. Occasionally, I get to talk face-to-face with the man it belongs to."

Grant's skin paled. "It's a real man?"

Tilting her head, she considered his question. "No, I wouldn't call Mika'il a man. He's much more than that."

"More than a man? Who is he?"

"I'm not sure I have the words to describe him. He's a warrior and a pacifist. He's a father and a brother. To a few people, he is everything." She squeezed his hand. "Don't worry. He won't hurt you. He isn't allowed to bother mortals." She used that word on purpose, wondering what Grant's reaction would be.

He stayed seated and relaxed. "You've used the word mortal before when you've talked about me and others. Does that mean you're not mortal? How old are you?"

"According to the government, I just celebrated my thirty-second birthday." She hedged.

"Screw the government. How old are you really?" He obviously wasn't going to let her dodge his question.

"I existed when God brought man into being. I watched as man took his first steps."

"That would make you..."

"Very old. No matter how you look at it and try to add it up." She took her plate to the sink. Bracing her hands against the counter, she stared out of the window. "I've seen civilizations come and go. Human devils basking in riches and human angels living in squalor. There isn't much about events in history that I can't tell you. I've lived and seen it all." She turned to see Grant studying her with narrowed eyes. "I've never lied to you about anything, Grant. Maybe I've hedged the truth on certain things, but I've never lied."

"I was just thinking how good you look for being thousands of years old." He smiled at her, then stood to move over to her. Wrapping his arms around her waist, he pulled her closer. "Danielle, I'm not sure I believe you, but I'm working on it. You've accused me of having a closed mind, but that's not true. I have to have an open mind to accept some of the things I've found in my digs. It's just going to take me time to absorb it." After leaning down, he kissed her forehead. "Let's get some sleep. You still need to rest and I need to take you to the lab tomorrow."

Nodding, she let him help her into the bedroom. She lay down and he climbed in with her. He curled up behind her, spooning her body with his. The tenderness of his touch brought sad tears to her eyes, not sure she could trust in him sticking around once the entire truth came out.

Chapter Nine

"Where did you get these?"

Grant traced the scars on her shoulder blades, making her skin twitch. The scars were still sensitive after all these centuries. She tried to move away from him, but there wasn't much space in her bathroom for the two of them. "They're from my old life."

"The life you were banished from." He traced the path of the scars with his tongue.

Tears filled her eyes and she fought back a sob. Now wasn't the time to weep like a baby. She'd had a long time to deal with the loss of her wings. Grant's gentle touch shouldn't affect her this deeply. "Yes. They took the very symbol of what I was from me."

"Your wings." His statement shocked her and she turned to look at him. He cupped her cheeks, swiping the tears off her skin. "Nevan told me you are a fallen angel."

"Look who's talking out of turn," she murmured.

"I'm right, aren't I? Those scars are where your wings once were."

Pushing away from him, she wandered into her bedroom then pulled on a shirt. She made her way to the kitchen for a cup of coffee. She didn't know how to handle this sudden about-face that Grant was pulling. With no proof other than herself, she didn't see how he could believe her—she wouldn't believe anyone if they came up with such a fantastic story. Well, she wouldn't if she were mortal. After pouring herself and Grant coffee, she handed him a cup while debating what to say.

"An angel's wings are the outward symbol of their spirit. They keep us apart from mortals. Without them, we aren't anything special or more important than any other being on earth." She took a sip of her coffee then grimaced as she continued, "When God banished us from Heaven, He made Mika'il take our wings. He didn't want us to have anything to remind us of what we once were. For many of the fallen, their minds were destroyed when their wings were taken."

Grant had set his cup down, listening to her intently. It was almost like he was trying to understand what she was telling him. She didn't know if that frightened or encouraged her.

"Why are you doing this? Why are you acting like you believe me?" She couldn't stop from asking.

Shrugging, he said, "I figured it wouldn't hurt to ask questions. That's the only way I'm going to learn the truth. You don't look or act crazy, so there must be some truth in what you're telling me."

"What does crazy look like? I've known people who look as normal as you and they've turned out to be sociopaths or psychotics. Insanity often manages to mask itself behind the façade of sanity without giving anything away."

"I know, but I don't feel like I should be worried about you. You're not going to hurt or kill me. I doubt you're in danger of melting down and shooting up schools. So maybe you are a fallen angel. I want to discover your past and figure out if we have any kind of future together."

She still didn't trust this drastic turnaround, but she could deal with his denials later. "You said you had to take me to the lab."

"Yeah. The grad students aren't working today and there's something I want you to see."

"Okay. Let's go."

After putting their cups in the sink, they left.

* * * *

Grant let them into the lab. He wiped his sweaty palms on his pants. He wasn't sure why he was nervous, but he was worried about Danielle's reaction when she saw the skeleton. Even though all the bones weren't there, she would still be able to tell what it looked like. Standing in the middle of the room, she stared at him.

"Go touch the vault door," he said. He remembered Nevan saying she would know exactly what he had if she ever got close to the vault.

She moved toward the door. Gasping, she almost went to her knees. "What did you bring back, Grant?"

He helped her to a chair then pushed her down to sit on it, before unlocking the door to wheel out the cart. The sheet was still over the bones, but he could see her eyes widen at the outlined shape of the skull. He uncovered it, then watched her.

"Oh my God." Danielle spoke in a hushed tone. "This is what they're looking for." Tears spilled down her cheeks as she sobbed.

"At first I thought it was just a very well made fake, but the more I tested it out in the field, the more I became convinced it might be real. I'd never heard of a winged humanoid species, especially in Peru." He stared down at the bones, a certain reverence beginning to fill his heart. If angels were real, then here was the proof.

"It's not all here. Some of the bones from his wings are missing." Reaching out a hand, she held it over the skeleton without touching it. "I wonder who he was."

"Unfortunately, one of the crates got misplaced. I'm not sure where it is. The shipping company is trying to track it down." He handed her a pair of cotton gloves. "If you're going to touch it, please use the gloves."

Nodding, she took them without looking up. "Brittany said Lucifer might be interested in what you've found."

"Lucifer as in the Devil?"

"Yes, he's the reason we all were banished. He incited us to rebel against God. The image you've created of the Devil is far more than Lucifer could ever think of being, but it's also less than what he truly is." Closing her eyes, she imagined beautiful white feathers covering the thin bones. She didn't know who this angel had been, but she mourned his passing all the same.

"It sounds like you've got an intimate knowledge of Lucifer." Grant moved closer to her.

"I've met him a time or two." She didn't elaborate. "Nevan knows about this?"

"Yes, he told me I should tell you. That's why we're here, along with the fact that since I didn't tell you, you ended up getting hurt. I don't want that to happen again."

"You do realize this complicates everything. My unrepentant brethren will come back searching for this and the criminals after those emeralds will be back as well. Something tells me the emeralds are in the missing crate with the bones. We're going to need help."

"What are you talking about? Nevan's doing his best."

Danielle reached into her coat pocket then pulled out her cell phone. "We can't leave the skeleton unattended. Bad things will happen if my brethren get a hold of it. Good thing I memorized Dominic's number."

"Hello?" someone with a whiskey-deep voice answered.

"Hello, Dominic. It's Danielle."

"Ah, *cherie*, it's wonderful to talk to you. I wanted to say thank you for all your help with our slight problem."

She couldn't help but smile at his downplaying the Vodou curse.

"You're welcome, but your thanks aren't needed. Mika'il has thanked me enough for all of you. I have a problem up here."

"I can't get up there until tomorrow morning at the earliest. Let me call someone who's closer. She can be there by tonight." There wasn't any hesitation in his voice.

She knew Dominic repaid debts and she guessed he figured helping save the woman he loved was a huge debt he had to take care of. "Thanks. I'll be at the Field

Museum. Whoever you send, have them meet me here and ask for me at the security desk."

"Fine. I'll see you tomorrow morning." Dominic hung up.

She snapped her phone shut before turning to see Grant watching her. "Someone will be here tonight and Dominic will be here tomorrow morning."

"Who's Dominic?"

"An Enforcer I met in New Orleans. I helped him out while I was down there working."

"An Enforcer? Isn't that like a Mafia hit man or something?" Grant looked uneasy.

"Not really. The Enforcers are more like angelic police officers."

"Angelic police officers?"

"Sit down." She waved him to a chair at one of the tables while she stayed next to the skeleton. For some reason, she felt a measure of peace in keeping a vigil over one of her brethren.

Grant cleared his throat and she looked up at him. "You were going to tell me what an Enforcer was."

"When we were banished, some of us asked—begged—for God to forgive us and allow us back into Heaven. For reasons known only to Him, He chose to ignore us."

"Why would He do that? Isn't He supposed to be a forgiving and loving God?"

Shrugging, Danielle slipped the gloves on before running her fingers over one of the tiny wing bones. "I almost drove myself crazy wondering the same thing until I figured out it isn't important for me to know why. I just need to accept the decision. God has His reasons and someday I might learn what they are. For right now, I try to live as normal a life as possible."

Shaking off the depression threatening to swamp her, she continued, "For some of the fallen, their own arrogance turned them away from forgiveness and they went insane. Those are the unrepentant. They've never asked God for anything and never will. Most of the unrepentant look at mortals as fodder for their own war. Without the Enforcers, they would destroy all mortals in a fit of rage."

"So the Enforcers protect humans?"

"Most of them do. Mika'il approached the Enforcers with the choice of keeping the unrepentant in check or being hunted down and destroyed like them. A majority chose to hunt down their fellow fallen and so they were branded with a cross on their chest."

"You don't have one," he pointed out.

"I don't. I told Mika'il I refused to become hunter or hunted. The one time I thought about being like God, I got banished from Heaven and my wings taken from me. I wouldn't play God with the lives of my brethren." Lifting one of the fragile wing bones, she held it up to the light. It gleamed a startling white under the harsh glare.

"Do you believe the Enforcers play God?"

She nodded. "Yes. They judge and punish those unrepentant who have fallen into the abyss. If that's not playing God, I don't know what is."

"Do the unrepentant look different from you? If I ever ran into one, would I be able to tell what he is?" Grant asked.

Danielle went over to sit next to him. Shaking her head, she said, "No, you wouldn't. They have managed to disguise their true selves from mortals. If you run into one that doesn't hide himself, look into his eyes. Instead of being bright blue like mine, his eyes will be dark, almost black. As the light leeches from their soul, they get crazier and soon it is more merciful for them to be destroyed, so I'm told, though I've never been able to work out that dilemma enough to justify the need."

Grant nodded, but she could see the confusion in his eyes. There was no way he could grasp everything at once. She would go easier on him, introducing him to her past slowly. She whispered a kiss over his lips.

"Go do some work, Grant. I have to go out for an hour or so, but I'll be back before whoever Dominic sends shows up."

"Okay. Where are you going?" He gave her a suspicious glare.

"I still have a business to run. Though I'd love to, I can't spend all my time here with you."

Laughing, he hugged her. "I could tie you up and keep you as my sex slave."

"That sounds like it might be fun." She kissed him again before pulling away. "I've got to go. Put the skeleton back in the vault and I'll be back before you know it."

Before she stripped off her gloves, she stroked a palm over the fragile skull, saying a silent goodbye.

* * * *

Grant answered the phone when it rang several hours later. "Dr Carson."

"Dr Carson, it's Jeffery up at the security desk. There's a couple here asking for Miss Weston. She hasn't returned yet."

"That's all right, Jeffery. I'll be up to get them." He hung up then stood.

Nervousness raced through him. It was stupid to worry about what they would think of him, but these were Danielle's brethren. When had the need to be judged worthy of her become so important to him? At the beginning, he had convinced himself that all he had been looking for with her was a couple of great nights in bed. Those feelings had changed. Now he wanted to stay in her presence and learn all there was to discover about her.

Making his way to the security desk, Grant saw a tall blonde woman and a huge dark-haired man talking in front of Sue, the Tyrannosaurus rex skeleton in the lobby of the museum. It was obvious they were a couple by the way the man's arm was wrapped around her waist and her head rested upon his chest. He didn't want to interrupt what looked like a private conversation, but he wanted them down in the lab in case Danielle got back soon. Clearing his throat, he approached them.

Whirling around, the man tensed like waiting for an attack. The woman faced Grant more calmly—her beautiful face held a smile though there was a hint of sadness in her brilliant blue eyes. He moved to the couple with a wary step.

"I'm Dr Grant Carson, the head archaeologist here at the Field." He held out his hand.

The woman took it, shaking with a firm grip. "I'm Celeste Montgomery and this is my husband, Adam. Dominic LaFontaine asked us to help out Danielle Weston."

After shaking hands with Adam, he gestured for them to follow him. "Yes, Danielle is working with me. I found something on my last dig she feels might cause some trouble. Well, in fact, it's already caused me a lot of trouble."

"What is it?" Celeste asked.

"I would prefer not to say anything until we're in my lab. I'll show you what I have and maybe Danielle will be back by then." His cell phone rang. "Excuse me."

Walking off a little ways from the Montgomerys, he answered the phone. "Carson."

"Hey, looks like those guys after the emeralds figured out who Danielle is," Nevan's voice grated over the phone.

"Is she okay?" Concern rushed through him.

"Sure she is. Her office has seen better days though. I guess they decided since you don't have the emeralds, she must. Trashed the place pretty good."

"Is she with you?" He needed to hear for himself she was okay.

"No. She told me to take care of things then headed out to meet you at the museum. She said she had some people to meet. Danielle called in more of her friends, didn't she?"

"Didn't she say anything to you about them? Two of them are here now and I believe more will be coming in tomorrow."

"I'm glad you finally told her about the skeleton. She needed to know, Carson. That's one of her brethren you have on that cart and it should be treated with respect." Warning sounded in Nevan's voice.

"Don't worry. I treat all my artifacts with respect."

"It's not just an artifact. It was once a person, just like you. How would you feel if someone dug up your body and put it on display?" A voice sounded in the background. "I've got to go. I'll try to stop by later on tonight. If I don't catch you at the lab, then I'll get you at Danielle's house." The detective hung up.

"Danielle's on her way here." He led them down to his lab. Opening the door, he was surprised when he saw Danielle sitting in one of the chairs. Ignoring Celeste and Adam, Grant rushed over to her and hugged her. "Are you okay? Nevan called me."

"I'm fine, Grant. They trashed the office pretty bad, but they were gone before I got there. I'm just glad my assistant had the day off." She glanced over his shoulder to where the others were standing. After gaining her feet, she went to them, offering her hand. "I'm Danielle Weston."

"We're the vanguard, you could say. Dominic will be arriving with William Bradford tomorrow. I'm Celeste and this is my husband, Adam."

Danielle was impressed, having heard of Celeste Montgomery. There were only two fallen on earth more powerful than Celeste, and Danielle really didn't want to run into either of them. "Where do you live, Celeste?"

"We're from Detroit. That's why we got tagged for this," Adam commented. Looking around the lab, his eyes glinted when he saw the gold armbands and the necklace. "So what's the problem?"

Celeste laughed at Grant's move to stand between Adam and the gold. "Don't worry, Dr Carson. Adam's a reformed thief. Now he robs people legally."

"It's hell on a life of crime to live with a fallen angel with morals." Adam grabbed Celeste and kissed her.

Danielle enjoyed seeing them acting like newlyweds. "We have two problems. The first problem seems to be that someone tried to smuggle ten million dollars' worth of emeralds into Chicago using Grant's artifacts as cover."

Adam's eyes gleamed at the mention of the jewels. "What's the problem with that?"

"It seems the shipment got misplaced. I'm missing an entire crate of artifacts, mostly bones. We think the emeralds are in that shipment. My lab and apartment have been broken into." Grant waved for them to sit.

Danielle sat next to Grant and the other two shared a chair with Celeste sitting on Adam's lap. "Grant was attacked two nights ago and now today, my office was trashed as well."

"Write down what shipping company you were using, Carson. I'll call some associates and see what we can find out about your crate." Adam set Celeste aside, then stood. He took the paper from Grant before heading into Grant's office, pulling out a cell phone on the way.

"Who's he calling?" Grant asked.

"His associates are best left unknown." Celeste smiled after her husband. "So what's the second problem?"

Danielle looked at Grant, gesturing toward the vault. "Show her what you found."

While Grant opened the door, she filled Celeste in. "Grant was digging at a new site in the mountains of Peru. He made a rather startling discovery." She handed the blonde Enforcer a pair of gloves. "In case you want to touch it."

Celeste gasped then blanched when Grant revealed the skeleton. At the same moment, Adam returned to pull her into his arms.

"What is it?" he asked.

"It has wings. It's one of our brethren, Celeste. He must have died before Mika'il could take his wings." Danielle stroked her gloved fingertip along the jawbone of the skull. "This is our second problem. One of the unrepentant has already been here looking for it. She didn't have time to search the entire lab because she would have found it for sure. Yesterday, she attacked me and nearly drained me of my power. She told me in an earlier meeting that Lucifer might be interested in this."

"Shit, there is no way we can deal with Lucifer. Have you contacted Mika'il yet?" Celeste took a wing bone and showed it to Adam.

"Not yet. My first thought after Grant showed it to me was to call for help. I knew I couldn't handle whatever was coming on my own. I'll try Mika'il now." She shut her eyes and drew upon her connection to the archangel.

"Mika'il, we need your help."

There was no answer. She frowned and tried again.

"Mika'il, we've got trouble here and we need your help."

First there wasn't an answer then faintly she heard, *"I'm sorry."*

"I'm sorry? What the hell does that mean?"

But he was gone.

Opening her eyes, she glanced at Celeste. "See if you can contact him. All I got was 'I'm sorry'."

Celeste closed her eyes and tried. A puzzled frown wrinkled her forehead. "I'm not getting anything. It's strange not having the connection with Mika'il. I mean, I have nothing, and that's never happened before."

"So is mine. What do you suppose he's sorry about?"

Sighing, Celeste shrugged. "I don't know. Hey, do you think we could talk about this tomorrow when the others get here? It's been a long day and a longer drive to get here."

"Sure. You're welcome to stay at my place while you're here. It's not the Waldorf, but it's clean," she offered while Grant put the cart away.

"We'll take you up on that. We could find a place if we tried, but I think it'll be better for everyone if we stick close to each other." Adam herded them out of the lab.

"Who's the Enforcer for Chicago?" Celeste looked around at the exhibits as they made their way to the exit.

"I don't hang out with that crowd normally, but it might be David Randolph. If Mika'il were around, he'd know for sure, though I've always gotten the feeling David didn't care much for mortals."

"Some are like that. They take their duty to protect mortals from the unrepentant—as you call them— very seriously, but they feel no urge to keep mortals from hurting each other. One less mortal is one they don't have to worry about." Celeste watched Adam flag down some cabs.

"Why does Mika'il allow that attitude?" Danielle couldn't help but inquire.

"Mika'il takes what he can get most of the time. None of us will ever win any gold stars for great attitudes. Right now, he's just happy there are more Enforcers than there are unrepentant, but some of the good guys are getting closer to the abyss every day." When two cabs pulled up, Celeste said, "Give our cabbie your address and we'll meet you there."

Danielle did that then they headed off.

"Have you ever met Celeste before?" Grant asked her as they rode toward her house.

"No, but I've heard of her. She's one of the most powerful fallen."

"Really? She looks capable enough. Who's more powerful than her?" He reached over and placed his hand on her thigh where the hem of her skirt met her flesh.

The heat of his hand traveled up her leg to rest on her mound. She was getting wet and he hadn't even started seducing her yet. "Lucifer and Christian. You know about Lucifer, but Christian stood behind only Mika'il and Lucifer in the Father's affection."

"How did he fall?" He crept his hand up in short, small swirling moves. Soon the tips of his fingers were resting against her pussy.

She spread her legs as wide as her skirt allowed. "No one knows except for Christian. He always tried to talk reason to us. He tried to fight the rebellion, but when the tide of the war was over, he stood on our side of the gate. One of the few whom God loved most of all had been barred from Heaven with the rest of us."

He slipped one finger over her clit with hard strokes. "Who do you think the skeleton is?"

Whimpering, she shifted her hips as he passed his fingers by her wet opening, then dipped in. "I don't know." It was getting harder to focus on what he wanted to talk about. "I've never heard of one of us disappearing."

He twisted slightly, shoving his finger in deeper. His cheeks were flushed and his breathing was quickening. With his other hand, he grabbed one of hers to cup his cock. She bit her lip to stop from crying out as he scraped over her sweet spot with each thrust of his finger. Danielle couldn't believe she was letting him do this in the back of a cab. Grant kept pushing in then pulling out, just alternating the speed and angle with each move. Finally, when she thought she couldn't take it anymore and would start begging him to take her, they pulled up in front of her house.

Grant paid the cabbie as she climbed out of the vehicle and stood on shaking legs. Celeste and

Adam's cab arrived a few minutes later while she was trying to unlock the door. Her body didn't want to let the lust drain from her and she could feel how slick her thighs were from her own juices. She might have to drag Grant into her bedroom for a little before-dinner sex.

"I know it's rather early still, but I was up all night working. I'm hoping it isn't too rude if I head off to bed," Celeste apologized.

"No problem. I'll show you to your room." She took them upstairs, to where her guest rooms were. "You can take this room and the bathroom is the third door down."

"Thanks. I'll stay up here and do some work of my own. We'll see you tomorrow morning." Adam shut the door firmly behind him.

They weren't going to get any argument from her—she was glad to be alone with that annoying man. She managed to get back downstairs with decorum, but the minute she saw Grant, she dragged him to her bedroom to finish what he'd started in the cab.

* * * *

It was still dark out when Grant woke up. A restless feeling drove him to climb out of bed before pulling on some clothes. Danielle murmured something, then buried her face in his pillow and went back to sleep. Opening the door, he tried to leave the room without making any more noise. He wandered down the hall, heading for the kitchen.

"Couldn't sleep either, huh?" a voice emitted from the shadows in the living room.

He tensed until he realized the voice belonged to Adam. "Yeah, I woke up and for some reason couldn't get back to sleep. Thought I'd get some water."

"Water? I need something stiffer than that when I wake up at night." Adam's harsh chuckle came from the dark. "Of course, I doubt your past is full of nightmares like mine."

He figured Adam was right. "Did you find the liquor?"

"Yeah, your lady has good taste in alcohol and possessions. Did she tell you the sculpture on her end table is a Michelangelo? And that she has a Da Vinci hanging in her hallway? Whole house is a fucking museum."

"No, I didn't know. How can you tell?"

"Used to make a living as a thief. I haven't done anything illegal in a while. I promised to clean up my act."

"Did Celeste make you promise that?"

"No, she would never have asked me that. It was her annoying archangel friend, Mika'il. When you don't want him around, you can't get rid of him, but when you need him, he can't be found. Looks like he's dumping this whole fucking mess in our ladies' laps. Fucking bastard."

Grant wondered if cursing the warrior angel was a wise move. "What did you think when Celeste told you she was a fallen angel?"

Laughing, Adam turned on a light. Waving the glass at a chair, he gestured for Grant to take a seat. "I thought she was fucking crazy. Most God damn beautiful woman I'd ever met and she's fucking crazier than a loon."

"What made you change your mind?"

"A demon, a priest and the sheer fact that I couldn't image my life without her. I had lived a lot of my life alone. It was never easy for me to trust, but after meeting her for the first time, I couldn't get her out of my mind. It was almost like it was meant to be." Adam grinned at him. "You probably think I'm an ass."

"A soul mate." Grant thought about the conversation he had with Meical about soul mates and Danielle.

"Yeah, a soul mate. That'd be a great romantic line, right? I'll have to remember that to use on Celeste. Of course, she might look at me like I've totally flipped. Celeste doesn't need a lot of romance and frilly things." Adam slugged down the rest of his drink, then yawned. "I think I'm going to head back upstairs and try to sleep."

After standing, Adam set his glass on the coffee table before walking out into the hallway. Grant joined him, and Adam reached out to slap him on the back.

"Man, you've come this far without screaming and running away. I think you're hooked. I know it's hard to believe in angels when so much of the world's screwed up, but you've got to open your mind to the fact that they're out there. They exist whether you believe in them or not. Just think of how much more miraculous the world will be when you start believing in things you can't see." Adam headed for the stairs. "I'm going back to my wife. If you love Danielle, nothing else is important."

He stood there for a moment, thinking. It was true. If he loved Danielle, then it shouldn't matter if she thought she was from Mars and looked like a little green man. It was her independence of thought and action that drew him to her. She lived her life the best she could under the circumstances and lived it on her terms. She never asked for help if she didn't need to. She had brought him into her heart. He would never find a better place to be.

After heading back to bed, he slid under the covers, then spooned her body with his. Wrapping his arms around her, he absorbed her warmth as he let her even breathing soothe him back to sleep.

Chapter Ten

Danielle was in the lab with the others when Dominic LaFontaine and William Bradford arrived with their fiancées. She gave Teresa Ryder, Dominic's girlfriend, a hug.

"You're looking better than the last time I saw you." She smiled at Teresa.

"I wanted to thank you as well." Teresa hugged her again.

"You don't have to. Both Dominic and Mika'il have thanked me enough. I did what I could to help out."

Dominic introduced William and Abby, then said, "Why am I here?"

"Grant found a skeleton in Peru." She gestured for Grant to bring out the bones.

Dominic and William gathered around the skeleton with Celeste and Danielle. Reaching out, the fallen angels took each other's hands and closed their eyes. A soft glow emanated from them to circle the bones. For several minutes, they stood that way then they broke apart to take seats around the lab.

"Where's the rest of the body?" William asked. Abby sat on his lap and he held her close.

Grant shrugged. "The crate it's in got lost along the way."

Adam spoke up. "I've got some associates making inquiries for me. We should find out by tonight where it is."

Dominic nodded. "How exactly did you find this?"

Grant went into his office. While he was gone, Dominic looked at Danielle. "Does your lover know what you are?"

"Yes, he does."

"Does he accept what you are?" Dominic asked.

Shrugging, she glanced toward Grant's office. "I'm not sure. He listens and reserves judgment, I think. The skeleton is the best proof to him that angels might be real."

"We had a talk last night. He's beginning to grasp what and who you are, Danielle. Just give him a little more time and he'll come around," Adam said.

She was surprised Adam would extend a hand to Grant, but she shouldn't have been. If anyone would be able to help Grant adjust to the truth, it would be someone who had lived through his own discovery.

Grant came out of his office with a couple of folders. They gathered around him as he started laying pictures out on the long table in the middle of the room.

"When we found the skeleton, it was in this kneeling position. It was in pristine condition. There wasn't any dirt or anything on it, which is what made me think it was a fake." He pointed to the first three pictures. They showed the skeleton in a kneeling position with the hands together as if in prayer.

"A fake? He was alive once just like you." Celeste must have spotted the slight smile on Danielle's face. "Okay, so he wasn't like you, but he was alive."

"I know. I did tests on the bones while we were in the field. They're real and very old. These armbands were found with them. I think the ancient Peruvians left them as offerings to the strange winged being." Grant pointed to the pictures that documented where the armbands were found in relation to the skeleton. Then he slid on some cotton gloves to bring the cleaned bands over for the group to see.

Danielle gasped as the cleaned gold revealed a winged man kneeling and pleading with another winged creature. "How did they know?"

"What are you talking about?" Grant asked.

"I think all of us were in this position when Mika'il came for our wings. We all pleaded with him not to take them." Dominic's blue eyes held sadness. Teresa rubbed his shoulder and kissed his cheek.

"What can we do?" Danielle stared down at the skeleton. "There's still been no answer from Mika'il and I don't think he'll come anyway."

Dominic agreed. "Mika'il stopped to see me last night. He's been ordered away from this situation." He held up a hand to forestall anyone asking him a question. "I don't know. I do know it's driving him crazy."

"It's not the unrepentants that scare me. Any one of us can handle them. What if Lucifer decides to get involved? We can't stop him, not even if all the Enforcers were here. Only Mika'il can withstand him," she pointed out.

"That's not true." Dominic studiously avoided making eye contact with anyone.

"Lucifer was one of the highest angels, the most beloved of God before his fall. Only an archangel would be able to face his powers."

"There's an Enforcer who could deal with Lucifer should the dark one decide to show his face. Christian Vosberg."

Celeste seemed hesitant. "Would he come, though?"

"That's the question, isn't it?" Dominic frowned.

"Why wouldn't he come if you asked?" Grant questioned.

Danielle sighed. "Christian's faith was strong and when he repented, he really believed God would forgive us. Imagine his shock and pain when the Father didn't. He's been slipping toward the darkness for a while. He lives in New York and the attacks there pushed him straight to the edge. He's been balancing there for years now."

"He's the one you're counting on to help you keep Lucifer from taking the skeleton? It seems to me you're fighting evil with someone who's just as evil," Abby spoke up.

"Christian isn't evil. He's broken," Dominic commented.

"Broken? How?" Grant asked.

"He had so much faith in God that when He turned from us, Christian's trust was broken. Once torn in half, faith is very hard to repair. I think we need him here, in case Lucifer shows up." Dominic looked each fallen in the eye. "Mika'il told me to do it. The archangel always has ulterior motives when he asks things like that, so I'll do it and hope he isn't wrong."

"Fine, but we have another problem. Not only does the missing crate contain the rest of the skeleton, it contains about ten million dollars' worth of emeralds, if our information is correct." Danielle knew they needed to know all the complications.

"Wow, this is all kinds of fucked up," William said.

"Tell me about it. Grant's been attacked once. The lab, his apartment and my office have all been broken into and trashed. Detective Largent, who's handling the case, says the guy's a professional, but that he has a temper and when he can't find what he's looking for, he gets mad." There wasn't any point in glossing over anything. The Enforcers were more than capable of taking care of themselves and their mortals.

"Adam." Celeste looked at her husband.

"I'm already on it, but having me ask questions might make them panic. I have a bit of a reputation," he said to answer Danielle's questioning stare.

Celeste's laughter pealed through the room. "A bit of a reputation? When I first met him, Adam was the boss of the largest gang in Detroit. He also pretty much ran all the crime going on in the city. If the people who stole those emeralds know Adam's in town and asking questions, they're probably shitting bricks by now."

"Well, you won't have to worry about anyone attacking you again, Grant. With all of us looking out for you, no mortal will get to you." Dominic stood up. "I'm going to go and call Christian."

Grant looked at each of them. "I need to get some work done. If you're all going to stay around, I'm going to put you to work."

All the fallen stood. Laughing, Danielle said, "I can take the ladies shopping, if they'd like that?"

"Oh, I know I would. How about you, Abby?" Teresa asked Abby, William's fiancée.

"Sure, I haven't been to Chicago before. I'd like to see the sights while we're here," Abby agreed.

William winced. "My wallet's getting skinnier as we speak."

Abby hit him as they all laughed. Danielle led the ladies out of the museum, and flagged down a cab. Adam had told them he was going to look for the men who wanted the emeralds while Dominic and William hung out at the museum.

* * * *

Several hours later, they met back at the museum lab. Adam, William and Dominic were helping Grant clean artifacts. The skeleton had been left out like no one could stand to hide it away again. Danielle stroked her hand over the skull as she walked by.

"Sit down, ladies," Adam ordered. All the women looked at him. "Please," he added.

"I'm working on instilling some manners in him," Celeste joked.

Seated, they waited for Adam to start.

"I went to a few areas of the city where smart angels fear to tread and made some discreet inquiries."

"What did you find out?" Grant took Danielle's hand.

"It's not good. The man doing the searching is Brad Diggston. He's the right-hand man for Carmen Martinez. Martinez is one of the most powerful crime bosses in Chicago. Not quite as powerful as the men I know, but he's dangerous and ruthless. Diggston has a reputation for having a temper and he's even more dangerous than Martinez because he doesn't think before he acts. He tends to get carried away and kill his victims before he gets what he needs from them."

"That isn't encouraging news, Adam." Dominic paced around the lab.

"I know, but I figured we needed to know what we're up against. Martinez contracted the theft of the emeralds. He has a buyer who's willing to pay good money for them. These particular jewels are a matched set. A ring, bracelet, necklace and earrings. They're natural, not created. It's extremely rare to find that many emeralds that match in size and clarity. The jewelry store had them insured for ten million, but they're worth twice that on the black market." Adam looked at each of them. "The bad thing is, the buyer gave Martinez half of the payment before delivery of the goods. That means Martinez must deliver them or he has to return the money. I can guarantee you, he doesn't have it. He owes other people, so he needs the rest of the payment."

"What you're telling us is Martinez won't give up until he gets those jewels." Grant squeezed Danielle's hand. "Are we going to tell Nevan?"

"Yes, he needs to know who's behind it. I'm not sure what he can do, but at least he'll know what to expect. I'll ask him to meet us at my house in an hour." She looked at Dominic. "Did you get a hold of Christian?"

"I left him a message. I haven't heard back from him. We'll know he's coming when he gets here." Dominic shrugged. "That's the best I can do. No one, not even Mika'il, tells him what to do."

"I understand."

"It's good that you do, because I don't like being made to come to Chicago. I fail to see why I need to be here."

The Enforcers and Danielle jumped. A blond man came into the room. He glanced at them all, towering over the other male fallen. When the man's dark blue gaze met Grant's, he felt tears well up in his eyes and he had to choke back a sob.

The stranger's eyes were heartbreaking. He had never seen such pain and sadness. He had the scary feeling Lucifer had arrived. Surprise raced through him when Dominic held out his hand.

"Christian."

"LaFontaine." The man's voice was low and musical.

Grant couldn't believe this was their only hope against the worst of the fallen angels. He could sense a darkness deep in Christian.

"Would you like me to introduce the others?" Dominic motioned to the other fallen in the room.

"Not really. Where's the skeleton?"

Grant gestured to the steel cart at the back of the lab. The Enforcer glided over before standing for a moment with his jaw clenched.

"It's Ferguson," the fallen said.

"How can you know?" Grant couldn't believe Christian would be able to tell who the angel was by looking at the bones.

"Where did you find him?"

"In the mountains of Peru."

Christian nodded. "Mika'il and I lost Ferguson in those mountains."

"You and Mika'il? You took his wings with the archangel?" Danielle accused.

Christian didn't move. His shoulders slumped, but he was silent. Grant had the feeling the Enforcer wouldn't ask for forgiveness.

"Can we trust you?" Adam asked Christian as he moved to stand next to Grant.

Christian swept his glance over the mortals in the room. A faint smile graced his face. Looking at the fallen, he nodded once. "You've chosen well. I'll be around if you need me."

He was gone.

"That went a little better than I thought." Dominic's grin was both rueful and relieved.

"He seemed like he was in a good mood." William shrugged.

"If that was a good mood, I'd hate to see him when he was angry." Adam shook his head, moving back to Celeste.

"You don't want to see him angry. To be honest, I've never seen him lose his temper. It's almost like he knows what he's capable of, so he won't risk it." Dominic glanced over at Teresa. "It's late and we need to get some rest."

"You're all welcome to stay at my house. I have more than enough room and Nevan will be meeting us there," Danielle offered.

* * * *

They had been at her house for thirty minutes when Nevan arrived. The second the detective saw the others in the room, he paled and Danielle was afraid he might turn around and leave. He glared at her.

"You didn't tell me there would be more of you here."

"I'm sorry, Nevan. I forgot." She put her hand on his arm, feeling how tense his muscles were. "If you want, Adam can take you in the kitchen and tell you what he knows."

Adam started to protest, but Celeste slugged him in the chest. Danielle tried to hide her smile at the man's indignant pout.

"I'd appreciate it. It's been a hell of a day and I can't fight the feeling that something else is going to happen." Nevan's face was drawn and a haunted look showed in his eyes.

"Sure. Adam Montgomery, this is Detective Nevan Largent. Adam is Celeste's husband." Danielle introduced them then let Grant take the two men to the kitchen.

"What's up with him?" Abby asked from her perch on William's lap.

"He's gifted, isn't he?" Dominic asked.

She nodded. "Being around us would be difficult for him on a good day. When he's as tired as he is now, he has no protection against the ghosts he sees around us."

"Shit. We should never have sent him with Adam." Celeste jumped to her feet.

"Why not?"

"Adam has some pretty serious ghosts hanging around him. His father killed his mother in front of him when he was young." Celeste was heading out of the room when Adam, Nevan and Grant came back.

Nevan was pasty white, but he smiled at the others and said, "I'll get in touch with the guys who work vice and the organized crime division. They'll be able to tell me more about Diggston and Martinez." He turned to shake Adam's hand. "Thanks for the leads, Mr Montgomery."

Danielle walked him to the door. "I apologize again, Nevan. I didn't know about Adam's past."

Shrugging, he shook his head. "You couldn't know. I'll be fine."

After shutting the door, she turned to find Grant standing behind her. He pulled her into his arms, kissing her on the forehead.

"I think we should all go to bed. It's been a long day and like Nevan said, I think something is going to happen. We need to be ready for it."

She agreed then showed the others where they could sleep. She was glad when she shut her bedroom door. Grant was already in bed so she slid in beside him. He rolled over and cuddled her close to him. *I could get used to this. It's nice to feel like someone else is in charge and protecting me instead of having to protecting myself.* Yet she was afraid she wouldn't be able to protect Grant from mortals or fallen.

* * * *

Later that night, Danielle lay in the dark, staring up at the ceiling. Grant's arms were wrapped around her but she couldn't shut her thoughts off enough to sleep. Slipping out of bed, she pulled on a robe before making her way to the kitchen.

She wasn't surprised to see Dominic already sitting at her table staring into a glass of whiskey. There was a full glass at the spot across from him.

"Did you know I couldn't sleep?" She sipped the liquor.

Shaking his head, he said, "I figured one of you would be out here. None of us sleep well at the best of times. When things are screwed up like this, we tend to think too much."

"Is that your problem?"

"Partly and also because Teresa still needs to rest, I thought I'd come out here instead of tossing and turning." His blue eyes pinned her. "You have a question."

She was glad it was Dominic in the kitchen. The other two Enforcers were nice, but he was the one she was closest to. "Do you remember the conversation we had about soul mates?"

Dominic thought for a moment then nodded. "You told me you didn't think God loved us enough to give us soul mates." He studied her for a second. "Have you changed your mind?"

Pushing her hair out of her face, she groaned. "I don't know. All I know is that I'd rather be with him than anywhere else and when we have sex, it blows my mind."

Dominic seemed to know what she was talking about. "A climax is never more powerful than when it happens in the arms of the person who was meant for you."

"I wondered if I was the only one who felt that way."

"No." William walked in, followed closely by Celeste. "We'll never truly be at peace here, but as long as we're held in the deepest soul of our lovers, then we'll find our moments of happiness."

Celeste sat next to her. "Also, it's not only in the arms of your lover, but in his eyes that you'll be able to glimpse Heaven."

"Mika'il said something to that effect in a conversation we had." She shook her head. "I don't know if Grant will be able to accept the entire truth of what we are and what that means to him."

"If he truly loves you, his heart will open his eyes to the truth in our world," Dominic said.

"He's leaning heavily on our side even now, Danielle," William encouraged her as he joined them at the table. He brought two more glasses and the bottle of whiskey.

"I know, and if the solid proof from the skeleton doesn't convince him, I'm sure your mortals will." She let William refill her glass.

"Adam said he and Grant had a chat last night. Your archaeologist asked Adam about our relationship," Celeste commented.

"What did Adam say?"

"That he was willing to accept me—even if I was crazy—when he realized he couldn't live without me."

"Abby and Teresa were much more accepting. Why is that?" Dominic ran his finger along the rim of his glass.

"I think, in their souls, women are closer to the spiritual world than men, except for your Detective Largent." Celeste slammed back her whiskey and had William pour her another.

"Poor Nevan. All his life, he's been tormented by what he sees. I'm amazed he's holding on to his sanity." She shook her head, remembering how tired and sick her friend had looked when he left.

"He'll meet someone someday who'll help him see his *sight* as the gift it is instead of the curse he believes it to be," Dominic predicted.

William raised his glass. "A toast to our loves. The other halves of our souls and the bits of Heaven they've returned to us."

The other three raised their glasses and they drank.

Chapter Eleven

Grant was startled awake by the shrill ringing of Danielle's phone. He lay in bed trying to calm his heart rate down while he listened to her answer.

"Hello... Nevan, what's wrong?" She reached back across the bed to touch his shoulder.

He could hear the worry in her voice, so he took her hand, holding tight.

"Oh no! We'll be right down. Has anyone contacted his family?"

A sick feeling settled into the pit of his stomach. Contacting family didn't sound good. Grant kissed her hand then slid out of bed. After grabbing his clothes, he yanked them on while trying to pay attention to her.

"You want all of us there?" She nodded at him and he headed out of the room to see if he could get the others up and moving.

Dominic, William and Celeste were already standing in the kitchen when he got there. The coffee pot was working and they stared at him with identical blue eyes. It was a little unnerving to see how alike those eyes were, yet each held a hint of the personality of the angel they inhabited. William's eyes sparkled with humor and Dominic's held a peace that he figured had been hard won. Celeste's eyes were serious and met his directly. She had strength of character in her gaze that spoke of honesty and determination.

"Was that Detective Largent?" Dominic asked as the fallen pulled out several coffee mugs.

"Yeah, I think he wants all of us to meet him somewhere." He took a mug then filled it with coffee. Taking a sip, he grunted at how strong the brew was.

"William made it." Celeste grinned. "The others are getting ready. We'll be able to leave in ten minutes."

"Good. There's been another break-in at the museum." Danielle walked in before taking his cup.

He didn't argue, just grabbed another one off the counter. "Shit. What more could the idiot damage?"

"It isn't damage to artifacts that he caused this time. He killed one of the guards." Tears shone in her eyes.

He wrapped her in his arms. Damn, this was getting out of hand. He hoped Montgomery found out where the crate had gone soon. He stared at the other fallen. "Why don't you do something about these guys?"

"We have to stay out of it. Unless unrepentants are involved, we can't interfere in the problems of mortals." Dominic shrugged at his growl. "Sure, that particular rule sucks, but there isn't much any of us can do about it."

Danielle pulled away from him as the other three mortals arrived to get their coffee before leaving.

* * * *

Danielle was watching Nevan look around the murder scene. She wanted to ask him what he saw, but didn't have the nerve to bother him.

"Why didn't you request my assistance?" David Randolph appeared in the room. Danielle assumed he was the head Enforcer for the Chicago area.

Nevan scowled at him, then continued to study the scene.

"He can see me?" he asked Danielle.

"And hear you," Nevan commented.

"Strange. I've never had a mortal see me if I didn't want him to." David stared at the detective.

"Stop it. Detective Largent has the *sight*. He's able to see spirits," Danielle explained.

"That has to suck. There's spirits all around us. How do you function?" he questioned Nevan.

"By ignoring them." Nevan knelt next to the body.

"Explain what's going on in my town, Danielle. Why is Chicago crawling with Enforcers?"

"You have no idea. You weren't too concerned when Grant got beat up the other night. I figured I wouldn't bother you with our problems. I called a few friends in for help." She glared at the fallen.

"It looks like they aren't very good at their jobs." David barely spared a glance at the dead guard. "Why did you bring Christian here?"

"We didn't have a choice. Are you going to stand up to Lucifer if he shows?" She smirked at the look of fear skating across David's face. "I didn't think so. Christian can and will stand up to him. That's why we asked him here."

Christian appeared and Nevan started.

"My heart might survive if you'd all arrive using the door like normal people," Nevan muttered.

Christian stared down at him for a moment, then looked at David through dark blue eyes. "It's about time you showed up, David. I'll head back to New York now."

David backed up. "Oh, that's okay. I wouldn't want you to waste a trip."

Christian's eyes narrowed and Danielle gestured for Nevan to move out of the way. The detective shook his head, staying put. There was a stubborn tilt to his chin, telling her he wasn't going to rearrange his crime scene for anyone.

"What do you mean no? It's not my job to keep Daystar out of your city. My inclination is to let him run rampant through Chicago."

"You can't," Danielle blurted.

Both sets of eyes turned her way, causing her to duck her head. Her big mouth was going to get her in trouble.

"Why not? No mortal is going to believe that skeleton is anything but a fake." Christian glanced down at Nevan again. "They don't have the imagination to believe in angels."

"Not if they knew what pains in the ass they are." Nevan nudged Christian's foot out of the way.

Christian grabbed Nevan's collar, dragging him to the tips of his toes. The detective joined gazes with the Enforcer—dark blue dueled with pale green. There wasn't any fear in Nevan's eyes. Somehow he must have known Christian wouldn't hurt him. Christian let go of him and Nevan knelt to take pictures of the body.

"You're the only one who can face Lucifer. It's best if you stick around." David tried to slide away.

Christian pinned him with his gaze. "Don't return unless we call for you. You're useless and your rather lax view on mortals could get you in trouble. Remember that."

"Yes, sir," David stammered before disappearing.

"Worthless piece of shit, if you ask me," Nevan commented as he stood, then gestured to the coroner's people who were waiting outside the room to take the body.

Danielle couldn't believe that Christian would choose to stay. Studying the legendary Enforcer, she saw lines cut into his face along the sides of his mouth. He looked as if he were in pain all the time. He caught her staring and she flushed. His smile was full of sadness, with a hint of insanity. She grabbed his arm when he turned to go.

"We will be forgiven one day. Heaven's gates won't be barred to us forever." She couldn't help it. The urgency to give Christian hope drove her to speak and touch him.

He glanced down at her hand and waited until she released him before he spoke. "I can only hope it won't be too late for some of us." He headed for the door after shooting an ironic look at Nevan. "I'll be back a little later."

She stared as Christian left, then turned to meet Nevan's gaze.

"You fallen all have problems, but that guy would keep a therapist busy for years with his." Nevan watched the crime scene guys carry the body bag out. "Okay, let's collect the others and go to the café. I'm hungry and I need to get some caffeine."

As they reached the café, Danielle noticed the rest of the group was there along with Grant. She was surprised when he leaned over to kiss her. He had done it before in front of her friends, but never out where colleagues could see. Did that mean he was willing to turn this into a serious relationship?

"It is a serious relationship, Danielle. If it wasn't, he would have left a long time ago." Dominic's voice skated through her mind.

Laughing, she realized he was right. A guy didn't stick around for casual sex when things got rough.

"Okay. First, I'll be leaving shortly to inform the deceased's family. I hate this part of it." Nevan stared down at his notebook for a moment.

She put an arm around his shoulders, giving him a quick hug. "Do you want me to go with you?"

Shaking his head, he looked up. "No, but thanks for the offer. So, have we found out anything else about this crate?"

Adam nodded. "I got a call about an hour ago. The crate was shipped to the Moffet Field Museum in Sunnyvale, California by accident. Here's the phone number and contact person's name. Carson, you should be the one calling them. See if you can get them to overnight it. If they have a problem with cost, I'll pay it."

"California? You've got to be kidding." Grant grabbed the paper and left to find some privacy.

"It's a state and it starts with a 'C'. We should be happy it's still in the country." Adam chuckled.

"So the crate's been found. What are we going to do to catch the men who did this?" Nevan included all the fallen in his gaze as he asked.

"If we catch Diggston, I can probably convince him to roll over on Martinez. Once we get the time and everything set up for the crate's arrival, I'll go drop a few interesting bits of information into the right ears. As soon as we know the bait's gotten to Martinez and Diggston, we'll set up a trap. They need to be taken care of. They're getting careless and if the police don't take them down, I can guarantee you that the crime bosses will." Adam shifted restlessly on his chair.

"That's what my contacts in vice and organized crime said as well. I don't want a crime war on my turf. We'll take this guy out soon and avoid the whole thing." Nevan caught Danielle's gaze and said, "Do you really think Lucifer is going to take time out of his 'taking over the world' plans to drop in here and steal this skeleton?"

Dominic answered before Danielle could say anything, "No one knows what Lucifer will do. He's crazy and cunning. If he thought it might further his cause, he'd be here in a minute and none of us would be able to do anything about it. The only ones who can make him back down are Christian and Mika'il. Together, we would be able to protect the mortals from him, but not the skeleton." Dominic looked at Teresa. "Even if I knew it meant the end of the world as we know it, I wouldn't let him hurt Teresa."

"No one would expect you to have to choose, Dominic. That's why we sucked it up and asked Christian to come here. None of us are comfortable around him, but we know what's at stake if that bastard Lucifer shows his face here." William took Abby's hand and glared at the others.

"The person at the Moffet museum is shipping the crate out today. We should be getting it delivered here by five tomorrow night." Grant came back, folding the paper to put in his pocket.

"Good. If we play our cards right, we can set our trap for. Montgomery, do you think your associates can spread the news that the crate will be in the lab after the museum closes?" Nevan asked.

Adam nodded. "I'll pay a visit to an old friend of mine. He'll make sure it gets to the right person."

Nevan stood. "I have to head back to the precinct. I'll get a hold of you when I have everything set up on my side."

"Detective, can I clean up my lab again?" Grant's voice held a hint of exasperation.

"Sure, Carson. My guys tried not to make a bigger mess than necessary, but they probably did track a lot of shit in there." The detective waved to them and left the café.

"Come on. We'll help you clean up," Danielle said as she joined Grant.

* * * *

Danielle and the others had been helping clean up Grant's lab for several hours. He had pulled the skeleton out of the vault when they'd got there to check and make sure nothing had happened to it. Sure, it was a bunch of bones, but at one time, it had been one of their brethren. The spirit might not be there anymore, yet they still felt obligated to treat the skeleton with respect.

She had been fighting a niggling memory that was trying to intrude on her consciousness. She studied the skeleton and armbands. "Grant, why did you pick this particular site to dig at?"

He was sitting at one of the lab tables, cleaning a beaded necklace. He frowned at her for interrupting him, but he answered, "A couple months before our field season started, a man came in. He said his name was Miquel Cruz. He owned the land where the dig was. He brought one of the armbands and explained a worker had found it. I was amazed. It is an almost perfect example of Pre-Columbian metal work. Mr Cruz had all the right papers signed and permission from the government for us to dig and bring the stuff back. He also funded the whole expedition."

"Have you seen him since?"

"No." He frowned. "Although the Meical guy I talked to at the bar reminded me of him."

She knew it. "In what way?"

"Their eyes were the same unusual silver color." He tensed when William jumped to his feet.

"The bastard knew the skeleton was there. He set this whole thing up," William growled.

"No. He knew Ferguson's body had to be somewhere nearby, but he was never sure where the angel had gone." Christian spoke from where he had appeared in the corner.

"So he came to Grant on purpose," Danielle suggested.

Christian shrugged, his dark eyes showing no emotion. "Everything the archangel does has a purpose and it is usually at the bidding of the Father."

"Wait, are you saying Mr Cruz was an angel?" Grant shook his head.

"Not just any angel. Miquel Cruz was Mika'il, the archangel and the most feared of God's Host," Dominic commented. "And more than likely Meical at the bar was the angel as well."

"He's always interfering," William complained.

"Mika'il interferes because he has to." Christian moved to the center of the room, his gaze touching everyone. "Don't judge or complain when you don't understand his suffering."

"Suffering? How does he suffer compared to us?" William faced off with Christian.

Everyone tensed as the two Enforcers stared at each other. Danielle wondered how Christian would tolerate what amounted to a challenge.

"He suffers. That's all I'll say. It's not time for you to know all the truths that exist." Christian turned to Danielle. "I'll be back tomorrow night. You all might want to take a moment to thank Mika'il. Without his interference, you wouldn't have the love that keeps you waking up in the morning."

After Christian disappeared, the other fallen descended on William.

"What the hell were you thinking?" Celeste slugged William in the chest.

"I wasn't thinking, obviously. I just get so tired of being manipulated by Mika'il." William glared at Celeste and rubbed his chest.

"These manipulations aren't his choice," Dominic pointed out. "He takes orders from a higher power. He lobbies God every minute of each day to allow us back in. I, for one, will never forget that, even on days when I'd rather strangle him than talk to him."

William hung his head. "I'm sorry. I know he does a lot to help us."

"As for challenging Christian?" Dominic slapped William upside the head. "What the hell were you thinking? If he chose to, there is no way we could have stopped him from hurting you. Tread carefully around him. Each day I see the darkness growing stronger in him. You do realize that if he ever goes over the edge, we'll be sent to kill him. Lucifer must never have all that power at his command."

Adam spoke up. "I think we're all tense waiting for the other shoe to drop. I think we need to go out and relax. Find a nice restaurant, go to a club or two and dance."

Danielle agreed with him. "I'll make reservations at Maggiano's for eight. That'll give us all enough time to get ready. You all feel like Italian?"

The rest agreed. She made the reservations while the others put away the skeleton. When they were all ready to go, everyone was laughing and looking forward to a relaxing night.

* * * *

Grant woke, reaching for the angel in his dream. Danielle touched his cheek.

"You're crying. What's wrong?"

He pulled her close and settled back. "When I found Ferguson's skeleton, I was overwhelmed with a feeling of déjà vu. It was as if I had been in that position before, but I don't ever remember being on my knees like he was. Also, there seemed to be almost desperation in the way his hands were pressed together. That night after we had documented and moved the bones, I fell into a deep sleep. Then I started dreaming." He fell silent.

"Dreaming about what?" She ran her hand over his chest in soothing strokes.

"I'm kneeling in the middle of a large white room. There's a desk at one end and two windows in the wall at the other end. In front of me stands an angel dressed in armor. He has dark hair and silver eyes."

She gasped. "Mika'il."

"Yes, but I didn't know that at the time. We don't talk. He just stands there staring down at me with the saddest expression. Then he disappears along with the room and I wake up crying. I always feel like I've lost something."

"What happened this time?"

"This time I knew his name, so I told him. He nodded and told me I had forgotten my name, but I'd remember when I got to Heaven."

"Remember your name? That's strange." She looked up at him with a frown.

"I know. He said my name was Grant for now and that I loved you."

Her blue eyes widened and she looked stunned. He cupped her cheek, smiling down at her. "He was right. I couldn't argue with him. I love you and it doesn't matter about all of this other shit. We'll get all these strangers out of here, then we'll focus on ourselves. There's so much I want to learn about you. Imagine all the history you've been through. I want to know everything."

Tears trailed down her cheeks and he wiped them away with his thumbs. He laid her back and leaned down to kiss her. He worshiped her lips with tender licks and soft nibbles. He took his time tasting every inch of her body. He kissed, teased and suckled her breasts until her nipples were hard and red. He moved down and dipped his tongue into her belly button causing her to giggle. When Grant passed over her pussy to start kissing her toes, Danielle pouted, but soon she was moaning as he trailed his tongue along the sensitive skin at the back of her knees. He nipped the silky skin on her inner thighs as she spread them.

He settled down between her legs and started to feast on her. He nibbled her clit with delicate nips. She pleaded with him to take her. He savored her, imprinting her taste and scent in his mind. With his tongue and fingers, he drove her over the edge and into her orgasm.

As she was coming down, he slid his cock into her warm pussy. Rocking in an easy movement, he showed her how much he loved her with his body and his lips. He told her of his love as he rode her into her second climax — this one was soft and tender.

Grant's climax snuck up on him, exploding throughout his body and nerves. He cried out his love to her as he spilled into her.

Chapter Twelve

"The crate's here," Grant told them all after he hung up the phone.

They had been wandering in and out of the museum while waiting for the bones and jewels to get there. They gathered around as the crate was brought in. Signing for it, Grant smiled at the look of anticipation on the others' faces. He was just as eager as they were to see the emeralds.

After the delivery men left, he gestured for Dominic and William to open the crate. They lowered the top to the floor. Everyone had cotton gloves on so they could handle the bones without worrying. He didn't want the oils from their hands destroying the skeleton. Nevan was standing by, keeping an eye on everything.

Each piece of the skeleton was unwrapped and checked out, but Abby was the one who hit the jackpot when she picked up a slender wing bone to unwrap it. A package fell out of the wrapping paper and Nevan grabbed it before any of the rest of them could get to it. They gathered around him as he stood at a table, carefully revealing what was hidden beneath the paper.

Abby gasped as the emeralds began to shine under the lab lights. "They look like my necklace." She pulled a heart-shaped pendant from under her shirt.

The clarity of the gems outshone anything Grant had ever seen. The stones themselves weren't large, but each was equal in size to the others in the set. Picking the ring up, Adam held it up to the light, studying it.

"I've seen some nice jewels in my life of crime and these are some of the nicest. I can see why the buyer would want them." His eyes gleamed.

"Give that to me," Nevan ordered, jerking the ring from Adam's hand. "Never trust a reformed thief. Never know what might pull them back to the dark side."

Adam glared at him, then smiled. "That's okay. I've got nicer jewels than that in my safe at home."

Celeste shook her head. "Can we get back to the business at hand? Now that we have the jewels, the trap is set and Adam's given them the bait. Should we all meet back here right before closing? We need to be in place before the museum empties for the night, so Diggston doesn't get suspicious if he's watching."

"The rest of you can come back if you want," Grant said. He pointed to the rest of the bones in the crate. "I need to finish unpacking these, then see about getting the skeleton laid out with the bones in the right places."

"I'll be here with some of my men around four-thirty. We'll come in separately and rendezvous here." Nevan waved to them before leaving to get his officers ready.

"We're taking Abby and Teresa to a ball game, but we'll be back in plenty of time," William said as he and Dominic led their fiancées out of the lab.

Adam and Celeste had made plans to meet up with some friends for lunch. Soon it was just Danielle and him. She smiled at him, then touched Ferguson's skull gently.

"You're so careful with him," she said.

"He might be dead, but he still deserves respect. I'd do the same with any skeleton I found." Looking down at the fragile wing bone he held in his hand, he admitted, "There seems to be something different about this one. It's almost like he's family. I don't want to do anything to destroy the bone or damage him in any way."

After setting the bone down, he reached in the crate for another one. With a nonchalance he didn't feel, he asked her, "Do you know what will happen to the skeleton once everything is taken care of?"

She shrugged. "I'm not sure. If Mika'il can come back, he'll probably take the bones with him. They'll be buried somewhere no one will ever find them. I'm not sure the world is ready for proof that angels exist."

"Wouldn't it be easier for you if people did believe in you?"

"I doubt it would. Mortals have been taught since man first thought about God that fallen angels are pure evil. There are no gray areas in their minds to accept the fact that fallen angels might be just like them. We have the unrepentant, the neutrals and the Enforcers. As you've seen with Christian, some of the Enforcers are only steps away from insanity, and not all the unrepentant are evil."

Grant could tell talking about her brethren bothered Danielle and he assumed it was because of Christian.

He decided to change the subject. "How long have you lived in Chicago?"

"I came in 1893 for the Columbian Exposition and never left. It was a great town, rowdy and bursting with life. I had lived in Virginia during the Civil War, risking my life to help runaway slaves. I needed a rest from Reconstruction." She pointed to a poster of the Chicago skyline on the wall. "I stayed and watched that skyline take shape. It's my city. The only place, besides Heaven, where I've ever felt at peace."

He understood how she felt because from the moment he stepped foot in the Field Museum, he'd wanted to work there. "I feel the same way about the museum."

"Things have changed lately. Now if I had to leave Chicago, I'd be fine. As long as I was with you, it wouldn't matter where I lived."

Her smile beckoned him and he kissed her. Pulling back, he said, "Let's go to the aquarium and grab lunch."

"Okay."

He secured the bones in the vault, then locked the lab. A plainclothes police officer stood guard at the end of the hallway. He nodded at them as they walked by.

"I meant to ask you. If fallen aren't supposed to interfere in the problems of mortals, why are your friends helping out?" He held her hand as they walked over to the Shedd's Aquarium.

"Some rules are made to be broken especially when the problem involves someone you care about. It's as simple as that, and I think Mika'il knew that when he made the silly rule." She waited until they were done paying before she continued, "Of course, he could have figured the best way to get us to help out is to tell us not to. We're a contrary bunch sometimes."

He chuckled. "I'd have never guessed."

"It's what got us in trouble in the first place."

They wandered around, looking at the tanks that held all the different fish. They didn't really talk about anything important, just causal things. He told her about his family. Mom and Dad were living in a retirement community down in Florida. His younger sister was working as a waitress out in L.A. waiting to be discovered. He told her how he had always wanted to be an archaeologist after visiting a museum that had an archaeologist on staff in his hometown in Michigan. The guy had made archaeology seem fun, even though at the time, he'd been disappointed that it wasn't more like the Indiana Jones movies. He'd become fascinated with the journey of discovering things left behind by ancient people. Never once through his long schooling to acquire his PhD had he ever think about changing his mind. Digging in the dirt was his idea of a great day.

When they got their food at the café and sat down to eat, his throat was sore and he realized he had done all the talking. After taking a sip from his drink, he smiled at her.

"Is there anything you want to tell me about yourself?"

Her eyes had been sparkling with laughter. Now the light died out, leaving only seriousness. "I've lived for so long, I can't begin to explain to you where I've been and what I've done."

"How did you get an original Da Vinci? It's not one I remember being listed in any books on him." He thought he'd help her out. He imagined thousands of centuries of life would get wound together.

"Leonardo drew it for me. I was living in Florence and happened to be a friend of the lady who sat for his famed *Mona Lisa*. I was always present when she sat for him. We got to be good friends. He was a genius and so far ahead of his time—if people knew everything he did, he would have been burned at the stake as a witch." She looked down at her food, then back up at him. "Leonardo knew what I was. Somehow he saw through the façade I showed to the world and saw the wings that I used to wear."

"The angel in the drawing? It's you." Thinking about it, the shape of the woman's face and the color of her eyes were just like Danielle's, but it was the heart wrenching sadness hidden in her gaze that he recognized.

"Yes. It was shortly before he finished the *Mona Lisa* that I decided to leave Florence. I had been there too long. It was time to move on and I hadn't planned on telling anyone I knew. I went with my friend to his studio for the last time. Right before we left, he pulled me aside and gave me the rolled parchment. He told me it was so I'd never forget what I once was and to keep me striving to retain what I'd lost." Tears shone in her eyes.

"And the statue on your end table? Adam told me it was a real Michelangelo."

"He didn't like the statue. Thought it was the worst piece of sculpture he'd ever done." Shaking her head, she grinned. "I met him early in his career. He was perfecting the magnificence you can see in every piece he has made. I begged him to allow me to keep it. He gave it to me after making me promise not to tell anyone it was one of his."

"You're telling me now."

"And Michelangelo has been dead for centuries. He won't be back to haunt me. A master craftsman has created each piece in my house. The quilts on the beds were hand-stitched two hundred years ago by women traveling out to settle the west. I know the stories attached to each piece because I was there and lived it with the people who made them."

"Have you ever been in love before?" He wasn't sure why he had to ask and he didn't know how he would react to the answer, but he had to know.

Danielle took his hand, brushing her lips over his knuckles. "Since I've been around so long, you would think my heart might have been broken before. No, I've never fallen in love with anyone. It's been easier to skim through life. My friendships might be strong, but I don't stick around long because people notice when you don't age like they do. My girlfriends here are wonderful. I've gotten to the point where I'm willing to risk a little to have people to talk to and hang out with. The ache when you lose a friend is a little smaller than the hole that's in your heart when you lose a loved one."

Relief raced through him then another thought hit him. "What happens when I die?"

Sorrow touched her eyes for a moment. "I go on without you, I guess. It'll hurt and I'll miss you every day for the rest of my life, but I wouldn't miss loving you to save myself from the pain. I figured that out while watching Dominic and Teresa overcome their problems. Love isn't love unless you're willing to risk having your heart broken."

"That sucks," he said.

"I know." Glancing down at her watch, she commented, "We need to get back. The others will be filtering in soon."

Nodding, he took their trash to throw away. While standing at the trashcan, he looked up and saw a tall, dark-haired man standing by the dolphin pool. As if he knew he was being watched, the man turned and looked up at him. Sunlight streamed through the glass walls and highlighted the silver of the man's eyes. With a smile and a nod of the head, the man disappeared. Grant met Danielle at the entrance of the aquarium.

"I think I just saw Mika'il," he told her as they made their way back through the park to the museum.

"I wouldn't doubt it. Just because he can't interfere doesn't mean he won't be around watching. He hovers like a mother hen sometimes. I've often gotten the feeling that Mika'il has another secret agenda that he's pursuing along with all these other adventures he puts us through." She smiled fondly. "Mika'il does his best to keep us out of trouble."

"Why did you rebel?"

"I listened to Lucifer's diatribes about angels being superior to mortals and how we needed to unify and show God that we were more precious to Him than humans. It was stupid, because God is like a parent who has several kids. Sure, He might have a favorite among them, but that doesn't mean He loves the others any less."

"I never thought of it that way." It made sense to him.

"I know, and none of us did either until it was too late." She looked at him and shrugged.

* * * *

As they walked in, Celeste and Adam were returning as well, and Celeste pointed out the dinosaur.

"When we got here the other day, I was telling Adam that I ran into one of those a long time ago."

Grant looked surprised and Danielle laughed.

"We've been around a long time, love." Danielle kissed his cheek.

"I know, but for some reason, I've never associated you with dinosaurs."

"We stayed out of their way and they ignored us. We didn't even register on their radar." She shook her head and exchanged a wry smile with Celeste. "It was tough living through the climate shift that killed them."

"Do you believe in evolution or creation?" Adam asked Grant with a smart-ass grin on his face.

"Well, before I found the skeleton and met Danielle, I'd tell you I was a strong believer in the evolution theory. Now, you've all proven that there is a God."

"God breathed life into man. What form man had when he took his first breath isn't important. You should all be thanking Him every day. He chose to give you life." Danielle winked at Grant.

He laughed. "You're right."

Nevan was talking to the plainclothes officer who had been guarding the door. He followed them in after Grant opened the lab.

"Davidson out there said no one came by while he was here. He's going to move into one of the rooms across the hall. My men have all moved into position as well. Where are the rest of your people, Danielle?"

She wasn't worried—they would show up before long. Grant had the skeleton pulled out and the crate opened up when Dominic and William appeared.

"We left the girls at your house, Danielle," William replied to her questioning look.

"Abby must be pissed at your rather high-handed way of shoving her out of danger," Celeste teased.

"She is, but I asked her to stay and watch over Teresa. My love isn't as recovered as she'd like us all to believe." Dominic's face softened when he spoke of his fiancée.

"It takes time for anyone to recover from a Vodou curse, LaFontaine. I'm sure you're proud of the way she's survived so far." Christian appeared and the tension in the room mounted.

"I am proud of her." Dominic's tone was relaxed.

Danielle was happy to see Dominic wasn't going to take offense to anything Christian said. She and Celeste pulled the broken Peruvian pottery out from the boxes Grant had put them in, and worked on piecing them back together.

Several hours passed this way until Nevan's radio squawked.

"Detective, the perp is coming in the south side door."

Everything except for the empty crate got put away and the lights were turned off. The mortals in the room hid in Grant's office and the fallen used their power to mask their presence from Diggston.

Within minutes, they heard a scraping noise at the door. It was obvious Diggston was trying to pick the lock. Danielle was standing next to Christian and felt the Enforcer shift his weight. Seconds later the door opened. A shadowy figure snuck into the lab, holding a penlight in front of him. He headed right for the crate. Nevan had returned the emeralds to the bone earlier because they wanted to catch Diggston holding the goods. The light rested on the edge of the crate and the perp started digging around, searching through the bones and packing paper.

Christian shifted again. She wondered if he was impatient to get this whole thing over with.

"Ah, here it is. Must have fallen out of the bone it was in." Diggston pulled the package out then grabbed the light. He carried it over to a table before unwrapping the paper. "Yep, they're all there and shining. The boss will have to stop bitching at me now."

Another shift and light exploded in the room. When it disappeared, he was surrounded by Nevan, Grant and Adam. The fallen hung back and Christian had disappeared. The criminal didn't argue while Nevan read him his rights and cuffed him. His watery gaze flicked to Adam and Diggston grew pale.

"I'm thinking the only vacation you're going to get is a long one behind bars, Diggston," Adam growled.

"Wait, I know all sorts of things about Martinez," Diggston pleaded.

"You should have thought of that before you killed the guard. There won't be any deals for you." Nevan glared at Diggston then dragged the man out. Danielle could hear the criminal protesting all the way down the hall.

"Where'd Christian go?" Dominic asked.

"I don't know, but I get the feeling he's responsible for the door unlocking and Diggston finding the emeralds so fast. Also the flash of light," Danielle said as Grant made sure none of the bones had been bothered.

"Why do you think he did it?" Celeste frowned.

"He'll do anything to facilitate his leaving Chicago sooner than later. He's not fond of being out of New

York." Dominic's crooked smile let her know he knew that was an understatement.

"Come on, it's late. I want to get some rest. We'll decide what we're going to do with the skeleton tomorrow." She pulled Grant away from the vault where he had placed the bones.

They caught cabs and headed to her place. As the vehicles deposited them on the sidewalk, a strange, uneasy feeling rushed over her. She dashed up the front steps with the other Enforcers right behind her.

Stunned, she stopped in the entry of the living room. Teresa was lying on the floor with Abby kneeling beside her. Christian stood over them. Dominic rushed to Teresa's side and William grabbed Abby's hand to pull her away.

Celeste faced Christian. "What's going on here? What have you done, Christian?"

"No." Abby jerked away from William then moved to stand between Christian and Celeste. "He didn't do anything. A woman showed up and attacked Teresa. I was trying to stop her, Dominic. I really did try," she pleaded with Dominic.

"He knows, Abby," Danielle said. She saw the cynical light in Christian's eyes.

"Then Christian showed up. He touched her and the woman screamed, then disappeared."

"Where did she go?" It could only have been Brittany.

"Brittany's gone. You don't have to worry about her bothering you anymore." Christian reached out to touch Abby's shoulder.

"Don't touch her," William blurted out.

Christian pulled his hand back slowly then stared at them. Dominic met his gaze as he rose to his feet, holding Teresa in his arms.

"Thank you, Christian." Dominic's voice was serious and honest.

The other Enforcer inclined his head a little. "I only did what I promised to do long ago. I haven't forgotten my promises yet." His dark blue eyes skated over to William. "Though I know there are those on both sides eagerly waiting for the day I do."

William had the grace to look guilty.

Grant stepped up to Christian. Holding out his hand, he said, "Thank you for all the help you've provided. I know it's hard for you to be away from your city. We'll have everything cleaned up tomorrow then you can go home. I'm sorry your reception hasn't always been good."

She wondered what Christian would do. It was no secret the Enforcer really didn't care for mortals, but she didn't think he would do anything more than ignore Grant. Surprise shot through her when he reached out and shook Grant's hand before Christian looked at her.

"You picked a good one, Danielle. All of you will need to meet me at the lab tomorrow morning. We'll take care of Ferguson's skeleton. Make sure your reserve of power is filled." Turning to glance at Dominic, he said, "Except for you, LaFontaine. What you have now will be enough. I need everyone, even the mortals and that detective of yours, Danielle."

"We'll be there," she promised.

He nodded and disappeared. They all went to their rooms—there wasn't anything else to say.

* * * *

"Why is everyone afraid of Christian?" Grant asked after they had lain in bed for an hour or so, staring at the ceiling.

Sighing, Danielle tucked her head under his chin to rest it on his chest. "Part of it is because we don't know his motives. Why did he choose to fall? He wasn't truly part of the rebellion. He tried to talk us out of it. Lucifer could never seduce him with talk of power or anything else. If he wasn't interested in power, why did he end up banished to earth? One of the many rumors about him is that he gave up his wings voluntarily. Mika'il didn't have to fight him for them."

"He seems so lonely." When the Enforcer had shaken his hand, Grant had seen a deep sorrow in Christian's dark eyes. "It's like he's behind a glass wall and doesn't know how to reach through it for help or a friend."

"Now he only has Mika'il as a friend and that doesn't make him feel better."

"Do you think he's going to lose his soul?" He shivered thinking about what that would mean to everyone.

She shook her head. "I don't think so. If he does, it'll be because he'll lose something more important to him if he didn't. He's stronger than we all have given him credit for. Now, what was it that Christian said about recharging my power?" She slid her hand down and cupped his cock.

A few minutes later, he was thanking God for Danielle as he came.

Chapter Thirteen

When they got to the museum and met up with Nevan, Christian had already pulled the bones out and had placed them in a pile on a table in the middle of the lab. Christian was holding the skull in his hand and a single tear had tracked down his cheek. Grant cleared his throat as they walked in.

Christian greeted them. "I know where the bones should go, so we're going to join our power together and send them there. It's the best place for them and no one will ever find Ferguson again."

"What about Mika'il?" Celeste asked.

"He isn't here. If he doesn't like where I send the skeleton, he can go and get it. I'm not going to worry about what he wants or doesn't want." Christian gestured for them to surround the table.

Grant didn't realize someone else was in the lab until after he had been pushed into a protective huddle with Abby, Teresa and Adam. Danielle stood in front of him in a circle formed by the other Enforcers. He wanted to protest, but then the stranger caught his gaze.

Broken perfection was the only description he could think of. The man's golden hair waved to his shoulders. His pale skin was without flaw, except for the faint scar on his left cheek in the shape of a cross. Yet one glance into the man's eyes... Grant knew a shattered soul when he saw one. The stranger's eyes were black bottomless pits. There were no pupils. It was hard to meet that stare because it felt like the man was draining his soul.

"You have no business here, Daystar."

Christian's voice broke the spell as he leaned against the table that held Ferguson's skeleton. There was no fear or tension in Christian's posture. A movement in the corner drew Grant's eyes and he saw Nevan frozen with a look of pure horror. He imagined the detective could see all the souls clinging to Lucifer.

Leaning forward, he whispered to Danielle, "You forgot Nevan."

"No, he'll be fine. His *sight* protects him from Lucifer's power, even with all the ghosts that haunted Lucifer." She spoke under her breath. "Now be quiet."

"What if I feel differently?" Lucifer's voice was beautiful, like a gospel choir singing hymns.

"It no longer matters what you feel or wish. You were banished and God turned His back on you like He did the rest of us. This angel suffered death because of you. He won't suffer anymore by your hands." Christian's dark blue eyes gleamed.

"Imagine what those pitiful mortals would think if we showed them the truth?" Lucifer nodded to where Grant and the others stood. "Imagine the power we could have."

"Your thirst for power has always been your downfall. You'll never get any power from his bones.

Let this one go, Daystar. There will be other fights for you to take on." Christian glanced down at the skull.

Church bells ringing on a clear day couldn't have been purer than Lucifer's laugh. "All right. To be honest, I have no real interest in that skeleton, but I heard someone was throwing my name around and I didn't want to disappoint anyone." He stared at the Enforcers and the humans behind them. "My time will come. I've been promised."

With that, Lucifer turned to go then he caught Nevan's eyes. His own eyes widened and a grin crossed his face. Nevan's face blanked and his green eyes closed as he dropped to his knees. His scream made Grant cringe and Christian slammed a fist into Daystar's face.

With the gaze broken, Nevan curled in a fetal position. Lucifer touched his split lip and looked at Christian with surprise in his eyes. "You hit me."

"Leave now. Don't torment him any longer." Christian was poised to counter any move Lucifer made.

"Why would I leave? I could take his soul if I truly wanted to. You left him unprotected. In your wisdom, you believed his gift would keep him safe. Foolish angels. No one is safe from me."

Before Grant consciously thought about what he was doing, he broke from the circle and ran to where Nevan lay on the floor. Stumbling, he placed his body between Lucifer and the detective as he pulled the gun from Nevan's shoulder holster. The air seemed to leave the room and he was aware everyone tensed, except Christian.

"You're a brave idiot, mortal. Do you really think a gun can stop me?"

He didn't say anything. There wasn't any point in arguing with Lucifer. He just kept the gun aimed at the fallen angel. A sharp touch in his mind made him cry out. He fought the urge to cup his head in his hands. A touch to his ankle eased the pressure slightly. He dropped his gaze for a quick glance to see Nevan's hand grasping his ankle.

Christian stepped between Lucifer and Grant. The Enforcer did nothing except meet the Lucifer's gaze. There was a break in Lucifer's composure as sweat beaded on his forehead. Grant held his breath.

Snarling, Lucifer broke first. "This isn't over between us, Christian." He disappeared.

Christian knelt beside Grant and Nevan. He touched the detective's shoulder, and Danielle hugged Grant.

"What the hell were you thinking?" she growled at him.

He stared at her then included all the other Enforcers in his gaze. "You left him alone, believing his gift would keep him safe. It didn't and he needed protection, so it was the best I could do."

"We forgot there is no protection from Lucifer except through the good will of God and the willing sacrifice of a mortal." Christian's voice was tired and his dark golden skin was sallow.

Nevan groaned and rolled over. "Is he gone?"

"Yes, Nevan." Christian helped the detective sit up, then after a few minutes, the Enforcer steadied him so he could stand. "You need to go and rest. I'll get you home."

"What about Ferguson?" William pointed to the bones.

"None of us are ready to do what I'm planning. Rest up today and we'll try again tomorrow." Christian stood close to help Nevan in case the man's strength failed him.

He waited until the detective and Christian left before he turned to look at the rest. "I'd say that was a pretty shitty start to the morning, wouldn't you? Let's find something fun to do today and we'll regroup tomorrow to send Ferguson to rest."

Everyone nodded.

* * * *

The next morning they stood in shocked silence, staring at the empty lab table.

"I didn't think things could get worse, but it looks like Lucifer came back," Danielle said.

"No, it wasn't Lucifer. He never returns to the scene of a defeat. It was another angel you all love to hate." Christian handed her a note.

"This has been the hardest thing I've ever done. Please forgive me for all you've had to go through. Thank you for taking such great care of Ferguson, Grant. I knew you were the best for the job. I've taken him to a better place where his soul might find some peace. Mika'il," she read out loud.

"Doesn't that just fit? We do all the work and he comes in to take the glory." William snorted.

Danielle didn't say anything. She really did think that it had been hard for Mika'il to sit back and let them handle everything. He cared so deeply for them and it hurt him when any of them were hurt.

"Thank you for Grant, Mika'il."

"I did nothing except give him a little push. He was always meant to be yours. Someday he might remember the truth of what you both once were."

"What do you mean by that?"

"Enjoy and love each other." Mika'il was gone.

Laughing, she decided he was making a joke at her expense. She turned to look at the others. "Let's grab lunch before everyone heads back to their homes."

Christian declined and disappeared, but the others agreed. As they filed out of the museum, she thought that it was great to have friends of her own kind. Grant wrapped his arm around her, pulling her close. The best part was having this man to love for the rest of their lives together.

About the Author

I've been writing for most of my life, but was first published in 2004. I believe everyone deserves love in all its forms. I write about women and men who find strength in loving each other. I live in the Midwest with my two cats, and when I'm not writing (which isn't very often) I read and watch movies.

Tiffany Aaron loves to hear from readers. You can find her contact information, website details and author profile page at http://www.totallybound.com.

Totally Bound Publishing